JEFFREY ROUND

Jeffrey Round is an award-winning writer, director, producer and songwriter. His first two books, *A Cage of Bones* and *The P'town Murders*, were listed on AfterElton's Top 100 Gay Books. *Lake On The Mountain*, the first Dan Sharp mystery, won a Lambda Award in 2013, while his short film *My Heart Belongs To Daddy* won awards for Best Director and Best Use of Music. He was founder and artistic director of Best Boys, a multi-media production company. He also directed the Toronto production of Agatha Christie's *The Mousetrap*, the world's longest-running stage show. His music has been recorded by soprano Lilac Caña. His blog, *A Writer's Half-Life*, is syndicated online. He lives in Toronto.

Visit his website:
www.JeffreyRound.com

Praise for the
Bradford Fairfax Murder Series

"*Death in Key West* is a suspenseful, campy, rollicking ride with the perfect blend of serious and silly. The mystery is well-crafted, the writing assured and the comedy relief is full of originality and wit." — RALPH HIGGINS, *Wayves Magazine*

"Round knows how to set the scene and throw around the bitchy one-liners. And he makes us take Brad and Zach's relationship seriously, which is really refreshing in a queer thriller." — SUSAN G COLE, *NOW Magazine*

"The author has concocted one quite spicy Conch Chowder. But the dish is never too hot for suave Bradford Fairfax and his blue-haired lover, Zach, to handle in this surprising sequel to *The P-Town Murders*." — DREWEY WAYNE GUNN, *The Gay Male Sleuth in Print and Film*

"Riotous lines … page-turning fun … it feels like a game of Clue with drag queens, thugs and crocodiles." — JAMES K MORAN, *Xtra! Magazine*

"Whether shaken or stirred, this exquisite cocktail is irresistible entertainment." — PAUL RUSSELL, *The Gay 100*

"Jeffrey Round is fast becoming one of my favorites. Witty, sly, and clever, there's a surprise in every chapter!" — GREG HERREN, *Murder in the Rue Chartres*

"I can't help but admire an author who poses as a corpse on the cover of his own novel. A breezy read that's hard to put down, I look forward to more Bradford Fairfax mysteries." — PAUL BELLINI, *FAB Magazine*

"I cannot recommend this book highly enough." — AMOS LASSEN, *Literary Pride*

Also by Jeffrey Round:

Books:

A Cage of Bones

**The P-Town Murders: A Bradford
Fairfax Mystery**

**Death In Key West: A Bradford
Fairfax Mystery**

The Honey Locust

Lake on the Mountain: A Dan Sharp Mystery

Pumpkin Eater: A Dan Sharp Mystery

Poetry:

In the Museum of Leonardo da Vinci

Forthcoming:

**Bon Ton Roulez: A Bradford
Fairfax Mystery**

The Jade Butterfly: A Dan Sharp Mystery

VANISHED IN VALLARTA

A Bradford Fairfax Murder Mystery

by Jeffrey Round

Rounder Publications

First Published in 2014 by Rounder Publications
10 9 8 7 6 5 4 3 2 1

Library and Archives Canada Cataloguing in Publication

Round, Jeffrey, author
Vanished in Vallarta / Jeffrey Round. —
(A Bradford Fairfax murder mystery series ; v. 3)
Issued in print and electronic formats.
ISBN 978-0-9810606-2-0 (pbk.)
ISBN 978-0-9810606-3-7 (ebook)

I. Title. II. Series: Round, Jeffrey.
Bradford Fairfax murder mystery ; v. 3.

PS8635.O8625V35 2014   C813'.6   C2014-900331-5
C2014-900349-8

Cover design: Shane McConnell
Black and White Cover Photograph: David Hawe
Back Cover Photograph: Box 77 (Author's Collection)
Interior text design: Shane McConnell

For Enrique

AN INTRODUCTION TO VANISHED IN VALLARTA

When I sat down to write *The P'Town Murders*, the first
of the Bradford Fairfax books, I had no idea there
would be more to come, let alone enough for a series.
By the time I was finished, however, I already had ideas
for a second, *Death In Key West*, and this book, the third.

An initial trip to Puerto Vallarta in 1997 opened my
eyes to the city's seductive allure, but it wasn't till a
second trip the following year that it opened its heart to
me. On that stay, I made the acquaintance of a man
who turned out to be Celine Dion's agent. This was at
the height of the Celine Dion-Barbra Streisand mega-
hit, *Tell Him*, and both divas seemed engaged in a battle
for supremacy in the gay world. That fact played nicely
into this book's themes, as you will discover.

While visiting the agent's rented villa in the hills above
town, I was impressed to discover that I had to cross a
long, narrow walkway to enter. (Like Brad, I have a fear
of heights, hence my clear memory of it.) On strolling
out back, I was even more impressed (and slightly
terrified) to learn we were suspended on a patio that
held a good-sized swimming pool. It's this place that I
describe as Brad and Zach's cozy abode during their PV
stay. Subsequent trips offered up additional details and
settings, such as the film set for John Huston's *The Night
of the Iguana*, which I also incorporated into my story.

More than fifteen years after that first visit, I now
wander around Puerto Vallarta as though it's a second
home, because it is. Yet there's always something new to

discover, given the constancy of change here. Not all of it is for the better. This year, for instance, I found that Casa Kimberly, actress Elizabeth Taylor's former home, had been gutted and is no longer open to the public. For now at least, her much-celebrated pink Bridge of Reconciliation remains.

The place where Celine's agent stayed, then one of the highest buildings in the hills, now reveals itself to be little more than halfway compared with recent developments, such is the growth the city has undergone in recent years. No doubt future vacation properties will eventually reach the very summit.

I have visited all the places I describe in the Bradford Fairfax books, but none has quite claimed me as Puerto Vallarta has. Long ago I fell in love with its sunsets and the white adobe villas honeycombing the hills, its pace of life and the warm welcome it offers the LGBTQ community. I'm sure that when I die a piece of my heart will remain here.

Jeffrey Round
Puerto Vallarta
December 2013

*What happens in Puerto Vallarta
stays in Puerto Vallarta.*

Mexican Tourist Brochure

VANISHED IN VALLARTA

1

It was coming on twilight—the lavender hour. A masked figure hugged the shadows beneath a cliff-top villa. Toned as a panther and poured into black Lycra, his muscular outline suggested he wasn't someone to be toyed with. Had anyone been watching, the man's swift movements and canny senses would have prevented him from being spotted, but in this secluded Puerto Vallarta neighborhood there were no watchers.

Blue eyes flashed up concrete pillars to an open-air deck high above. Nestled in the hills and surrounded by jungle, the dwelling appeared impregnable. Anyone wanting access from below faced a death-defying climb up a sheer wall of rock, while entry from above was possible only by crossing a treacherous walkway wired with a deadly electric charge. A small helicopter might have touched down on the upper deck or a practiced paratrooper could have landed directly on the roof, but the element of surprise would have been lost. And surprise was a must.

A light blinked on above. The figure shrank against the wall. He waited breathlessly as seconds passed, but nothing further ensued. Get on with it, he told himself. There were worse places to die.

He glanced up. If he scaled the support beams to the deck, he would have direct access to the house, but he risked being seen. If that happened, it was a long way back down—even longer when you were being shot at. On the other hand, if he attempted to cross the walkway, one false move with those wires and he'd fry like a mess of *chicharrones*. It was an awkward moment, but the walkway won out. Somehow the threat of electrocution seemed preferable to falling to his death.

From a crouching position, he aimed a grappling gun and fired a streamer of nylon overhead. The hook tugged securely and he began hauling himself up. From that vantage point, the villa resembled a Mayan fortress, complete with stone-carved turtles, jaguars and jacaranda blossoms. Suspended mid-air, the intruder stopped momentarily to remove a pen-like object from his lapel, aiming it at a grimacing monkey head. The beam sliced through the monkey's eye, neatly disarming the electric charge. Laser was such a beautiful thing.

Next, he swung confidently onto the walkway and crept to the front door: bolted. Now what? Forcing it would undoubtedly trip an alarm within. He looked up. There was only one thing left to do—go higher. The roof was a long way above, but there was no turning back. Now things promised to get interesting.

He had to work fast. Anyone approaching along the road would catch sight of him. Not to mention anyone exiting the villa. He aimed his grappling gun and fired—once, twice, three times. Each time the hook slid over the tiles and back down. What to do? Think! To the right, a chimney jutted up. His next shot caught on the lip. He secured the rope and began to pull. Halfway up, he realized he was holding his breath. Just don't look down, he told himself. One day he would conquer his fear of heights—but not today. He exhaled and continued to climb. Another few seconds and he'd grasped the roof edge. Whew! So far so good.

He pulled himself panting onto the red tiles that radiated warmth in the evening sun. Now, he found himself face to face with a roof dweller. A fat pigeon watched him warily, its bright yellow eyes following his progress. For a second, each regarded the other with extreme suspicion.

A glance back along the bougainvillea-lined roadway assured the interloper he was safe for the time being. Still, he had to hurry. He crawled cautiously up to the peak and peered down at the patio with its deck chairs and pool rippling in the breeze. The city lay spread out in the distance. Now what? Dropping directly onto the patio might prove a fatal choice if anyone had heard his stealthy movements along the tiles.

Below and to the left lay a small Juliet balcony. From there, he could use his grappling gun to reach the patio without being seen. He began to ease his way down. All went well until a tile slipped. He reached out, grabbing blindly as he slid over the edge. The last thing he saw was the pigeon's yellow eye winking at him.

He hit the balcony with a thud as his grappling gun went clattering down into the gorge. He tensed, waiting for a reaction. From inside came the sound of a dance beat. The only other sound was the banging of his heart as he peered at the jagged rocks below. Not a pretty way to die.

He looked around. With growing panic, he realized the patio was too far to reach without his grappling gun. Here he was, stranded on a balcony overlooking beautiful Puerto Vallarta without water or food. When the sun hit him tomorrow, he would fry, though chances were he would be discovered before then. It was one of the most desperate situations he'd ever encountered. He was stuck.

Or was he?

He reached out and tried the door handle. The door opened onto a darkened interior.

Whew!

The villa had character, and had obviously been designed by someone who fancied himself a Mexican Frank Lloyd Wright. Contoured arches gave way onto tiled hallways; exotic flowers and seductively lit *objets d'art* nestled in sculpted niches. Clearly, his intended victim was a man of taste.

The figure stopped beside a door and leaned his head to the frame. The dance music beat on inside. He paused to take stock of the situation: it all seemed too easy. That he might merely open this door and surprise his opponent in an unguarded moment was too good to be true. His enemy was a wily young man known for his cunning and rumoured to have strange powers and unusual abilities. It was even said he possessed a sixth sense that let him see through solid objects. Was he watching now?

The intruder's hand slid over the doorknob. Dare he chance it? He didn't have much choice. But wait! Just in time, he recalled a second entrance indicated on the stolen set of blueprints. He padded softly down the hall and turned the corner. Yes! There was the other door. Through a keyhole, he glimpsed his prey relaxing on the bed and reading a book. The boy was stunning: sleek muscles, aquamarine eyes, strawberry lips and ... blue hair! Someone had been extremely clever in their choice of secret agent. With such obvious sex appeal and boyish good looks, anyone might be taken in by him. Almost anyone.

The watcher felt his resolve weakening. No—that could never happen. His will had been hardened into a formidable diamond for exactly this moment. It wouldn't fail him now. He'd take what he came for.

And after that?

After that remained to be seen. Perhaps he'd show his opponent mercy. Perhaps not.

Inside the room, the young man suddenly closed his book and sat up. He looked around as though something had alerted him. Standing at the window, he cast his gaze over the city. Perhaps he was waiting for a lover or a fellow agent. Or possibly he had sensed the intruder who at that moment was propelling himself through the open door and bounding silently across the floor.

In a flash, the masked figure collided with the boy. A fierce struggle ensued. The boy was agile and strong, but the intruder had the advantage of surprise. He soon had the young man's arms deftly pinned behind his back, securing them with a knotted pillowcase.

"The jewels of the Madonna! Where are they?" he demanded.

The boy shook his head. "I don't know what you're talking about."

He slapped the boy's face. "Tell me what I want to know!"

His captive glared. The boy's chest heaved and strained against the fabric of his T-shirt. "I won't tell you a thing."

The intruder smirked. "You have no idea what a rough ride you're in for if you don't cooperate."

The kid glanced over at the patio. "I think you're the one who might end up being surprised."

Blue eyes flashed behind the mask. "Waiting for someone?"

"Wouldn't you like to know?"

A quick push sent the youngster stumbling across the room where he collided with a dresser.

"You won't get away with this!" the boy shouted, struggling to right himself.

The intruder shoved him hard again. "Tell me what I want to know before I get rough for real."

"I won't tell you a thing!"

A knife flashed. The blade eased down the boy's T-shirt and the thin cotton sprang apart. A fresh scratch oozed where the boy had struck his chest when he fell. The masked man trailed a finger through the blood, smearing it across the boy's glistening abdominals.

"Red looks good on you. It sets off your blue hair." He reached around to the boy's backside. "Beautiful," he murmured, giving a squeeze.

"Get your hands off me! You just wait till my partner shows."

The intruder laughed. "Your work partner or your personal partner?"

The boy glared, but said nothing.

The masked figure smirked. "No matter. I've already taken care of Mr. Fairfax."

A worried look crossed the boy's face.

The intruder leaned in, but quickly pulled back when the boy snapped with his teeth. "All right! If you want it rough, I can be rough!" He picked his opponent up bodily and threw him onto the bed. "So you want to play with the big boys, do you?"

He hoisted the boy's legs over his shoulders. Rape was always an effective tactic. So persuasive. Far less messy than breaking arms and legs.

"This is your last chance. Tell me what I want to know!"

"Never!"

"Never is a long time," the man said.

A zipper was yanked down, shorts peeled off. The boy gasped and steeled himself.

"Where are the jewels?" the man demanded.

"I won't tell you anything!" the boy panted.

The intruder forced himself in as the boy mumbled a feeble protest. Strictly speaking, these were not standard operating procedures, but sometimes the masked figure resorted to unusual tactics to subdue his foe. He thrust again and again, breathlessly, till he felt the familiar headlong rush of ecstasy. Spent, he looked down to see the boy spurting across his chest and shoulder.

Mission accomplished.

The intruder slowly pulled off his mask, smoothing his reddish hair back into place.

The boy looked up, a smile on his face. "The jewels of the Madonna?" Zach said. "Are you having another *Tosca* fetish? I thought you said Puccini was for the blue-rinse set."

Bradford Fairfax leaned back and grinned at his partner. "Yeah, well, when it's Callas, it's much more than Puccini. She makes everything sound great."

"I hate to ask, but would you mind untying my hands? They're starting to ache."

Brad's face registered surprise. "I thought you'd have got free of that sad excuse for a knot by now. Good thing I wasn't a real intruder or you'd have been done for."

Zach grinned. "Is this really the kind of tactic I'm going to have to use against the enemy one day?"

"You'll be in the unit soon, Zachary Tyler," Brad said, untying him. "You have to do whatever it takes to seduce—I mean, subdue—your man."

Zach had yet to undergo the rigorous physical and psychological conditioning that was a prerequisite for joining Box 77, the only known title for the surreptitious security organization Brad worked for. He'd applied against Brad's wishes, but with the full recommendation of Box 77's shadowy director, Grace. She considered Zach's abilities—intellectual as well as intuitive—to be not only highly unusual, but also highly desirable from a director's standpoint. If all her agents had such super-human skills, she would find herself with one of the most formidable security forces in the world, not to mention on whatever other plane of existence there might conceivably be.

"Have you ever had to do anything like this before?" Zach asked.

A fleeting memory made Brad smile. There had been that time in Provincetown when he'd been overcome by a burly Mongolian assassin stalking the Dalai Lama. Except Brad had been on the receiving end of things then.

"Nah—not really," he said. "And now that I have you around, I hope I never will. But in the meantime, it's good training for both of us."

Zach sat up, rubbing his wrists. "Let's survey the damage. How did you get in?"

"Balcony door," Brad said. "You left it unlocked."

"Drat!" Zach shook his head. "I thought you'd come up the back wall. When I used my Remote Viewing, I was sure I saw you climbing."

"You did, but I came up under the walkway and over the roof."

Zach's face registered surprise. "Really? The back route is so much easier. Not to mention safer. What made you choose the front?"

Brad help up a finger. "Know your opponent. I'm afraid of heights, remember? That electric charge might seem daunting to most people, but to me it's far less terrifying than the thought of falling hundreds of feet to certain death. But I zapped the wires just in case."

Zach shook his head. "Hundreds of feet? It's only twenty feet from the patio to the ground out back."

Brad harrumphed. "Well, it certainly seemed

higher."

Zach shook his head. "Anyway, that electric charge is meant to deter pigeons, not humans. You probably wouldn't even have felt it."

Brad tried to hide his disappointment. "Next you'll be saying you didn't really try to resist when I attacked."

Zach winked. "Don't worry, I would've let you take advantage of me no matter what."

"Very sporting, but not in your best interest," Brad reminded him. "I still can't believe you can have an orgasm without touching yourself."

"It's the Tantric training. But it takes a really hot intruder to take advantage of me." Zach picked up the remnants of his knife-slashed T-shirt. "Guess someone'll be taking me shopping, right?"

"Sorry about that. I wanted to throw a little realism into the scene."

"It's okay." Zach looked up sheepishly. "I kind of enjoyed being thrown around."

Brad eyed him. "I don't want to have to beat you up regularly for sex."

"What if I hold out?" Zach said, his eyebrows arching coyly.

"Then I might have to take matters into my own hands again."

"Ooh! I like it when you threaten me!"

Brad leaned down for a kiss, but quickly pulled back. "No biting!"

Zach grinned. "Promise."

"Now that all the fun and games are over, what do we do about the security problems?" Zach asked. "Is it something to worry about?"

Brad's eyes swept the room. Obviously there were weaknesses in the villa's safety design. "I think we're okay for now," he said. "I'll reconnect the wires, but I should let headquarters know one of their cadets-in-training was man-handled by another agent after a breach in the system."

"Make sure you tell them I was willing," Zach said, putting on his clothes and heading out to the kitchen. "I wouldn't want to have to break you out of prison next."

Brad peeled off his Lycra suit, changing into shorts and a T-shirt. Out on deck, Zach handed him a margarita. He took the glass, scanning the horizon. His eyes lingered over the splendour of Banderas Bay and the mountains ringing the city. The last rays of the setting sun spilled gold across the white adobe walls honeycombed on the hillside. It was the sunsets Brad had fallen in love with on his first visit to Puerto Vallarta. Since then, hardly a year had gone by that he hadn't returned to the Pacific paradise for a respite while winter raged back home. This year was the first time he'd brought Zach. Since their arrival, however, clouds had covered the horizon a little before six each evening, spoiling the promised spectacle. Today was different. At last, they could say they'd experienced Vallarta in its full glory.

Brad checked his watch and looked up.

"Any sign of our boy?" Zach asked.

"Not yet," Brad said, at the exact moment they heard a familiar *whuff-whuffing* from above.

The sound intensified as a chopper shot into view over the mountaintop.

"Right on time!" Brad cried.

They kept their eyes trained on the helicopter as a dark shape dropped from its bottom and pivoted downward. Within seconds, a parachute blossomed and a figure streamed to earth feet-first, holding briefly in their field of vision before plummeting from sight.

2

Garbo's was in full swing when they arrived. The air was heavy with cigarette smoke and dusky notes issuing from the throat of the reigning diva. As piano bars went, it was one of Puerto Vallarta's finest, offering a seductive blend of Latin music, foreign intrigue and the irresistible tang of sex. Languages were as diverse as looks as men lined up at the bar keeping their eyes peeled for anything that might promise more than just the usual fun night on the town.

A waif-like waiter wafted by. Brad ordered a chocolate martini for himself and a Blue Curaçao for Zach. "To match your hair," he said with a wink. He checked his watch and looked around the bar.

"How will we know him?" Zach asked.

"Grace said he'd be wearing a very unusual hat."

A glance around the room revealed at least a dozen heads sporting a variety of baseball caps cocked at various angles. The degree of tilt seemed to offer a clue as to the wearer's view to life: rakish, coy, shy, haughty, sulky, indifferent. So much to be said with a cap! Another customer wore a raspberry beret, while three others had donned cowboy hats for the evening. Further inspection revealed a purple fez with appliquéd rhinestones, a green Jackie O pillbox number sporting an assortment of feathers, a rubber bathing cap encrusted with glow-in-the-dark stars, and two postmodern Carmen Mirandas seated near the piano. The first bore a unique concoction of vegetables, while the other had gone in for a marine theme—papier-mâché fish and a squid tangled up in seaweed.

"Unusual hat?" Zach said. He arched his eyebrows and surveyed the room. "Has Grace ever been in a gay bar?"

Their waiter, a Mexican twink with a winning smile and highly delectable ears, returned balancing a tray of glasses. Brad tipped him handsomely and watched his nubile bottom glide back through the crowd. Coupled or not, in Puerto Vallarta love-lust came with every drink order.

The twosome sat at a corner table with a good view of the room. They relaxed as the chanteuse warbled a set of Brazilian love songs to the driving patter of a blind piano player.

"Very cool," Zach pronounced, his head bouncing with the restless rhythms.

An ebullient group came through the door, their laughter reaching to the very back of the bar. The leader was an attractive older man with silver hair tucked neatly beneath a sailing cap. From across the room, he caught Bradford's eye and winked.

"Looks like you've got an admirer," Zach said. "Could this be our contact?"

Brad smiled and lifted his glass to the man. "He looks a bit old, but you never know."

The man detached himself from his group and headed to their table.

"You boys have such beautiful smiles." He extended a hand. "Sebastian Mathers."

They shook as Brad and Zach introduced themselves.

"A pleasure," Sebastian said. "What brings you to PV?"

"The three S's," Brad replied. "Sun, sand and surf. How about you?"

"The fourth S." Sebastian tipped his cap. "Sailing. I just arrived from up-coast."

Brad waited expectantly, but Sebastian was not forthcoming with the code phrase that would have identified him as their contact. The trio exchanged small talk about bars and restaurants in the city by the bay. The conversation soon extended to other cities and countries. By his own estimation, Sebastian seemed to have travelled nearly everywhere on his yacht.

"Everywhere but Tibet," he concluded.

"I've been there!" Zach said.

Sebastian looked impressed. "Then we'll all have to go together. You can be our tour guide. Can we get there by boat?" he said with a wink.

At that moment, Sebastian's youthful group called out to him with one voice: "Oh, da-a-addy!" The waiter had arrived with a bill. The silver-haired captain glanced over his shoulder and gave them a "Hold On" signal. He turned back to Brad and Zach. "Are you boys in town for a while?"

"We're here for a couple of weeks, at least," Brad said. "It's hard to say just yet how long we're staying."

"Ah! You're men of leisure, like me. You must come for a sail on my boat sometime."

"Love to," Brad said. "How do we find you?"

Sebastian made a wide sweep of his arm that seemed to include most of Banderas Bay. "I'm right out there most days. And when I'm not, I'm just a hop, skip and a swell down the coast at one resort town or another." He glanced around the bar. "At night you can usually find me at one of PV's watering holes. Garbo's is my favorite, 'cause all the beautiful boys come here eventually. Like you two."

Sebastian's group signalled to him again. "Duty calls," he said, tipping his hat and returning to his friends.

One look confirmed Sebastian's comment—the bar was indeed full of beautiful men. Three tables over a spectacular pair of muscle tykes—one blonde, the other dark—sat gazing into each other's eyes, desire etched on their youthful faces. With one glance, it was clear to see they were blissfully in love and enjoying their night on the town in one of the world's most magical resorts. *I'm old enough to know that Beauty isn't Truth,* Brad reminded himself, *but it sure makes for one hell of an attractive date for the evening.*

In the middle of the room, a redhead half-heartedly resisted the fawnings of a beefy party boy and a tall skinny man wearing a billowy blouse and a Mad Hatter top hat. The pair had nearly coaxed the man's T-shirt over his shoulders. Within seconds they'd removed it completely, revealing a nicely pumped torso. A trail of fleece ran from the redhead's pectorals down to his navel, where it swirled briefly before disappearing into his waistband. He could easily have been an off-duty model for *Men's Fitness*.

"Swoon!" shouted the tall skinny man, twirling the redhead's T-shirt overhead.

The other boy started in on the man's belt buckle and soon had his pants down around his knees. A skimpy pair of briefs—outlining a sizeable package and a nicely sculpted butt—gleamed in the bar's dim light.

"I'm a doctor!" the redhead wailed. "I can't be seen doing things like this in public!"

"Then let's go back to your hotel. We'll do them there!" the beefy boy called out.

Half the room turned to watch the doctor, now wearing only his briefs and a scandalized smile. Scandalized or not, he made no attempt to restore his attire to its proper state. In fact, he looked as though he hoped some-one might make him do even more things he shouldn't be seen doing in public.

The thin man in the top hat appeared to have lost interest in the game. He glided over to a cluster of men standing nearby. With a fey hand to his cheek, he called out. "Did you hear the news? Celine Dion's in town! Ska-*ream!*"

The group was soon aflutter on learning the sultry French-Canadian diva was practically in their midst. Brad watched as the man in the billowy shirt skirted from group to group, badgering and annoying each one in turn. Eve-rywhere you went these days, Brad noted, there seemed to be a tall skinny guy who bugged everybody and made his own sound effects.

At that moment, the man looked over and caught Brad's glance. He seemed to take Brad's bemused smile for an invitation. He strode over, sleeves fluttering, and latched onto Brad's shoulder, towering over him like a transvestite scarecrow.

"I take it you're a Celine fan?" Brad asked, looking up into the wide-set blue eyes.

"The biggest ever!" the scarecrow replied. "Gush!" He removed his hat and held out his hand. "Jarod Scythes—like the Grim Reaper."

"Brad Fairfax ... Zach Tyler." They shook.

Jarod squeezed his palms together in a manner remi-niscent of Lillian Gish portraying happiness. "Wouldn't you just love to be on Celine's yacht right now, enjoying a moonlight sail and sipping margaritas while yummy Mexi-can boys did unspeakable things to your unmentionables?" Jarod cried. "Big sigh!"

"Sounds delightful," Brad said.

Jarod's eyes lighted on Zach. "You have blue hair!

Egad!"

"It's the Curaçao," Zach said, holding up his drink.

"How extraordinary! I shall have some."

At that moment, the singer notched up several keys as the bar rippled with excitement. The room had become very hot and crowded.

"What are you boys doing here in the land of cocaine and cactus?" Jarod asked.

"Just enjoying a little break from the snow back home," Brad said. "And you?"

Jarod waved his arms about as though conjuring an entire landscape. "Looking for foreign intrigue," he said. "I'm trying to cultivate a reputation as a man of mystery!"

"Vallarta's definitely the place for it," Brad said.

"So they say!" Jarod's eyes flashed like Theda Bara oozing seduction. Just then, something on the far side of the room caught his attention. His sleeves billowed and he was off again, a sailboat in motion. "Toodles!" he cried, tipping his hat as he steered through the crowd.

Brad exchanged a glance with Zach. "I don't know about the mystery part, but he's certainly an oddball."

"He's probably working off a lot of repression back home," Zach said.

Brad looked around. Sebastian and his troupe of merrymakers had disappeared. So had the love-struck, look-a-like couple. New faces came through the door every few seconds as the party burbled on. Greetings were exchanged and introductions made. Martinis were stirred, shaken, folded, risottoed and poured. The heat intensified as the crowd crammed even closer and the chanteuse grew sultrier, aiming her seductive lyrics over the heads of the men who eyed one another and prayed that the exotic-looking profile they were staring at two tables away wouldn't turn out to be just another accountant from Boise.

Brad was finishing his drink when a veritable Adonis entered the bar. The air stilled and heads swivelled toward the newcomer as though a magnet had yanked them all in one direction. Here was Dolph Lundgren's younger, butcher brother. The son of GI Joe crossed with a six-pack of circuit boys in heat. These were cheekbones you could sharpen an axe on, colossal chest muscles that rippled beneath a silk shirt like a sultry breeze on a Spanish isle. But something told Brad this guy was an impostor in the land of Wynken, Blynken and Nod. There was a skittish cast to his features, a wariness that said, "What have I got myself into now?" where there should have been mute, undying certainty about his godhood status. "I'm not gay," his look pleaded as he glanced nervously about, aware that all eyes—*men's* eyes—had locked directly onto him. Even in the dark, his blush radiated across the room.

He hesitated then reached down self-consciously and tugged something from his hip pocket. Brad watched in fascination as he placed a velvet-trimmed Santa Claus hat on his head, the long white tassel hanging down over his shoulders. *Very* unusual, Brad noted.

"Contact," he murmured to Zach.

Zach nodded. "I take it back. Grace *has* been in gay bars."

They watched the man scan the room till his eyes met theirs. Brad inclined his head while maintaining eye contact. He waited for Dolph to make the first move.

At that moment, a waiter approached them balancing a tray of drinks. This wasn't the waiter of the nubile bottom Brad had watched so attentively earlier on. This one was older and more muscular. He kept his eyes averted as he handed over a second round of drinks.

Brad turned to Zach. "Did you ask for these?"

Zach shook his head. Brad shrugged and reached into his pocket to pay the man, but the waiter had already begun to retreat across the crowded room.

"Hey, wait!" he called out.

The man stopped and glanced back with heavily lidded eyes. The whites were red-tinged and almost demonic looking. Brad reached out to Zach's upraised arm and lowered the glass.

"Don't drink that," he said. He held his glass out to the waiter. "I think there's something wrong with this. Will you taste it?"

Panic spread across the man's face. "No speak English." He turned abruptly and headed for the bar.

Brad took a stride forward and bumped headlong into the man in the Santa Claus cap.

The man forced a smile. "I got some toys fer yer box," he said with a finely honed Tennessee twang. "Perhaps y'all'd like to take delivery?"

Brad stopped, his eyes following the quickly vanishing waiter. "Great," he said. "My box number is 77."

The man nodded with relief. "Ayuh."

Over the man's shoulder, Brad saw the waiter slip into the kitchen. "We saw your sleigh coming down earlier. Good drop, Santa."

The man hesitated. "I think I mighta been followed," he said. "Can we all step outdoors?"

Brad nodded. "Give me a minute and I'll catch up with you. I've got a little problem too. Turn right outside the doors and head up the steps. I'll meet you at the top of the hill."

The man looked relieved to be quitting the premises. The crowd seemed to swallow him up as he headed for the exit.

Brad turned to Zach. "Let's find that waiter."

A surprised bartender watched as they pushed past him and into the kitchen. Their original waiter lay on the floor, his eyelids quivering as though he'd been drugged or knocked out. A back door opened onto an alleyway.

"Stay with him!" Brad shouted to Zach, as he sprang to the doorway.

Bradford raced down the alley and around to the front of the bar. The fake waiter had vanished, but there on the ground was a Santa's cap with a long white tassel. A dark stain led away from the cap. Brad followed it with growing trepidation.

He hadn't far to go. Around the next corner, the drawling agent lay sprawled in a slowly spreading pool of blood. Brad knelt and felt for a pulse. It was faint. The man's eyes opened. He tried to speak, but he was choking.

"Take it easy," Brad said.

He lifted the man's head. Blood streamed from a wound in his abdomen. Down the street, someone screamed.

"Who are you?" Brad asked.

"Si—*Silver*," the man gasped.

"Agent Silver?"

The man's hand reached inside his jacket. "Give this to…"

His head fell back as a small gasp escaped him.

A crowd had gathered. People spilled out of the clubs lining the street. Brad heard someone yelling for help. He felt inside the man's jacket and gripped something hard and thin, a little larger than his palm. He slipped it into his own pocket.

Brad stood and walked quickly up the street. He took out his cell phone as he went, dialling a number he'd used only once before in a similar situation. The line picked up somewhere far away.

"Agent deactivated," he said softly.

3

"He said his name was Silver." Brad stood on the balcony of the hillside villa, talking on his cell phone. Fireworks were going off in the distance, illuminating the bay in sudden streamers of colour.

"Silver?" Grace said. "That's not who I sent to meet you."

Brad pulled a slim, bloodstained case from his pocket.

"What did he look like?" she snapped.

"Young, crew cut. Military type."

"Attractive? Muscular? Tennessee twang?"

"That's him."

"Hmmm," she pronounced meditatively. "That was Panther, my parachutist. Maybe he had something to deliver to somebody named Silver. Or possibly he was confused."

Brad listened to his boss turning over the possibilities. He wondered what she felt at times like these—remorse over the loss of a life or simply annoyance at the problems she faced with her agent's demise? With his very last breath, a dying man had been loyal to his organization. He hadn't asked Brad to take a message to a loved one or tell his mother he'd been thinking of her as he died. He'd simply tried to convey the urgency he felt in fulfilling his duty. Did that mean anything to Grace?

"He wanted me to give something to somebody," Brad added. He looked down at the bloodied case with the photograph of a popular singer on it. "I don't think I found much of anything, though."

"Much of anything being…?"

"A CD. A Celine Dion CD, to be precise."

There was a silence. "Intriguing," Grace said at last.

Brad wondered how much she would reveal to him about what was going on. What passed through Grace's mind was anybody's guess. She was like an iceberg—cold, silent, opaque. Only a small percentage of her was discernible, while the greater portion remained unseen.

"I don't know what to tell you, Red. You'll have to keep your eyes open and your ears to the ground. Something must be up or our man wouldn't have been taken out like that. Maybe his killer already got whatever he wanted you to deliver. At present I have no idea why he was killed or who's responsible. You're going to have to find out for me."

"I'll do my best."

"I suggest you get that boy of yours working on it. He has phenomenal talents. He aced the Remote Viewing examination. I can't wait till the CIA learns they teach those skills for free in Tibet when they've spent billions training their agents here."

Brad could hear her gloating. "What do you want us to do for now?" he asked.

"Don't do anything for now. Let me clear this mess up first. I'll get back to you." She clicked off.

Zach stood watching him from the doorway. "What did she say?"

"Not much. I'm still in the dark about what's going on here. What did you find?"

"Twelve French songs…"

"Anything else?"

"Something intriguing. Come and see."

He followed Zach inside and stood looking over his shoulder. The laptop screen showed a photograph of the pop chanteuse alongside a list of song titles. At first Brad couldn't see anything unusual, but he soon detected the faint glow around a handful of letters embedded in the words.

"There are five of them," Zach pointed out. "B—E—I—R—L."

"Any idea what they spell?"

"Nothing in English, is my guess," Zach said.

"How about French?"

"Or Spanish."

They both looked again and at the same moment cried, "Libre!"

"It's the same word in both languages," Brad said. "But what does it refer to? Is it in any of the song titles?"

They searched, but could find nothing corresponding to the word.

"Click on one of the tracks," Brad suggested.

Zach did so and Dion's voice crooned a lilting lullaby.

Brad cocked his ears and listened. "Not Maria Callas," he opined at last, with a shake of his head.

"In both French and Spanish the word 'libre' denotes the idea of being liberated," Zach said. "But in English, the word means something more like 'no cost' or 'gratis.' As in free software, free beer…"

They were both looking at the tag 'Bonus Track' at the bottom of the play-list.

Bradford shrugged. "Be my guest," he said.

Zach clicked on the words and looked up with a smile of satisfaction. "It's a map!"

"So where's the buried treasure?" Brad said, examining the image.

"This is the coastline around Banderas Bay, with what appears to be a short travel itinerary," Zach said. "Other than that, there's nothing that would make you think it was unusual…"

"…except for the unusual fact that it's been buried on a CD handed to me by a dying secret agent," Brad finished.

"Exactly!"

"And what do we make of that?"

Zach thought for a moment. "Somebody doesn't want his or her location known."

"Right—at least not to the wrong people. I think we need to find out why."

Zach cocked his head. "Why isn't Grace telling us more about what's going on down here?"

"If I knew why Grace did anything, I'd be a happier man."

Brad was used to his boss's caustic manner, but her extreme reticence in this latest matter was unusual. In the past few weeks, she'd been as close-lipped as he'd ever known her to be. All he knew was that they'd been sent suddenly to Puerto Vallarta to make contact with another agent. From there, they were to have learned more about the operation. But that agent was now dead and his boss was not forthcoming about anything. It occurred to Brad that he might be just one agent in a chain, each of whom had a part to play. It was also possible that no one person at Box 77—Grace included—knew the entire story. If so, there was no doubt a very good reason for that too. Still, Brad's instincts said there was more here than met the eye. And with murder added to the mix, there was every reason to want to see the larger picture. Warning bells were clanging loud and clear.

The full scope of Box 77 was and would probably

always remain a mystery. Its mandate was clear: to counter any threat that challenged the tenuous balance of world peace—or at least what little of it there was—though where the organization got its cases from and who assigned them, he couldn't say. All Brad knew was that Box 77 took orders from no government body and remained financially independent.

In the meantime, here he was with his blue-haired *amor* in one of the world's sexiest gay resorts with no end of sun, sand and surf. And while Zach would normally have been excluded from tactical operations, he was officially on his way to becoming a full-fledged member of Box 77. For that reason, Grace had seen fit to include him. He'd co-incidentally elected to begin his training with a special initiation ceremony—a Vision Quest—that would take place in the Mexican desert. Brad wasn't sure exactly what this entailed, but Zach would no doubt fill him in when the time came.

Brad looked over at his partner. He was definitely growing up. When they first met, Zach had been all of nineteen, still more boy than man. He'd shaved once a week at most and almost never attended a gym. Now, three years later, his abs were ripped, his biceps bulging and a dusting of hair had appeared on his chest over the past few months. Against all odds, Zach was now a clearly defined part of Brad's life.

Love.

Secret agents were supposed to be immune to such things, but someone had decided to make an exception in this case. The rules of engagement, however, were about to change in a very big way. Things had been fine when Zach was just a regular citizen of the free world, but Brad had no idea what might happen next.

Zach's pre-training qualifications had been a bit

obscure, not to mention exotic. While on retreat in Tibet and India, he'd met an elite group of monks who claimed him as the reincarnation of a spiritually-advanced 16th century lama. From what Brad understood, Zach's training had enhanced some natural abilities in line with a similar course the CIA offered its recruits under the name "Remote Viewing." According to Zach, Remote Viewing was nothing more than a fancy term for "intuition," but trained to a very high degree in a way that endowed the practitioner with tactically useful extra-sensory abilities of the sort ridiculed by the public for decades, yet secretly taught by various security agencies, including the CIA, who cultivated such skills for their own nefarious purposes.

Zach had yet to undergo the months of rigorous training required to join Box 77. Not only were those months intense and gruelling, Brad knew from his own initiation, but they were also extremely secretive. Though Brad suspected he'd been in Peru, he'd never been sure. He recalled a long flight on a plane with blacked-out windows, followed by a slow crawl in an all-terrain vehicle through dense vegetation and, finally, a lengthy blindfolded walk to a location with no visible access roads. The heat and vegetation were tropical—there'd been no doubt about that. Rocky hills ringed the camp, while waterfalls were plentiful, but he might just as easily have been in Africa or Borneo. A single daylong trek yielded breathtaking views of jungle-covered mountains that went on for miles, but offered no clue where he might have been.

In any case, sightseeing had been low on his list of priorities. The training was no picnic. What he'd learned during this period were the four phases of tactical operation: planning, reconnaissance, action, and extraction. First you planned and then you counter-planned and then you counter-planned some more, because it was a given that things would not go as expected. Next you observed, listened and learned as much about your sphere of operation as possible, getting as close to the heart of things as you could. Finally, you moved in and did whatever you had to do and then you vanished, leaving no trace behind.

It was that simple. Or maybe not.

Of the twenty-four willing, determined and highly capable men and women who started out, eighteen had dropped out, one after another, leaving six superbly honed recruits, their minds and bodies sharpened beyond measure, who had bonded so closely the ties might never be broken. In fact, Brad was sure only death could break those bonds, as happened on at least one occasion.

From that point on, there was no turning back. His training had left him a different man entirely from the one he'd been before. And he wondered now, not without a tinge of worry, and not for the first time, just who Zach might be on his return.

Zach yawned. "Bed?" he asked.

Brad was lost in thought. After a moment, he nodded. "You go ahead. I'll join you soon."

He waited till Zach got in bed and turned out the light before heading back out to the balcony. Music wafted up from far below. The wind was just beginning to cool. A night breeze grazed his skin, as though enticing him away from the patio and out over the sleeping city, tempting him to fly. Puerto Vallarta lay before him, a velvet cape encrusted with stars. It seemed to emanate from the blackness of the ocean and the soft crescent of sand surrounding Banderas Bay. This was one of the most seductive cities he'd ever known. It was also the scene of a recent murder. No matter how he looked at it, that now involved him and, by extension, Zach. Whatever lay ahead promised to be tricky, possibly even treacherous. Yet again, Brad felt unsettled at not knowing why they were in PV. That alone was reason to fear whatever challenges faced them.

At least he and Zach were there together in this. That much was good. He breathed deeply, searching inside himself for that elusive tickle of contentment he'd felt lately. Yes, there it was, underlying everything—a voice whispering that this was completeness, that rarest sense of being fully alive, here and now, with someone to share his life and love. Slowly, he felt his misgivings drop away. They would get through this. No matter what obstacles they faced, and no matter how much Zach changed in the days to come, he resolved that nothing would pull them apart. And whether Grace did or did not feel remorse over the fate of her agents, including Agent Red, it would not shake Bradford's world or change him in any way. Come what may, he and Zach would face it together.

For a split second he had an almost overpowering sensation of being watched. Maybe it was God or some invisible eye winking down at him from somewhere out in the universe or just a night bird flying overhead, but he felt that someone or something was aware of his presence as he stood there in the darkness contemplating his life and fate. And then, just as suddenly, it vanished. A new sensation came surging in, making him feel in some intangible way as though he owned everything he could see before him.

He looked up. Clouds wheeled overhead like night phantoms, obscuring the stars, but only momentarily. A spectacular moon rose over the horizon. If he could reach his hand high enough, he might just touch it…

4

Just before dawn, two sleepy boys woke to what sounded like a trash compactor gearing up to crush something large and virtually indestructible. In Puerto Vallarta, no matter how secluded your guesthouse, you were never far from a rooster. Brad wrapped his arms around Zach, pulling him close and rubbing his belly.

Zach moaned with pleasure. "What time did you come to bed? I must have fallen asleep waiting."

"It was late. I had things to think about."

"Like?"

"Like—why Celine Dion?"

"Oh, the CD!" Zach sat up. "Simple—because no one would suspect anything unusual of a pop song compilation, whereas if you'd found a CD of Buddhist monks chanting you might stop and look at it twice."

Brad nodded. "I always overlook the obvious, don't I?"

Zach grinned.

"Grace said I was to put you to work on this. She said she's never seen anyone do as well as you in the prelim exams. Apparently your Remote Viewing technique is more advanced than the CIA's."

Zach shrugged. "It should be—it's thousands of years older than theirs. It comes from Tibet and before that probably from Atlantis."

Brad shook his head. "Atlantis?"

"The Atlanteans were way ahead of their time. They

built the pyramids, of course."

"Pyramids? As in Egypt?"

"Sure. Everyone knows that."

"How exotic," Brad said. "So where did you get these powers?"

"We all have them in latent form, but they need to be developed. I learned a few tricks while I was in Tibet. The most important thing is to learn how to open your chakras properly."

Brad blinked.

"Chakra is a Sanskrit word that translates roughly as 'spinning wheel.' Chakras are energy vortices."

"And where do we find these chakras?"

"On our bodies. Each one corresponds to one of the seven endocrine glands. The only problem is, most people can't see them."

"The glands?"

"No, silly—the chakras."

"And since we can't see them, we know they exist how?"

"We can't prove their existence scientifically, because they're spiritual energy centres. Being a physical-based knowledge, western science hasn't developed sufficiently to measure them. And what it can't measure, it won't accept as a reality. The closest it gets is with the Kirlian electro-magnetic photographs of auras."

"So I repeat—how do we know that chakras exist?"

"How do we know the mind exists? Or an emotion? Can you show me either one?"

"No, but if I pick up a chair and smash it against a wall, you'd probably guess I was angry."

"Or drunk. But that's deductive reasoning, not proof of an emotion. What you'd really be expressing is the effect of an emotion, which leads us to postulate that emotions exist. Of course, we can measure things like blood pressure, but you still can't *see* an emotion. Nevertheless, we know they exist because we've all felt them. In Tibet I learned to see chakras when I meditate. And while I can't show you a chakra, I can show you what I can do with them. For instance, when I close my eyes and concentrate, it's like I'm seeing your body in X-ray vision, but with a full-colour spectrum."

He passed a hand over Brad's chest. "In this area"—he pressed down on Brad's forearm just below the elbow—"I see the aura as green, which tells me you've bruised yourself here…"

"You're right. I banged it during our espionage game yesterday. But why green?"

"Because green is the vibratory frequency that body tissue gives off when it's healing. A bone fracture would be more serious and might generate a red frequency."

"But how do you locate it?"

Zach's eyes opened. "I don't. My subconscious shows me what to look for."

"Wait, wait, wait … back up a moment. How does your subconscious know what to do?"

Zach shrugged. "I tell it what to look for. The subconscious is connected with the Universal Mind…"

"Oh, the Universal Mind!"

"…which of course has access to everything that's ever happened and ever will. It's like a giant, invisible library. Once you know that, it's just like trying to locate a memory. If it's there, it will come to you. It would take forever to explain more than that."

Brad rolled his eyes. "Oh, my poor head!"

"It's okay. You'll learn to trust it in time."

Brad grinned. "I trust you, anyway."

"That's a start."

"And it's a good thing I do, because otherwise I might think you were nuts."

"Time for a chakra lesson." Zach rolled on top of Brad and straddled his chest with his legs. "There are seven main chakras. The Bible refers to these as the Book with Seven Seals, only it's supposed to be something scary and all End-Of-Time-ish. But it's not." He placed a hand on top of Brad's head. "This is your crown chakra. It connects with your higher spiritual centres. When it's correctly balanced, it gives off a white-violet vibration."

He placed a fingertip between Brad's eyebrows. "This is your third eye. It deals with telepathy and extra-sensory communication. Usually it's indigo, while your throat"—his hand crept downwards—"is blue, like the sky. The throat chakra deals with communication."

"What happens if my chakra colours aren't what they're supposed to be?"

"If they're too light or too dark, it means they're under- or over-developed. If they're a different colour altogether, it might indicate you're going through some sort of change or turmoil. For instance, if you had a sore throat I might see the energy around your throat chakra as brown and muddied. But when your energy is balanced the chakras show up brilliantly, like the colours of the rainbow—red, orange, yellow, green, blue, indigo and violet."

"The same rainbow as the gay nation?"

"You got it."

"So we really are the chosen people."

"Some would say so." Zach's hand continued down Brad's chest. "Here's your heart chakra. It's a vibrant emerald green. This tells me you're emotionally open and loving." He smiled and closed his eyes again, searching out Brad's anatomy with his hands. "Right here—the solar plexus—is your 'sun centre.' If you think of your body as a map of the universe, this is where the sun would lie, right in the middle of everything."

Zach drew a finger down Brad's abdomen, below and to the left of his navel. "This is your sacral chakra. It rules creativity and reproduction. Yours is a very bright orange."

"What does that mean?"

Zach opened his eyes and smiled. "It means you're highly sexually charged."

"*Quel surprise!* You're sitting on it at the moment."

"And finally"—he reached around to Brad's tailbone—"this is your root chakra. It's red. It touches on core values and belief systems. It's our tribal chakra. In a sense, it's where we come from before we learn to be individuals."

"Okay, so now I know my colours. What does it all mean?"

"When you meditate on the colours—literally envisioning them in your chakras—then you open and develop their latent energies. Ten minutes a day is all it takes—starting from the crown chakra and descending to the root, then back up again."

"And if I'm successful?"

"You'll start to see images. That's the coded language of the chakras. For instance, when I first opened my crown chakra, I saw a flower blooming. My teacher said it was the thousand-petalled lotus—a sign I was doing the meditations correctly."

"And the purpose of it all?"

"With the CIA, the purpose was to use it for a spying tool. That's why Grace is so impressed with what I can do." Zach's eyes were glowing as he stared down at

Brad. "For everyone else, it elevates our consciousness level. Increased self-awareness on the part of each individual also raises the planetary vibration. And bingo! Before you know it, there'll be peace on earth and the end of wars and suffering. We'll feed the hungry, cure the sick and house the homeless. Life could be a blast down here on planet earth if we'd all work on raising our vibratory patterns."

"That's a pretty tall order. Is there anything else? Something a little more day-to-day practical, maybe?"

Zach cocked his head. "If you meditate daily, it will increase your telepathic abilities, give you clairvoyant dreams and psychic insight. You'll shake hands with someone and know immediately if they have good or bad intentions toward you."

"That would be handy," Brad said.

Zach nodded. "You'll also know who's going to be a loyal lover and who's going to break your heart and leave you stranded—that sort of thing. Some people develop healing abilities. That's what happened in my case. Others develop artistically. If you're financially inclined, you might get a sense for which stocks to invest in and which to avoid. The images and symbols give clues to everything. Not long after we met, I placed my hand on your heart chakra one night when you were sleeping and I saw a lion. I knew then that in love you were strong, fierce and loyal."

Brad's jaw dropped. "You cheated!"

"I just took a shortcut to find out who you were." Zach winked. "I like to use my abilities to their fullest. Besides, I'd already fallen in love with you. I wanted to know what kind of ride I was in for."

"And you say anyone can do this?"

Zach nodded. "It's a skill, not a talent. But you have to practice. If Shirley McLaine can do it, so can you."

"In terms of symbols," Brad said, "what does a lizard mean?"

"A lizard symbolizes death and resurrection."

"Why death and resurrection?"

"Because lizards hibernate in the cold seasons, so ancient cultures believed they died in fall and came back to life when winter passed. Why do you ask?"

"Because there's one staring down at us from the ceiling," Brad said.

Zach turned to view the grey reptile looking back at them. It blinked and scurried away.

Brad ran his hands along the inside of Zach's thighs, massaging them until the beginning of a respectable erection pointed at him. "And what does a snake mean?"

Zach grinned. "It means my orange chakra is happy to see you."

Brad raised himself up on his elbows. "Come here. I think I need to examine this in close-up."

Half an hour later, Brad lay in a deck chair watching Zach paddle back and forth across the pool. His swim finished, Zach emerged dripping in the faint morning light. Brad saw him stoop and pick something up.

"Look," Zach said, holding out a white-and-grey striped feather. "I think we were visited by an owl last night."

Brad turned the feather in his hand, studying the interlinking bristles from point to tip, where the quill narrowed and ran free to its end.

"Owls are a symbol of wisdom," Zach said.

"What sort of wisdom?"

"In native cultures they represent shamanic wisdom. They also denote the ability to come and go secretively, without being seen."

"First death and resurrection. Now shamanic wisdom," Brad mused quietly. "And the day has hardly begun."

Zach went inside to dress. Brad sat there holding the feather, looking down over the awakening city. He was in the same spot fifteen minutes later when Zach returned and put a steaming cup of coffee in his hand.

"It never occurred to me before that symbols can have real power," Brad said, looking down at the feather. "This one took me back a long way."

"It triggered some memories?"

Brad shook his head. "More than memories. It triggered a whole raft of emotions."

Zach nodded. "It's not surprising. Symbols connect us directly with the sub-conscious, where memories are stored. They can be very powerful stimulants. Wave a flag in front of a political prisoner and watch how he reacts."

After a leisurely breakfast, they packed their gear into beach bags and headed out over the walkway. Brad paused briefly to look at the rocks below. It hadn't been very difficult for him to breach the house's security system yesterday, all things considered. As the gate clanged shut behind them, he wondered just how safe they were if someone really wanted to get in.

5

Half an hour later, Brad and Zach found themselves crossing the gleaming white sands of Playa de los Muertos.
Every gay men who hadn't stayed out too late the previous night was now busy spreading towels, donning bathing suits, absorbing suntan lotion, ordering *cervezas* and
staking a claim to as much beach as he could get. Turf
wars here were legendary. Brad watched the others from
beneath the shade of an umbrella, amazed by the urge to
become as dark as possible, health warnings to the contrary. Perched around him were men of all hues, ranging
in shade from the paper white of the newly arrived,
through the coppery red of the overdone gringos on their
seven-day sun binges, to the nutty brown of the natives
who wandered the beach plying their trades as sellers of
arts and crafts, instant tattoos, hats, *hamacas*, clothing, jew-
ellery, musical instruments, pedicures, manicures, massages,
fresh fruit, pastries, the lost etchings of Leonardo, and
tantalizing skewers of grilled seafood.

Dreamy clouds hovered over the gleaming strip of
hotels in the famed *Zona Romantica*. At the heart of it stood
the world-renowned Blue Parrot Hotel. The Parrot was
the place to stay for anyone determined to be as close to
the beach as possible. The only way you might get any
closer—apart from sleeping overnight on the sands—was
to stay in one of the many colourful pleasure boats tethered just offshore.

From his sling-back chair, Brad commanded a view

of the entire beach. He'd donned a long-sleeved shirt and full-length cotton trousers as a precaution against the sun. On a small side table, he lined up bottles of suntan lotion, skin creams, digestive aids, headache tablets and bicarbonate of soda, giving the waiter careful instructions on what sort of glass he required his drink to come in. *Sin hielo*. Without ice, *gracias*. The humble *E. coli* bacteria came in many guises, he well knew. Zach, on the other hand, ate a skewer of grilled shrimp, downed it with a cool glass of ice water, and proceeded to peel off everything but his bathing trunks, to the admiring glance of every man in the vicinity.

Anyone who's been to Puerto Vallarta knows that Playa de los Muertos is as famous for its spectacular beauty as for its spectacular dangers. As usual, gay men had claimed the most visually stunning location as far from everything and everyone else as possible, though in truth there was little competition for this secluded stretch of sand. It hadn't been christened "Beach of the Dead" for nothing. While affording excellent body surfing, the waves could be deadly as they pummelled unwary swimmers against the treacherous shore over and over again, until they weakened and sometimes drowned. Accidents involving broken bones and dislocated limbs, while preferable to drowning, were not uncommon. The waves that day seemed especially turbulent.

"Not a day to go swimming alone, I suspect," someone remarked over Brad's shoulder.

They turned to see their silver-haired admirer from the night before. Sebastian beamed down at them, hair neatly tucked beneath his captain's cap. Off to the right, his rowdy troupe were busy unfurling their towels on a patch of sand in full sun, far from the protective covering of umbrellas or shady palapas.

"Greetings!" Zach called.

Sebastian glanced curiously at Brad's full-clad figure. "Are you cold?" he asked.

Brad shook his head. "Just playing it safe," he said. "I don't want to get burned my first day on the beach."

Sebastian chuckled. "Not much chance of that." He surveyed the mini pharmacy, picking up a bottle of suntan lotion. "I didn't know it came in 150 SPF."

"Why worry?" Brad replied.

"Good looking crop today," Sebastian said as he scanned the bodies lying on the beach. "How did you boys make out last night? I bet those smiles of yours were popular with the bar crowd."

Brad's mind returned to the happenings of the previous evening. "Popular" was not the word he would have chosen. "Your offer of a sail was still the best one we got all night," he said.

"Glad to hear it! I gather I missed some excitement after I left. Was there really a shooting?"

"It was a knifing, I believe. In fact, someone got killed."

Sebastian gave them a sober look. "Drug wars, I'd bet. Probably the Federales. They're not the nicest guys you'll ever run into. You don't want to cross them," he said darkly.

Brad knew about the Federales and their reputation for rough justice. And while he didn't doubt that some of them took the law into their own hands, he couldn't think why a Federal officer would kill an international agent on a mission of peace. Still, in Puerto Vallarta anything was possible.

Sebastian turned his gaze to the bright vista before them, covering his brow with a hand and pointing across the water. "See the rainbow flag on that two-master? That's me." He gave a nod over his shoulder. "I also keep a permanent suite at the Blue Parrot for late-night emergencies, but if you don't find me on the beach, just get a water taxi and come out and join me. You're welcome on board any time."

"Oh, da-a-addy!" someone called out. "Credit card, please!"

Sebastian looked over at his vagabond gang where a waiter held up a bill. "Be right there!" He turned back to Brad and Zach. "Don't forget my offer," he said, before trudging over the sand to join his group.

Chairs were filling up all around them. Any later and they might not have found seats. Waiters ran back and forth across the burning sands, taking orders and dodging the Chiclet Chicos, the three- and four-year-old waifs who plied their wares to the friendly, the sympathetic and the plain hung-over, trading smiles and chewing gum for a handful of pesos and the right to suffer in peace.

Off to the right, Brad recognized the ultra-hot look-a-like couple from the martini bar the previous night. They were salt and pepper, chocolate and vanilla, mint and julep. By daylight, the only discernable difference in their looks was that one was blonde and the other dark. In fact, they might have been twins. The pair lay on identical lounge chairs, their buff legs entwined like oversized pretzels. They wore identical swimsuits over identical thirty-inch waists, but in different colours. One crotch bulged orange and the other blue.

The pair were spectacular specimens of manhood by any standard, but there was one standard in particular in which they excelled: that of the hair department. It adorned their heads, legs, arms, chests and even butts. And while the hirsute man need not be of any particular nationality, it may be observed that Brazilian men (and a few Brazilian women) seem naturally blessed in that department. And, as many gay men will tell you, neither too little nor too much hair will suffice when it comes to the search for the perfect man.

Wherein lies the appeal, we might well ask? In a mere dusting or a deep shadow? In a massive forest or a golfer's green? Do you lust for a shag carpet gliding over pecs of iron or a thin trail unfurling across a taught solar plexus and encircling the navel? Such questions, of course, are hotly debated by the connoisseur. Will a small bristling hedge on the shoulders suffice or do you crave a mighty field of wheat across the chest in which to lose yourself with abandon? A hairy head or a shiny one? Full facial mask or a mere hint of peach fuzz? Massive arms gilded in fur and legs girded like a ridgeback or toes adorned in a frosty finery with knuckles festooned in bristling spears? Eyebrows and nose hairs like a yeti or as smooth as a baby's bottom? Such are the telling details when it comes to hair.

Some will even admit to having such an intense fetish for hirsutedness that the hair factor assumes an even greater importance in its erotic appeal than other more obvious attributes. There's no end to the variations it can acquire. For a man who craves a plethora of hair cannot abide a smooth man nor a smooth fetishist sleep with his more hairy brethren. "My brother Esau is an hairy man," cried Jacob, as he girded himself in goatskins to fool their father, Isaac. "But I am a smooth man." And thus he stole his brother's birthright. So it went in biblical days, and so it goeth in some circles even now.

The right amount of hair can be all-important, as many of us know. Brad knew of one happily married couple in his younger days, a pretty pair who'd met during the grunge music heyday, both fully bearded. They were happy, travelled everywhere together, and were seldom seen apart. Fans of both REM and Nirvana, alas, they found they had to part once the fad was over and each had shaved his epoch-defining features down to a receding chin and backward creeping hairline as respectability and middle age beckoned, neither being able to recognize his partner afterwards. Sadly, for want of hair, all attraction was lost.

As for the Brazilians, the pair was neither too hairy nor too smooth, having just the right amount of hair to make for the perfect man. At least, so far as Bradford was concerned, our hero being inclined to enact the part of Goldilocks in pronouncing them just right! To each his own, as they say.

Taking his eyes off the pair for a second, Brad recognized within a fifty-foot span at least a dozen faces from the previous evening. It seemed the crowd from Garbo's had simply rematerialized, but with fewer clothes, on the beach that morning.

He turned to Zach. "Do you think it's a coincidence that all those people who were at the bar last night at the time of the murder are now here on the beach?"

"They can't all have been involved," Zach replied.

"Maybe not, but while we're sitting here we should be on the lookout for anything suspicious."

Directly behind them, a voice cried out: "Gasp! It's the beautiful boys from last night at Garbo's!"

Brad turned, expecting to find that someone had spotted the look-a-like lovers. Instead, he saw Jarod Scythes bearing down on him and Zach.

"Good morning!" Brad called out as the thin man approached.

Jarod had divested himself of the previous evening's top hat and billowy smock. His hair was a wispy blonde fleece. He'd come decked out in knee-length shorts and a sleeveless T-shirt, which only emphasized his scrawny build among all the muscle-bound dudes lying on the beach.

"I'm exhausted!" Jarod exclaimed, plunking himself down in a chair.

"Been here long?" Brad asked.

"Just got here!" He looked around and spotted the look-a-like pair a few chairs over. "Are those boys lovers or brothers?" he asked.

"Maybe both," said Zach.

Jarod looked pleasantly outraged. "Hush or I'll have you declawed!" He turned his gaze across the bay and pointed out a three-masted schooner gleaming in the sun. "Oh, look! That's Celine Dion's yacht. See the big, red maple leaf on the flag?" He leapt up, waving madly and throwing kisses across the water. "Bonjour, Celine! I love you, baby. Big smacks!"

Brad glanced up as a waiter arrived with a tray of drinks. "That's a very nice looking piece of equipment," he said, glancing past the waiter's crotch to the boat. "I bet it really moves."

Jarod gave Brad a quick up-and-down with his eyes. "God help us—an actual *naïvette*."

The waiter placed three perspiring glasses on the table. Jarod popped the lid on a plastic vial, dumped three pills into his hand and swallowed before chasing them down with his beer. He caught Brad's inquisitive gaze and held out the vial. "Paxil?"

Brad frowned. "Do you really need those things?"

"Couldn't get through the day without them," Jarod said, casting an ironic glance at Brad's mini-pharmacy. "To each his own, as they say."

Brad shook his head. "Don't you find anti-depressants just decrease the lows at the expense of the highs?"

Jarod grimaced. "Do you really think I need the highs?"

Brad mulled this over. "I just think anti-depressants interfere with your real personality."

Jarod rolled his eyes and tossed him a baleful glance. "Isn't that the point?"

He turned his attention back to the look-a-like lovers who sat slipping their tongues into each other's mouths. The winsome pair now occupied a single chair, with the dark haired boy sprawled suggestively in the lap of his blonde partner.

"Now what do you think their story is?" Jarod asked. "My theory is they're escaped bank robbers from Brazil or one of those sexy, dirty countries where people live in filthy heaps on the street and you have to kill someone to get ahead."

Brad pondered this. "You're right," he said, after a moment. "You don't need the highs."

A short native woman came by shouldering a load of blankets and woven bags. She eyed Jarod and headed straight for him, holding up her wares with both hands while balancing a pile on her shoulders.

"Ten dollar for you!" she cried.

Jarod sprang up, hands on hips, and glared at her. "I just bought two of those miserable rags from you yesterday for $20 each!"

"Oh, yeah, but today Friday."

Jarod's gaze narrowed. "And just what is the difference between today and yesterday?" he demanded.

"Tonight party-party," she said with a wink. "Me no want carry home all these."

"Harrumph!" Jarod harrumphed, and plunked back down onto the chair.

The vendor continued spreading her wares, deftly

displaying several burgundy bags with a distinctive white stripe running horizontally along the sides. "These my very best," she said. "No bargain—always twenty dollar. Very special."

"Those *are* nice," Jarod admitted, his gaze lingering over the weave. "And I do need a bag to pack my moisturizers in."

She pointed over to the look-a-like lovers. "They buy one yesterday," she declared, indicating an identical bag bulging at the boys' feet.

On seeing they'd become the focus of attention, the pair glared and pulled their bag closer as though to ensure its safety.

Jarod turned back to the vendor. His face softened. "They are awfully nice." He picked one up and glanced over at Brad. "I can't resist," he said. "Once I touch it, I'm a goner." He turned back to the seller. "OK," he said. "I'll take one."

"Not two?" the woman asked.

"No!" he shrieked.

"OK." She handed him his bag and took the $20 bill. She turned to Brad. "You need bag?"

"Not today, gracias."

"For you, fifteen dollar."

"What?" Jarod shrieked. "I'll kill you, you shameless hussy!"

She smiled. "Hey, you like party-party?" she asked.

"Of course I like party-party!" Jarod snapped, unwilling to be so easily diverted from his exasperation.

"Then maybe you like this!" The woman flipped her apron, revealing an over-sized foam-rubber dildo strapped to her waist.

Jarod screamed for real. "You horrible woman! That's so disgusting! I *love* you."

She began piling her wares back on her shoulders. "Maybe I look for you tonight then," she said, with a little shake of her hips.

"Not if you're wearing that thing," Jarod said. "What's your name, sweetheart?"

"Me Angie. What your name?"

"Jarod Scythes, like the Grim Reaper."

She regarded him critically, shaking her head. "Too long," she pronounced gravely. "Anyway, tonight I look for you. We party-party." She winked and gave another little shake of her hips as she went off with her wares.

Jarod turned to Brad and Zach. "Can you believe that woman?" he shrieked. "She's outrageous!"

A few feet away a bronzed Adonis seemed to be stripping for the entire beach. The man had removed all but a tiny strip of bathing suit. The sands seemed to gather at his feet, pulling in a considerable number of sun-bathers with them.

"Pitter-patter, pitter-patter!" Jarod said, with a hand palpitating over his heart. "If I could only look like that. But I will soon. My operation is next week."

"What operation?" Brad asked.

"Facelift. It's my third. I come down here because they're cheaper. You've never seen anyone wield a knife like a Mexican plastic surgeon."

Ironically, Jarod hardly looked old enough to require plastic surgery. Brad glanced back at the demi-god, who had begun rubbing lotion all over his bulging muscles.

"I doubt a facelift will make you look like that," he said, "but a few weeks in the gym lifting weights might be a good start."

Jarod's face assumed an expression he might have held in reserve for two-dollar underwear. "Darling! Nobody goes to the gym any more. It's all plastic nowadays!"

"How old are you anyway?" Brad asked.

"Thirty-five." Jarod hid his face. "Cringe!"

Which is exactly what you look like, thought Brad, though he refrained from saying so. "If you don't mind my asking, how long have you been having these operations?"

"I had the first one when I turned thirty, but they botched it. I came away with a mixture of 'happy-sad.' Everything above my eyebrows said 'happy' and everything below said 'sad.' They got it right the second time around. 'Happy' is now my default expression. There are only three basic looks I can manage anymore: 'happy,' 'mildly outraged' and 'impulse shopper's remorse.'" He glanced down at his new bag. "The last one really comes in handy."

"As you said, 'To each his own.'"

Jarod scrutinized him with a knowing look. "I'm sure they could do something for you while you're here. Your eyelids are looking a bit droopy."

Brad brought a finger to his eyelids. They suddenly felt puffy and tired.

Jarod checked his watch. "Darlings, I must fly! Drop by and see me sometime." He nodded toward the Blue Parrot's imposing facade. "I'm staying right over there, but I'm here at the beach every morning and at Garbo's every night. It's an easy social schedule." He picked up his new bag and towel and raced across the sand.

Brad turned to Zach. "Are my eyelids really droopy?"

Zach looked him over. "Don't worry. I love you anyway."

Brad turned up the collar on his shirt. "It's the sun," he declared. "I've been coming to this place too long. It's dangerous."

Just then a parasail landed a few feet away, throwing a spray of sand in their direction. The parachute collapsed in a tangled heap as two *chicos* pounced on it, dragging it off to prepare for the next daredevil. Brad eyed them warily, brushing the sand off his collection of pharmaceuticals.

"Don't tell me," Zach said. "You'd never go up in one of those."

"Not willingly," Brad agreed. "I see no point in risking life and limb for a cheap thrill."

"Guess I'll be doing all the fun things alone on this trip."

The morning passed with the sublime indifference of life by the sea. They watched the endless throngs of tourists, the passing sailboats and the waves rolling up on shore, while gulls screamed overhead and vanished around the next point of land in search of dinner or other gulls to scream at.

By midday Brad was on his fourth margarita. His grin was getting goofier and more relaxed. He'd finally shed most of his clothing.

"I think I've had enough beach," he said at last. "Time for a siesta."

"You go—I'll catch up," Zach said. "I want one more swim."

Brad eyed the waves. "Never swim alone," he cautioned. "I could stay and keep an eye out for you, if you like."

"I'll be okay. I've got about fifty companions right out there," Zach said, indicating the bay full of swimmers. "Don't worry. I'll be careful."

Brad rolled up his belongings and made his way across the sand, wincing with every step. He'd forgot to put lotion on the bottom of his feet. From Calle Olas Altas he turned and climbed the one-hundred-and-twelve steps to Calle Pino Suárez, counting each one as his thighs burned with effort. He thought of Jarod and his gym-free scheme to become a muscle-stud. If only it were that easy, he thought.

At the top of the rise he stopped and leaned over the railing with its unimpeded view of Banderas Bay. The water glittered so brightly it hurt to look directly at it. In the distance, boats moved like toy sails. He could just make out Sebastian's schooner. A mother whale cavorted with its calf while a tourist ship tacked toward them for a closer look. What could be more peaceful?

He continued on to Avenida Insurgentes, keeping to the side of the busy roadway. Several taxis tooted their horns, but he waved them on. He'd just turned up Calle Pulpito, where the road snaked between the hillsides, when another taxi headed toward him. It slowed and came to a stop.

The window rolled down. The driver smiled behind his sunglasses. "Señor, I think you need a ride. You look *muy caliente*."

"No, gracias," Brad said over his shoulder. "I can make it."

"No, señor. You need to get in my car."

A gun was aimed at his midriff. Brad put up his hands.

"Put your hands down, idiot. You're attracting attention."

Brad lowered his hands. There was nowhere to run. If the driver fired at this range, he'd be blown apart. The man removed his sunglasses. His eyes were a glittering green with red-tinged rims. It was the phoney waiter from Garbo's.

"What do you want?" Brad demanded.

"I want to give you a little ride," said the man, whose English had clearly improved since the previous night.

Before Brad could respond, a white VW skidded to a halt in a cloud of dust across the road. A shot rang out. For a second, Brad thought he was being ambushed. Instead of finding himself dead, however, he watched in slow motion as the taxi's windshield shattered and the cabdriver whirled to face the shooter. Instinctively, Brad leapt for the ditch.

Seconds passed in what seemed like hours. Three more shots were fired as time sped up again. The taxi spun its wheels and screeched off with the VW in hot pursuit. Brad had just enough time to look up and catch a glimpse of the other driver's face before both cars vanished in a cloud of dust like the finale to some magic disappearing act.

Brad scrambled out of the ditch and began to run. At the top of the hill, he stopped and turned. The water still sparkled peacefully under the blazing sun. He could make out tiny beach umbrellas and miniature figures moving across the sands of Playa de los Muertos. It was all so far away it didn't seem real.

Bradford wiped the dust from his clothes and caught his breath. Sweat dripped down his back and legs. He brushed the hair from his forehead. Someone just saved my life, he thought. He recalled the red-ringed eyes of the taxi driver and the gun he'd been threatened with. No doubt about it, it had been the same waiter from Garbo's the night before. Who knows where he'd be on his way to now if he'd been forced into the taxi.

The other driver's face flashed before his eyes again.

That face had given him an even greater chill. It belonged to a dead man.

Death and resurrection.

51

6

Brad listened to Grace talk as he paced back and forth through the living room. Her voice was slightly more animated than usual, but not much.

"You're telling me there was a dead agent on your tail?"

"I saw him right across the street. I'm sure it was him!"

"How sure is sure?"

Brad held the phone at arm's length and glared at it. He was as spooked as he was exasperated. Had the driver of the white VW really been the same man he saw get knifed into oblivion four years earlier on a Paris street corner? Or was he just going nuts?

"I'm as sure as I can be in a crazy business like this!" he exploded.

"Okay, settle down, Red. I'm taking you seriously. I just don't know what to make of it."

"And neither do I."

"Obviously not. And where was our young blue-haired friend through all this?"

Brad glanced out the window to the balcony where Zach sat tracking Wi-Fi hotspots on his laptop. "Swimming," Brad said. "I left him at the beach. He just got back."

"Tsk-tsk. Never swim alone. Isn't that what they say?" Grace chided.

For a second, Brad wondered if she ever really took

him seriously.

Grace continued. "One agent has been killed and a second shot at—not to mention a possible attempted poisoning of the two of you last night—and now a third one reappears from the dead. Whatever is going on down there?"

"That's what I'd like to know," Brad said, agonizingly aware that Grace had yet to tell him why he was in Puerto Vallarta.

"By the way," she continued. "Did you retrieve those drink glasses from the bar the other night? We should do a trace analysis for poison."

Brad slapped his forehead. In the wake of the shooting, he'd forgot to go back. And with the way Mexicans obsessively cleaned up after any crime lest it upset the tourist industry, there was no chance they'd find any evidence intact now.

"No," he admitted. "I didn't."

"You're slipping, Red."

"Sorry." Brad shook his head, wondering how he'd redeem himself this time. "What about the map we found on the CD? It must have something to do with why we're here."

"Yes," Grace said, drawing a breath. "It looks like things are progressing faster than I anticipated."

"What things?"

"We-e-ell, there's the rub," she said, as laconically as any saddle-weary Texan. "I know only so much about what's going on, and I'm authorized to tell even less, but…"

"But if your current agents are starting to die on you, and former agents are returning from the dead, it might make sense to let someone in just a little about what's really going on."

"Yes. But what really *is* going on? That's what I'm starting to wonder."

Brad wasn't enjoying this game of cat-and-mouse one bit. For a second, he was tempted to chuck his cell phone over the wall and let it plunge all twenty feet to the rocks below. "Well, you'd better give me something to go on," he said pointedly.

Grace sighed. "All right. I'll tell you what I can."

Bradford waited, alert.

"Can you see the bay from where you are, Red?"

"Clear as day," Brad replied, shielding his eyes from the water's glare.

"Then you can probably see a nice little three-masted schooner anchored somewhere in the middle of the harbour. It's not huge, but it's powerfully built and probably sports a Canadian flag, if you were to see it up close. Or maybe a Quebec flag."

Something was starting to click. "You aren't talking about Celine Dion's boat, are you?"

"You sure are a smart cookie, Red," Grace said. "No doubt the beach was all abuzz with the news this morning?"

"I heard a comment or three."

"Well, here's the thing. We—meaning you, me, and any other Box 77 agents currently down there—need to make sure nothing unpleasant happens to the little lady..."

There was that Texas twang again. Was she pulling his leg? He wouldn't have been surprised to hear her whistle *Shenandoah*.

"Meaning?"

"Meaning we've had word someone might be out to kidnap Mlle. Dion and we don't want anything dastardly to happen to a nice girl from Quebec who just likes to sing her heart out."

Brad was flummoxed. "We're protecting Celine Dion?"

"Not exactly 'protecting' her—we're just looking out for her well-being. Anything wrong with that?"

"Isn't that a bit of an unusual assignment for us?"

"Our mandate—at least, as much as an organization that doesn't exist can be said to have a mandate—is to help maintain what these days is rather ironically referred to as 'global peace.' Looking out for the safety of celebrities might seem a bit unusual for us, but I can assure you it would cause an international incident of substantial proportions for someone of Celine's stature to be abducted ... or worse. It's not the first time something like this has had me worried."

Brad recalled similar threats made against the pugnacious Australian movie star, Russell Crowe. The FBI had eventually been called in to guarantee his safety. Was that what she had in mind?

Grace hemmed and hawed. "Let's just say Celine is a *beloved* figure," she replied. "Whereas some might say Crowe is a loud-mouthed, mewling baboon of an actor. I certainly wouldn't want to be in the same room with him if he had a phone in his hand. And let's face it—not a few people would mind if he got dismantled a bit."

"So other than looking out for suspicious types trying to kidnap Celine Dion, what else are we doing here?"

Grace paused. "That's about all I know."

Brad chewed on that for a moment. He had a suspicion she was still holding out on him. "All you know or all you can tell me? What's really going on down here?"

"Shadowy things, Red. That's all I can say."

Brad didn't like the sound of that one bit.

Grace continued. "Panther was supposed to have been your connection, but what he was going to tell you and who this mysterious Agent Silver might be, I haven't a clue. I suspect it has something to do with the CD you found on him. Otherwise, the boys upstairs have kept me in the dark as much as anybody else on this one."

"Surely there has to be more to this than a simple celebrity kidnapping threat? And what the hell has my dead ex-partner got to do with it all?"

"If you figure that out, I'd like to be the first to know, Red."

The call clicked to an end. Brad sat there, wondering what was so shadowy that his own director couldn't let him in on it. It sounded ominous.

Outside on the balcony, Zach sat looking triumphant. "I can latch onto five unsecured Wi-Fi connections out here," he announced. "I can also connect to a secure hook-up from a hotel just down the hill. I was able to hack in because it has an easy password: OFFICE. We can always use that if the others aren't up and running—that's assuming we'll ever need to hack into anybody else's system."

"Sometimes you really scare me," Brad said. He cocked his head. "But mostly in a good way."

Zach watched him for a moment. "Are you all right? I mean, apart from the fact that you just got shot at by a dead guy?"

Brad gave him a half-hearted grin. "Actually, the dead guy just saved my life. Our boss, on the other hand, is doing her best to keep me in the dark about what we're really doing here." He pointed to the yacht. "Apparently we're to make sure no one tries to kidnap Celine Dion while she sails up and down the coast."

Zach's eyebrows knotted. "Who would want to hurt Celine?"

Brad shrugged. "Who knows? Could be a revenge

thing. Maybe someone went a little nuts listening to that *Titanic* theme song one time too many." He nodded at the laptop. "I think we should have another look at that map."

Zach pulled up the file. They scrutinized the coastline around Vallarta, where it stretched south as far as Torrecillas and north past Sayulita.

"Where does this itinerary put us right now?" Brad asked.

"According to this, it's Vallarta all morning. Things start to move again at 2 p.m. Later, it mentions three small islands known as Los Arcos and a town called Mismaloya."

"We'd better get down there pronto. Does the coastal road extend that far?" Brad asked.

"Barely. The highway turns inland a little further down at Boca de Tomatlán." Zach looked at Brad. "Do you have any idea what this is about?"

"Maybe," Brad said, checking his watch. "It's one-thirty now. We'll know in about an hour and a half if I'm right."

7

Brad and Zach jumped on board the bus as it slowed briefly, stirring up a cloud of dust before swerving off again. The interior was crowded with *paisanos* and a handful of *turistas*. At the back, a posse of youthful faces grinned at the newcomers, bucking for adoption or, barring that, a handful of pesos as the bus bounced and shuddered along. The seats were bare metal and the road so old and rugged it might have been handed down directly from the Maya. Each bump tossed the passengers into the air for a fraction of a second before resettling them at unusual angles and in new relations to their travelling companions. For good measure, crates of oranges were used to seat a few overstock riders in the aisles. At least this route didn't cart live chickens.

Mismaloya lay twenty miles down the winding coast. The bus passed colourful haciendas dotting the hillsides—pleasure palaces paid for in American dollars and hidden in the palm-covered recesses of the foothills. Cars passing in the opposite lane beeped their horns while the bus driver honked back and shouted enthusiastic greetings out the window. Why concentrate on driving when you could be having fun?

Brad kept on the lookout for a sign that they were being tailed, but he saw nothing suspicious. After half an hour, the bus approached a concrete bridge where a trickle of water ran beneath the road. Just up ahead, the highway abandoned the coast and headed south down through the

Sierra Madres.

The bus slowed to a stop and the door creaked open. All heads turned to watch as the two gringos staggered out into the mid-afternoon heat, trying to re-establish their sense of balance. Not far off, waves washed up on a pristine beach bordering a tiny fishing village. The settlement was little more than a sandbar with a few adobe huts surrounded by bougainvillea. In the distance, a giant iguana guarded the beach like some prehistoric monster from a '50s Japanese horror flick.

Zach looked up. "Wow! Are we in Disneyworld?"

Brad smiled. "Nearly. I suppose it won't hurt to do a little sightseeing, will it?"

They crossed the beach and headed for the metal sculpture poised at the entrance to the former film set of John Huston's *The Night of the Iguana.*

"I saw it as a kid," Brad explained. "Richard Burton played a lecherous defrocked priest who fled to Mexico and became a tour guide. But I couldn't understand why he kept chasing after young girls when there were all these gorgeous, semi-naked Mexican boys running around."

Though a few buildings had been maintained, much of the set was in an advanced state of decay. Once, however, it had been the focus of world attention. If it hadn't been for Mismaloya and director Huston, Puerto Vallarta might have remained just another charming, unspoiled seaside village.

For centuries, native lore had prophesied the arrival of two waves of long-legged, light-skinned gods to the tropical paradise. One would deliver death, the other a sort of rebirth. The first was clearly the Spanish conquistadors, bringing unheralded destruction, hideous diseases and a shoddy new religion that liked to play favourites. The second wave was a little kinder to everyone involved, arriving a few centuries after the first invasion with the appearance of a white-haired film director and his obstreperous band of movie stars.

Once Huston and his noisy lot descended on the shores of Banderas Bay, nothing was the same. Their presence brought an international spotlight to Puerto Vallarta, turning it forever after into a place where the celebrated might vacation when the Mediterranean just seemed too far to go for a fling. Fortunately, beautiful cities outlast even the most beautiful movie stars. A stunning geography eclipses even fame. The movie's glamorous actors, along with their celebrated affairs and messy artistic squabbles, have all but faded into memory, while Puerto Vallarta's fame remains. Such are the whims and whimsies of the gods of creation.

Once or twice, Brad turned to look over his shoulder as they passed between dense groves of palms or skirted the ruins of the once-impressive stone structures. While he might not have Zach's Remote Viewing capabilities, his sixth sense was definitely acting up, leaving him yet again with an eerie feeling of being watched from afar.

He was about to put it down to paranoia when suddenly the look-a-like lovers appeared on the path dead ahead, clutching their burgundy bag with its telltale stripe. What exactly, Brad wondered, did the pair have tucked away in there? The beautiful twosome passed by, their eyes narrowed in suspicion, nodding brusquely as they went about their business.

Once they were out of earshot, Brad turned to Zach. "What do you make of that?"

"You know what they say," Zach replied. "There's no such thing as a coincidence. But my guess is that if I shook their hands I wouldn't be impressed with whatever vibrations I felt."

When they turned to look back, the pair disappeared into the foliage on a side path. Brad and Zach continued their explorations, but did not run into the couple a second time. This was surprising, given that the entire site was little larger than a football field. In fact, *not* running into someone would be less likely than running into them over and over again.

Having exhausted his curiosity about the faded glory of an all but forgotten Hollywood legend, Brad turned his attention to the task at hand. "I guess we should go back to the village and see what's happening," he said, a trifle regretful that nothing more had come of the visit.

It was nearing three o'clock. A fleet of fishing boats could be seen heading in to Mismaloya with the day's catch. Down on the beach, an overeager bar owner rushed to offer them his best table. His left eye was marbled, its sightless pupil eerily reflecting the sun. At that hour, all the tables were unoccupied. Brad declined the man's offer, but asked about the possibility of getting a water-taxi for the afternoon.

The man cocked his head. "I am also a water-taxi driver," he said, revealing a talent for entrepreneurship. His good eye scanned the empty beach. "I don't have so many customer today. I can take you, if you like."

"I would like."

"Okay, let's go," he said. "How much you pay for, señor?" the man asked, almost as an after-thought.

"One hundred dollars for the afternoon."

A smile lit up his face. "Okay!" he said. "That's a lot of *cervezas* I have to sell for that much dollars."

He removed his apron and put a lock on the bar. They followed him to a worn-looking skiff tethered to a post just up the beach. Brad eyed the rickety boat and wondered aloud about its seaworthiness, but the man assured him his craft was a veteran of years of safe transit. They clambered aboard and with a gentle shove the boat headed into the bay.

With the sun overhead, the water was sparklingly clear. Zach motioned to Brad and pointed down. The dark outline of a hammerhead shark ominously skirted the ocean bottom twenty feet below. The fearsome-looking creature was easily eight feet long.

The boat owner looked down and shrugged. "*Es un niño*," he said. A baby.

"Actually," Zach said, "sharks aren't nearly as dangerous as everyone makes them out to be. Although they're fairly aggressive predators, their feeding habits are not usually human-oriented. That hammerhead, for instance, is mostly a bottom feeder. If you got close up, you'd see it has a very small mouth. It would be hard-pressed to take on a human for lunch. Animals are very practical when it comes to eating."

Brad's eyebrows rose. "Are you talking from experience?"

"Actually, yes. I swam in an isolated pen with half a dozen sharks once. You pay a guy in Thailand five dollars and he drops you into the enclosure. When you first see them lurking below, something instinctive kicks in and your brain screams out that you're in danger, but if you stick around long enough, you realize they're all cowering at the bottom. They're more afraid of us than we are of them. Under those conditions, nobody's going to attack anybody."

I'll take your word for it," Brad said, his skepticism tempered by the knowledge that Zach's stories were always based on fact.

"Sharks use electro-sensors in their heads to feed.

They pick up subtle vibrations in the water telling them where the fish are from miles away. It's a primitive form of Remote Viewing." Zach grinned. "In the case of hammerheads, the sensors are distributed through the hammer. It also helps them orient themselves by the earth's magnetic fields, enhanced by the superior conducting qualities of water."

"I guess they wouldn't have much use for a GPS."

They reached the open sea and their taxi driver turned to them. "*¿A dónde vamos, señores?*"

Brad pointed to the three huge rocks jutting up in the distance. "*A Los Arcos, por favor.*"

The prow turned and headed directly for the islands. As they approached the forbidding looking outcrop, the buzzing of thousands of seabirds grew till the noise was almost deafening. They could make out numerous caves and nooks that served as nesting grounds.

Everywhere, the water was populated by snorkelers and scuba divers. They'd been there less than fifteen minutes when the elegant schooner with the red-and-white maple leaf flag sailed proudly into view.

"Right on schedule," Brad said quietly.

Zach produced his binoculars and swept the prow. "Look at this!" he said excitedly.

Brad took the glasses and focused on the boat. Flanked by a pair of *fleur-de-lis* and painted in blue lettering across the prow was the word "Libre."

"Bingo!" Brad said.

The vessel slowed and stopped. They watched for several minutes, but there was no visible activity on deck. No one slipped overboard to swim in the busy waters. The boat dipped gently on the sun-dappled swells. Nothing appeared to be happening. That's odd, thought Brad. Why come to a snorkelling paradise and not jump in the ocean or at least sit on deck and enjoy the view?

The sun grew hotter and the air stilled. Voices carried across the water as new vessels arrived every few minutes. The waves teamed with flippers and blow spouts. Brad continued to scan with the binoculars. A sailboat sporting a rainbow flag appeared. It bore the legend *Rainbow Warrior* on its prow. On deck, a gaggle of boys pranced to a loud beat spilling from the speakers. Definitely one of the tribe, Brad thought. His binoculars caught an attractive older man with silvery hair at the helm. He could almost have fallen overboard. It was Sebastian Mathers.

"We've got company," Brad said.

At that moment, the *Libre* went into action. An engine purred. The ship turned abruptly and headed straight for the up-thrust of Los Arcos. Just when it seemed the sailboat might smash into the nearest of the islands, it disappeared through an archway in the rock that had been hidden by the angle of view. Seconds later, it emerged gracefully on the far side. There was still no one in sight. Whoever was in charge was steering from inside.

The ship continued past the two farthest islands. Sebastian's boat had picked up speed as well. It veered sharply toward the *Libre*. Brad watched in fascination as the distance between the two shrank until they appeared to be on a collision course. What were their captains thinking? Would Brad be forced to go to the rescue? If the *Libre* were rammed and Celine forced off her boat, it would be a perfect opportunity for someone to kidnap her. Was this what Grace had been warning him about? He'd been assigned to protect Celine, and it looked as though she was about to be abducted right from under his nose.

"*¡Dios!*" cried their half-blind skipper, watching the two ships.

At the last moment, the collision was barely avoided

with some skilful handling on the part of both captains. The worst that came about was a sharp dip and thrust on the swells as the ships passed within inches of one another.

"That was close!" Brad exclaimed, still wondering whether it had been intentional.

He kept his binoculars trained on the vessels. At last a figure appeared on the deck of the *Libre*. The two captains were having a storm of a conversation, shaking fists and yelling as their boats swept past one another. What I wouldn't give to have an audio plant on board right now, Brad thought.

Celine's boat headed off into the open water before turning back toward Banderas Bay. She seemed to be curtailing her run instead of going on to Mismaloya, as the schedule indicated. Brad kept watch, but no other boats approached or followed the *Libre*.

The *Rainbow Warrior* circled the farthest of the outcroppings and anchored there. Brad watched a while longer before signalling to return to shore. Their skipper dutifully turned the skiff around and headed back to Mismaloya.

The afternoon was winding down as they disembarked. They thanked the man and promised to return for his specialty, "*Ron y coca.*"

Whatever else the afternoon may have accomplished, one thing was clear: the itinerary embedded on the CD was for the *Libre*. But who had hidden it there and what Agent Panther was doing with it when he was killed were still up for grabs. Had the map been intended for Brad so that he could follow the ship's progress and make sure the Canadian chanteuse remained free from harm? And was it mere coincidence that Sebastian and his party boys had ended up there at exactly the same time as the *Libre*? More important, what had set those two boats on a near-collision course?

These and other thoughts plagued Brad on the ride back to Puerto Vallarta. He still had no idea who Agent Silver was. As for the green-eyed Mexican, it seemed fairly certain he had knifed Panther on the street outside Garbo's in order to get hold of the map with its hidden itinerary. In that case, it was probable the poison drinks had been intended to prevent Agent Red from collecting the CD. Presumably, that was also why the green-eyed man tried to kidnap Brad the following morning.

To add to the mix, however, someone who looked very much like his former partner—or to be precise, his formerly-deceased partner—had prevented whatever had been about to happen to him. Brad was sure it had been him. But how could it be? Dead men didn't come back to life!

Or did they?

His code name had been Little Wing. An ironic tag, because there'd been nothing *little* about the boy. Brad could vouch for that. In the end, however, all he really knew for sure was that Little Wing had been a half-blood Cherokee. The face came back to him: those searching black eyes, the high, flat cheekbones. They'd met during training sessions for Box 77 and bonded during the gruelling regimen. Little Wing's physical capabilities had been astounding—mere pain didn't faze him; no test of strength was too great for him. He never once cracked under the intense psychological pressure. He was a mountain of muscle, yet he could be as gentle and tender as a newborn kitten. As far as Brad was concerned, he'd been the best of all the new recruits, bar none.

Brad thought all this as the bus flashed along the highway from Mismaloya back to Puerto Vallarta. He looked down to where Zach leaned his head against his shoulder, the boy's slumber interrupted momentarily each time the bus hit a bump. The afternoon sun had been too much for him.

Brad's thoughts returned to his former partner. Yes—he and Little Wing had bonded. But more than bond, they'd become lovers in a secret relationship that flourished under the noses of everyone at the training camp. They'd been taught to scheme and double-cross and think for themselves, and that was just what they'd done, night after night, without anyone's being the wiser. In the presence of others, they barely acknowledged one another, but the dark of night told another story altogether.

When their training was over, fate saw to it that they were assigned to work together. In fact they'd made a fantastic team, successfully tackling one difficult assignment after another. There'd been something special about their work together—every one of their superiors had said so.

Then came Paris.

Brad hadn't allowed himself to think of that night for a very long time. Because after all this time, it still haunted him more than anything since the death of his father when Brad was fifteen. Yet he could still recall every detail of that evening—the risky tail through the rainy streets of Montmartre, the knife blade flashing under the streetlamps, the body falling to the sidewalk. And, finally, Brad's hands covered in blood as Little Wing died in his arms.

Or so he'd believed.

8

The Blue Parrot was an exclusive five-star hotel of the sort only dreamed of by pre-Stonewall gays and lesbians. Catering to men and women of all sexes, it boasted a world renowned restaurant, a 24-hour gym with an Olympic-sized pool, emergency mental-health facilities, a team of massage therapists, an in-house agony aunt, and a famed rooftop nightclub designed for world-class romance and non-stop fun. Mondays and Tuesdays were reserved for naked bingo, Wednesdays for camp movies, and Thursdays for karaoke, while the weekends featured some of the most innovative drag acts in the known world.

It was because of the latter, Brad knew, that the Parrot would be one of the best sources of gossip—for whither the Drag Queen goeth, news followeth. News of the seamy and juicy sort. And while the things that a drag queen doesn't know—Cartesian logic systems, semantic reasoning, ontology engineering, and other etceteras—could not exactly be called negligible on the spectrum of available information, what a drag queen *does* know is guaranteed to be of scintillating interest. Especially to the people who don't want it known. And besides, Brad reasoned, the Blue Parrot made an excellent passion fruit daiquiri.

Flyers handed out on the beach boasted of an "extrabaganza" at the Parrot that very evening. The star entertainer, one "Esmeralda, True Mayan Princess," was noted as a DQ of "unusual abilities." The printout failed to specify what those abilities consisted of, save that

Esmeralda was considered the "Sylvia Browne of Drag."
(But wait! Brad thought. Isn't that a tautology?)

All Brad could recall of Sylvia Browne was that she
was some sort of New Age guru with more wigs than
Cher, more husbands than Liz Taylor, a penchant for commanding attention like Madonna, and a flair for fashion
that would put Madame de Pompadour in the shade. Just
what sort of shtick would this be, then? Did Esmeralda
read palms in a Mayan headdress or levitate in a tutu while
lip-synching to *Que Sera, Sera*? No matter, Brad thought—
there were still those daiquiris to look forward to.

Thus it was that Brad and Zach found themselves
exiting the elevator onto the Blue Parrot's much-lauded
rooftop. But being at the entrance to something is not the
same as being invited inside, as any celebrity spotter will
tell you. Like many an elite resort, the Parrot was run by a
highly efficient SS squad. Hitler's personal bodyguards
could have been fashioned from this crowd of sleek, taut
and toned hit-men masquerading as bouncers and waiters.

Brad and Zach stood patiently waiting to be granted
entry as the sun set over the hills and the lights of Vallarta
twinkled into relief. Over the next half-hour, they found
themselves shunted from side to side when they weren't
being ignored outright. One after another, a dozen sec-
ond-rate celebrity-look-a-likes were ushered in by the air-
kissing doorman while gloating at those in line as they
passed into the roof's inner circle. There's no fascist like a
minority fascist, Brad noted, recalling sadly how the ma-
jority of Hitler's elite had been gay. With grim amuse-
ment, he watched the white-haired staff with eyes so blue
and cheekbones so perfectly sculpted you'd think Marlene
Dietrich had sired them all. Even the few native Mexicans
in the hotel's employ managed to look oddly Teutonic,

moving and speaking with such gruff efficiency that the hotel might have belonged on the Maximilianstrasse.

Every few minutes, the elevator door opened to admit a new crowd of fabulous beauties. Standing in the midst of this jostling stream of constant arrivals was like trying to have a picnic on a runway with jet planes landing. It took a considerable bribe on Bradford's part before the *maitre'd* would even allow their presence to register on his Scale of Estimable Beings. Once inside the club perimeters, however, they quickly joined the elite. The crowd that evening was a fairly upscale—some might even say *swank*—gathering of well-to-do gays and lesbians. The smell of money hung in the air. The sheer ratio of pesos-per-square-inch rubbing thighs with the *nouveau pobre* who followed them was considerable. Had there been a fire, a lot of people would have found themselves pulling out their wallets in vain to purchase an escape ladder or maybe a tab of E to help them enjoy their last moments on earth.

Brad and Zach split up, making their way through the crowd. Sniff around as he might, however, Brad was unable to find anyone who gave off even the slightest whiff of *scandale* when he mentioned Panther's death. True, everyone had heard of the murder—in a town like Vallarta that was unavoidable. And of course everyone had theories about it. A Perez Hilton wannabe claimed a jealous Latina girlfriend had caught Panther with his gay lover, while someone else said the Federales wanted him out of the drug trade permanently. Still others believed the beach Mafia had caught him horning in on their territory, which controlled both gambling and the sale of exotic beach towels.

One pathetic soul, who would have placed first in a Truman Capote look-a-like contest even if Capote had been in the house, declared Panther had had an affair with

Brad Pitt and that Brad had had him silenced for fear of being outed to Angelina. The same man also claimed to have been Panther's Sugar Daddy. ("But please don't tell anyone. I'm in mourning," he cried.) This, Brad knew, was impossible because a) Panther had almost certainly been straight, and b) he'd parachuted into town a few scant hours before his death. The teller of the tale had likewise been vague as to when the alleged affair had taken place. Brad recalled reading a juicy biography of James Dean and thinking that if he added up all the people in the book who claimed to have slept with the actor—who'd died at the age of twenty-four—he would have to have lived to twice that age to accomplish even half of what his legend reported.

So far, Brad reasoned, the people he'd talked to were mere waiters, bartenders and hotel guests, so the information he ferreted out was dismissible. His real targets—the drag queens—were backstage preparing for the evening's show. He would have to wait until he could speak to one or two of them in private afterward. Maybe then he would uncover something important.

After half an hour and a couple of daiquiris, they'd still learned almost nothing, though Zach received two marriage proposals in the process. Just when it seemed they had talked to everyone worth questioning, the elevator opened to emit a blast of sound and colour presaging the arrival of Sebastian Mathers and his ebullient bunch. The gregarious ship's captain was much tanned and sounding even more buoyant than usual.

Without waiting to be admitted formally, Sebastian and his motley crew simply pushed their way into the club. Once in, his group raced to stake out a table nearest the stage.

"Howdy, friends!" the captain called, on spotting

Brad and Zach.

"How was your day?" Zach greeted.

Sebastian beamed. "Awesome! We had a terrific sail down the coast to Los Arcos this afternoon. It was really something—a clear sky, nice wind up. Everything was going rather well until we had a bit of a set-to with another ship. The captain—a foreigner, of course—wasn't watching where he was going and almost put his prow through my side."

Brad wondered if Sebastian would have altered his tale had he realized that Brad and Zach had watched the same events unfold in a very different light.

The captain veered off to another subject. "Are you boys here to see Esmeralda?"

"Yes," Brad replied. "Have you heard anything about the show?"

"I sure have," he said. For a moment, Brad thought Sebastian actually twinkled. "In fact, I witnessed it last week. I say 'witnessed' because that's about the only possible word for a spectacle like this."

"Is it good?" Brad asked hopefully.

"'Good?'" Sebastian repeated. "I'm not sure if 'good' covers it. 'Unmissable' is what some have called it, though phrases like 'earth-shattering' and 'mind-blowing' come to mind. We might be witnessing the evolution of drag as we know it!"

"I'll take that as an unqualified recommendation," Brad responded.

"They say she's a Mayan princess," Zach added.

"That and more," Sebastian agreed. "But I don't want to spoil it for you."

He excused himself and went off to join his group, who were busy ordering drinks at the table they'd commandeered on the far side of the terrace.

Glancing around, Brad recognized a number of people in the audience. He was quickly becoming acquainted with Vallarta's moveable collection of faces that appeared everywhere there was an event of significance, and a few that managed to be in two or three places at once. Turn a corner and there was the cute guy in the pink Stetson you'd just seen at a trendy café a moment before, only now ten steps ahead of you. How did they do that?

Brad noted the look-a-like lovers four tables over, the blonde straddling the dark-haired boy. It was like an X-rated mirror trick. Now *they* could certainly be in two places at once, he realized. At least with the right hat, anyway. The pair had obviously returned from Mismaloya and were clutching their burgundy bag between them. Brad was getting more and more curious as to what might be so valuable that they always had to have their hands on it.

They sipped from a single cocktail with two straws, occasionally looking over to slip one another the tongue while twisting their torsos to achieve maximum body contact. Perhaps, Brad thought, they performed as one of those contortionist acts where people manipulated their bodies into impossible shapes and those stupefyingly hard-to-reproduce-at-home sexual poses. It would certainly make a unique porn act, beating out Thai prostitutes who simultaneously ejected ping-pong balls and smoked cigarettes with their so-called "private parts." In any event, it promised to be worth the ticket price, if it came to that.

A tall figure skated through the crowd, sleeves billowing like sails. Jarod's eyes lit on Brad and Zach as he headed for their table.

"*Bli-i-i-iss!*" he cried, his fingers waggling in the air. "What a coincidence! Here we all are again!"

He plopped himself down and leaned in, elbows

on the table. "I had the most wonderful afternoon!" he confided. "I was on that man's boat"—he pointed over at Sebastian—"and who do you think we should run into but Celine and her yacht! Literally! We almost rammed her side!"

Brad was on the verge of saying he'd witnessed the event, but thought better of it.

"I was absolutely thrilled at being so close to my favourite diva of all time! Even if we'd killed her, it would have been worth it. Of course, we didn't actually see her. In fact, she may not even have been on board at all, but still…! It gave me goose bumps. *Sh-i-i-i-i-ver!*" he bleated.

"Sounds exciting," Brad said. "Zach and I spent a quiet day on the beach in Mismaloya."

"With Liz and Dick and Ava and Deborah! How thrilling! Did you go to the Iguana set? Was it beautiful?"

"It was a devastated ruin…" Zach answered.

"Just like Liz!"

Brad said, "We brought greetings from you, of course."

"Then I hope you were well received. If not, I'll be sure to put in a complaint."

At that moment, a spotlight threw the stage into relief and the crowd hushed as a figure in top hat and tails emerged from behind the curtain.

"It's great to see everybody tonight!" the MC called out. "Now I promise not to bore you with a lot of chit-chat, because I know you didn't come to see me." Here he held out the microphone as though anticipating a protest, though none followed. "Well, you could at least pretend you cared," he pouted. "Never mind! Esmeralda's back-stage getting beautiful for you"—this comment did in fact elicit spontaneous cheers—"but first I'd like to bring out a quartet of gals we all know and love."

A fanfare sounded and the impresario slipped off-stage as Barbra, Cher, Celine and Madonna took centre stage. Waves of applause erupted as hit number followed hit number. It was surprising how little effort it took to give an impression of any performer, except that these gals were a little more vivid than some of their real-life counterparts. Take Celine, for instance, Brad thought. That nose and chin line were almost too real. How did they carry off these sleight-of-hand impersonations so well? They must have had very malleable cheekbones, not to mention waistlines. And this Celine's lip-synching was flaw-less, even in French.

"Bless!" exclaimed Jarod. "Wouldn't you just bet it was the real Celine?"

"It certainly does look like her," Brad agreed.

"But wouldn't it be funny if it really was?"

That gave Brad pause. He watched the prancing diva in the elegant gown with the slit up one leg. The sparkling diamond on her chest certainly looked real too. What if this *was* the real Celine? What better place to hide than right under everyone's nose? It would be a brilliant ruse, if a trifle unrealistic. Or maybe a trifle too realistic. Which was it? Could you have your diva and kidnap her too?

Brad recalled a dinner date at a small diner in Toronto, of all places, where he'd been sitting quietly eating when the house band had been joined by Liza Minnelli. She sat through a quick set before going back to her seat and finishing her meal. The whole thing had seemed star-tlingly unreal. But Minnelli probably hadn't had a kidnap-ping threat over her head at the time.

Maybe Celine was capable of an impromptu din-ner performance too. Didn't her family own some sort of fast food outlet in Quebec? But nah! Brad thought. It couldn't be her. On the other hand, if this was the real Celine then was it mere coincidence that Sebastian Mathers had showed up yet again in the same place at the very same time? Maybe. Still, Brad had no reason to suspect Mathers of anything—at least no more than he did Jarod Scythes or the look-a-likes. It was the green-eyed Mexican he needed to watch out for.

Brad signalled to the waiter, another dazzling member of Hitler's elite, for a third daiquiri. In truth, he had only a minimal interest in drag acts, no matter how good the impersonation. If this was to be the sum of the evening's entertainment, it was going to be a long night.

The fabulous foursome soon finished their act and slipped behind the curtain. The impresario reappeared.

"Thank you, ladies," he said to the retreating figures. He clapped with one hand against the microphone, making a loud thumping noise and varying the rhythm for effect. "That's as musical as I get," he told the crowd, who remained stonily silent. He glared at them. "Still not here to see me, I take it? Well, just remember who owns this place."

A very large lesbian guffawed.

"Thank you, Mother," the MC said. He glanced over his shoulder to see a pair of feet positioning themselves behind the curtain. "For those of you who know her, she needs no introduction. For those of you who have never experienced the phenomenon of Esmeralda, all I can say is get ready because here ... they ... come!"

The MC stepped back.

The crowd roared and stomped its approval as a creature bearing a strict resemblance to an Andean Condor schlepped onto the stage. She wore a Vera Wang skirt with a helter-skelter top and a cock-eyed bust that seemed to glare at the crowd in a vaguely threatening manner. As she stood and gazed over the audience, her eyes glittered like an iguana's beneath bat-sized eyelashes. The applause grew.

She was formidably ugly, yet there was something undeniably regal about her, like some half-forgotten Anastasia—neglected and disenfranchised—who had been unable to forget her own aristocratic legacy and must in some small way live up to it every single day of her life, the indignity of having to exist in the ordinary world notwithstanding.

The applause slowed and finally stopped. But Esmeralda just stood there in her gaudy outfit, gazing coolly over the crowd. Here, Brad thought, was the classic drag queen: a cross between the beautiful and the butch, the sweet and the insane, Tallulah Bankhead and the Battleship Potemkin. But just what, he wondered, was so extraordinary about Esmeralda, True Mayan Princess?

He looked over at Zach who smiled and shrugged in return.

9

"*Buenas noches*," Esmeralda intoned, in a voice suggestive of rusty bed springs at an orgy or the jailer at an insane asylum scraping his keys against the bars of the cells. "And good evening to the rest of you."

The MC had not deserted the stage, as he had with the previous act. Instead, he'd taken his place a few paces behind Esmeralda, who glanced over her shoulder at him.

"Shall we begin?" he asked.

Esmeralda nodded and turned back to the audience, one foot planted dead ahead, the other pointed stage right, as if she might make a sudden run for cover. Then raising one arm, she closed both eyes as though waiting for a music cue. None was forthcoming. The crowd sat subdued and silent for nearly a minute. Literally. Nothing. Happened. Technical difficulties, Brad decided, wondering which would turn up first, his daiquiri or Esmeralda's missing music.

All at once Esmeralda twitched, as though invisible hands had just given her a full-body chiropractic adjustment. The audience tensed. At the second twitch, someone in the front row screamed. With a sharp intake of breath, Esmeralda's eyes flew open. A hush came over the crowd.

The MC suddenly stepped forward. "Spirit, say who you are!" he commanded.

There was another convulsion as Esmeralda's condor-like features gave way to those of a gamin. "Why, I'm not sure," said a girlish voice totally unlike Esmeralda's guttural growl. "I think my name is Dorothy. I'm … I'm looking for a little dog. Have you seen one?"

"It's Judy Garland!" someone screamed.

"Where have you come from, Dorothy?"

"Why, from Kansas! You see, there was a storm and I—"

"Why are you here, Dorothy?" the MC interrupted.

"I don't know! I don't really want to be here. Oh, if I could only go home…!"

The body contorted again and the waifish Judy seemed to grow old before their eyes. It was still Judy, though her voice had deepened. "I … I just wanna sheetherainbows again," she said in a pleading whine. "They shaid there'd be rainbows over here, but I haven't sheen one for years…"

"We love you, Judy!" someone shouted, and the crowd roared its assent.

Judy turned to the audience. "Could shembody gimme un drink?" she continued, looking more than a little wobbly on her feet. "I'll sing for ya!" She gazed around sadly, but no sound came from her voice. "I forget the lyrics," she said at last. "Maybe jess a little drink furst." She looked up at the MC, reaching out to him. "You look like a nice man. Cujew help me out?"

The MC looked her up and down with an expression of pity. "Sad spirit, we will pray for you. Go, Dorothy, and be at peace."

Brad turned to Zach. "What's happening here?"

"It's a séance," Jarod screamed. "Isn't it fab?"

"I think technically it's a trance channelling session," Zach said. "That's what happens when a person is able to vacate his personality and let other personalities—sometimes discarnate ones, meaning those of the dead—come in to fill the void temporarily. It's called 'crossing over' in some circles."

Dorothy melted away as Esmeralda transformed again. Her cheekbones grew long and dramatic as her eyes became giant and liquid. Now she seemed to tower over the stage, commanding far more height than either Judy or Esmeralda had possessed.

"Say, spirit, who are you?" said the impresario.

"My name is Joan," came a silvery reply as unlike the previous voice as that had been from Esmeralda's. "Who has summoned me?"

"Joan who?"

There was a pause as the figure struck an indignant pose. "Joan *who?* Joan Crawford, of course!" she barked. "Who the hell are you and what kind of pathetic way is that to greet a star?"

"My profound apologies, Miss Crawford."

"That's more like it."

"Ask her if Bette's with her!" someone yelled.

La Crawford's eyes flared. "Of course that tramp is here! She follows me everywhere. And she's still over-act-ing!"

Someone guffawed.

Joan said, "I see you know whereof I speak."

Esmeralda's eyelashes batted wide and a hand clamped onto her hip. "Watch it, bi-*itch*!" came a familiar bleat. "Or I'll push you down those sta-*airs* again!"

"It's Bette Davis!" someone shrieked, as the figure on-stage twitched and writhed in an agony of misfired synapses rarely seen on-screen since the golden age of Hollywood.

"As Baby Jane Hudson!" someone added.

The figure curtsied. "None other. Glad you could make it to my sha-*owl*"

"*Your* show?" boomed La Crawford. "Why Bette, I thought you'd learned your lesson when you died."

"Dear Jo-*oan*! You died in *Johnny Guitar*," said Bette. "And numerous other atrocities. I just crossed over for the enterta-*ain*-ment value."

The audience guffawed. Bette turned to the MC. "Say, you're a cutie! I'd kiss you but I just wa-*ashed* my hair."

"I'd kiss you too, Miss Davis, but I'm gay," the MC replied.

"Oh? You're ga-*ay*? Is that so-o?"

"Surely you approve of gay liberation, Miss Davis?"

Bette's lips drew back in a sneer. "That depends. What's in it for me?"

The crowd roared its approval.

"Wow, this is amazing!" Brad said.

"Isn't she great?" Jarod enthused. "You never know who's going to come out of her next. Last weekend she channelled Leonardo DiCaprio spending a night in a Bangkok jail with six underage hookers."

Brad's eyebrows rose an inch. "I'd like to have seen that."

They turned back to the stage where someone claiming to be the boy King Tutankhamun had taken over with the antics of a 14th century BC Buster Keaton. After he left, Esther Williams tried to swim across the stage.

Bradford took the opportunity to look around. Sebastian and his entourage were wholeheartedly enjoying the spectacle. Even the look-a-like lovers had separated themselves long enough to give Esmeralda their nearly undivided attention. An hour passed as A-list celebrities followed B-movie actors in a parade of the fatuous, the famous and the downright peculiar. Finally, they watched in astonishment as Esmeralda curled herself into a ball, moaning and writhing as though she were about to give birth. Suddenly, she spewed what looked like papaya salad over the audience, who reacted with a curious combination of disgust and gratitude.

"Say, spirit, who are you now?" the MC cried.

Esmeralda's eyes stared over the crowd, but they were clearly no longer the eyes of Esmeralda. "I am the Near-Immediate Future of Mankind!" a voice boomed darkly. "Beware! Your selfish ways lead to doom!"

Without further warning, she exploded in a puff of pink feathers, leaving a faintly sulphuric smell hanging in the air. The audience clapped and cheered, but Esmeralda had vanished.

"Gosh. Looks like we haven't got a chance!" Zach exclaimed.

"Oh, dear! I wonder how 'immediate' she meant?" Jarod said. "I hope not before my facelift!"

"From the looks of it, I'd say it's pretty imminent," Brad replied, and rose from his seat. "I'll be back!"

He rushed onto the empty stage. Grabbing the curtains with both hands, he yanked them back. He was startled to see nothing behind them but night sky. The stage ended a foot from the rooftop edge. He looked down. Wind blew through his hair while from the darkness below came the pounding of the surf. Where had Esmeralda gone? Then he spotted a stage door opening onto a passageway off to the left.

Bradford followed an echoing hallway past a series of identical doors till he heard voices.

"Why are you so mean to me?" someone asked.

"I'm mean to a lot of people, darling—you're not special," came Esmeralda's distinctive rasp.

"But I'm offering you Vegas!" the other voice pleaded. "We'll headline together!"

"Darling, I don't want Vegas. I don't *need* Vegas! You show biz people wouldn't know real talent if it walked all over you in spiked heels."

"I want to make you a star!" the voice insisted.

"I *am* a star!" Something smashed against a wall. "Now get out!" Esmeralda shrieked.

Brad shrank back into the shadows as footsteps approached. The door opened and Celine's double stepped out and walked swiftly away. Brad took a breath then marched up to the door and knocked.

"*¿Quién es?*" Esmeralda called out brightly.

"*Soy un admirador,*" Brad said trippingly.

"*¡Ah! ¡Pase!*"

Brad opened the door and entered. The shattered remains of a vase lay on the floor. Tarantula eyelashes greeted him in the mirror.

"Hello, handsome," Esmeralda said, flinging a snakeskin boa over her shoulder. "*¿Qué pasa?*"

She turned to the mirror and removed her wig. Beneath it, she was completely bald, making her look even more condor-like. Here was the real Mayan princess, all feathers and headdresses and slinky scales. Brad tried to recall the name of that Mayan god, the snake with feathers that impressed so many people who otherwise couldn't care one whit for mythology.

"That was an amazing performance," Brad said.

"*Gracias,*" came the reply, wheezing like a car engine that wouldn't quite turn over. "But I'm sure you didn't come here to tell me that. Are you offering me Vegas too?"

"N-no!" Brad stammered. "Please don't throw anything!"

"What then? Atlantic City? Broadway, perhaps?"

"Actually," Brad began, "I wondered if it's possible … can you request a specific person to come through? A dead person, I mean."

"Sometimes," Esmeralda said. "But the spirits don't always cooperate. They can be nasty bitches too, you know."

"Do they have to be famous or can ordinary people come through?"

Esmeralda waved a hand dismissively. "Darling, I come from the *barrios*. Money isn't an issue. Anybody can come through me so long as they promise not to take up permanent residence. I hold the only valid passport to this body."

Brad swallowed. "What do you need—a name? A birthdate?" He was thinking of Agent Panther. If Esmeralda could summon him, maybe his spirit could tell Brad who killed him.

"Usually just a name will do," Esmeralda said. "The Universal Mind knows all."

"The Universal Mind?" Brad said, thinking he'd heard that phrase somewhere recently.

"Sure, everyone knows that," said Esmeralda with a shrug. "If a spirit wants to come through, it will."

"It's as easy as that?"

Esmeralda's nostrils flared. "Easy? You think what I do is *easy*?" Her eyes cast about the dressing table for something to throw. Thankfully, there were no more vases within reach.

"Sorry!" Brad exclaimed. "I didn't mean it like that."

Esmeralda smoothed her ruffled feathers back in place, regarding him in the mirror. " Come back Sunday— I'll see what I can do for you."

10

The rooster woke them before dawn again. Even half-awake, Brad was feeling amorous. His hand snaked under the covers. I know what a rooster symbolizes, he thought. Apparently Zach felt the same

"Cock-a-doodle-do," Brad whispered in Zach's ear.

"Speaking of birds," Zach said. "I just dreamed I saw you flying through the air with your own set of wings."

"As if that'll ever happen with my fear of heights," Brad said. "Unless they happen to be the wings tattooed on my abdomen."

Half an hour later, they slipped out of bed and dressed. Feeling nostalgic, Brad donned a favourite T-shirt sporting a bison and the name of a city far to the north. The shirt was a prized possession, a gift from an old flame from Indiana with a taut lasso and a penchant for bull riding.

Zach, meanwhile, had prepped a knapsack with food and water for a reconnaissance hike around Puerto Vallarta. Though it was still early, the morning light was already blinding when they stepped outside. Their explorations took them into the mountains above the city, where water shrivelled in the sun and anything resembling a road dwindled to a narrow dirt path. This wasn't the flashy Beverly Hills-style neighbourhood above the touristy *Zona Romantica* where their villa was located. Here the buildings were piecemeal adobe constructions grafted to the mountainside, with yards scrabbled out of uneven patches

85

of dirt and dotted with boulders and a few ragged trees.

Scrawny dogs set off a chain of alarm at their approach, but the people they met were welcoming, offering suggestions for sightseeing and advice on how to avoid being bitten by the mangy *perros* dogging their footsteps. Clearly, this wasn't a neighbourhood anyone could stumble into accidentally or go unnoticed. Judging by the surprised faces they met, visitors to this altitude were not an everyday occurrence. Especially not white-faced gringo visitors.

They reached a summit and stopped to gaze over the town. Without realizing it, they'd stepped onto a roof half-covered by sand and pebbles. Looking down over the edge, they saw a small yard filled with colourful weaves and native handiwork. A door opened below. Someone emerged and flashed a smile.

"Hey! You guys come for party-party?" Angie beamed up at them, hands on hips, looking every bit the dime-store huckster here as on the beach below. She motioned for them to join her on her tiny patio where they drank lemonade and shared jokes.

"Okay, José," she said, after checking her watch for the third time. ("Surely that isn't a *real* Rolex," Brad whispered to Zach when Angie was distracted. "See the continuous motion second hand?" Zach replied. "It's real.") Angie gathered up their glasses and shook their hands. "Okay, cowboys. Me go work now. See you below. We party-party again sometime."

They left Angie and continued their climb to a giant wooden *cruce* overlooking the city. The view was spectacular. Power grids loomed in the distance like a postmodern crucifixion. At the top, they paused for breath beneath a jacaranda tree. Zach grabbed Brad's arm.

"Look!"

A blue butterfly with an eight-inch wingspan glittered ethereally over the gulch yawning below them.

"It's a Morpho," Zach said. "Otherwise known as the Blue Butterfly of Love. The dorsal side of their wings is actually iridescent, which is why they look metallic."

"It's incredible," Brad said, watching as it flashed in the sun. "I've never seen anything quite like it."

"There's a legend among the Amazonians that when you see a Blue Morpho you're near your true love."

"It must be true," Brad said, pulling Zach close and kissing him. "And it just happens to match your hair."

"Of course, there's another side to the legend that says if you follow a Morpho into the jungle in search of love, you'll never return."

Brad shook his head. "Don't you just hate how there always has to be a moral to everything?"

They watched until the butterfly floated gently out of sight before turning back to the world below. If they'd glanced over their shoulders at that moment, they might have seen a figure following at a distance, skirting the sides of houses and vanishing behind oleander bushes whenever they turned for a look.

Following the dusty trail back downhill, they approached a small Franciscan mission. It was like something out of time, built long before cars or planes or Zapatista uprisings. An old padre sat grooming a burro in the courtyard. His face was shrunken, his skin cracked like dried earth. The man's eyes were twinkling black coals. He might have been in his nineties or possibly older. He brought a finger to his face and touched his cheekbone. He smiled and nodded, as though they'd done something unusual. It was the light colour of their eyes that attracted him.

"*Buen día*," Brad called out.

The man held a finger before his mouth and shook his head. This monk had taken a vow of silence. He offered them water in tin cups dipped into a bucket. They drank in silence and nodded their thanks before moving on. The mission's bell tower cast its long shadow over the mountainside under the morning sun. It boomed once as they passed beneath.

With all the water and lemonade, Brad was beginning to feel an overwhelming call of nature. He scanned the streets for a public building, but nothing presented itself. Up ahead, a pink footbridge spanned the road. Brad looked up and down the deserted avenues before deciding to take his chances relieving himself against the walls of a nearby building.

"What would the Buddha say about urinating on someone's house?" he asked over his shoulder.

Zach cocked his head. "I think he'd be cool about it. He'd probably say something like, 'The stream of life is endless.' I'm sure he understood the necessity of peeing on someone's house occasionally."

Brad had just finished when they heard footsteps approaching. He hurriedly zipped himself into his shorts.

"Eeeek!" someone screamed. "You just pissed on Liz Bloody Taylor's house, you total barbarian!"

They turned to see Jarod coming toward them. He pointed at a sign that read *Casa Kimberly*.

"Don't you even know where you are? Are you such a philistine that you would piss on the house of the most beautiful woman of all time?" Then he shrugged. "Oh, what the hell! I'm sure she was used to it after being married to Dick Burton all those years. Which reminds me of a good piece of advice my mother gave me: don't pretend it's raining when someone's pissing on your head."

"Are you serious?" Brad asked.

"Absolutely—she said that. My mother was a very wise woman."

"No. I mean, is this really Liz Taylor's house?"

"The one and only, doll-face!" Jarod indicated the pink bridge overhead. "That's the Bridge of Reconciliation. When Dick got drunk and abusive, Liz used to lock him on the other side of it and not let him back across till he was sober. It's a museum now, but the original furniture is still here. You can even spend the night in their actual bed. Imagine, sleeping in Liz Taylor's bed and getting fucked by the hunk of your dreams. You'd almost imagine you were her!"

"And afterwards you could drink from one of Burton's seven bars," Zach added, looking up from a sign he'd been reading. "It says he installed one in nearly every room, so he wouldn't have to go looking if he woke up thirsty."

"It's true," Jarod said. "There are seven functional bars and I can describe them all. I'm an expert. I've been inside thirty-seven times."

Brad shook his head. "Gosh, I can't even think of a witty response to that."

Jarod looked him up and down. "Your T-shirt says 'Calgary.' That's witty enough."

Without waiting to be asked, Jarod joined them, providing an amusing if unorthodox commentary as they went along. Their walk took them into uncharted territory, along the banks of the Río Cuale through the poorer section of town. Here, the houses were even more unkempt and derelict than the ones on the hilltop. Junked cars and rusted heaps of scrap cluttered the yards. Scrawny cats followed them everywhere. The Cuale thinned as it drew closer to the mountain. In the dry season the river was little more than a dirty rivulet stagnating alongside the road.

Jarod stopped to regard the neighbourhood. "I just love squalor! It has such a poignant, down-at-heels charm, don't you think?"

"Probably more so if you don't live in it," Brad said.

Jarod shot him a glance. "Well, aren't you just a killjoy? Maybe we should find you another movie star's house to piss on."

A pack of teenage boys kicking a soccer ball along the dusty street turned to watch as they passed. Jarod smiled disarmingly. One of them flipped him the bird.

"Ouch!" he said. "I must have got my expressions mixed up."

They turned down a side street into what appeared to be some sort of lurking zone. Everywhere they looked, flamboyantly dressed Latinos skulked in corners, watching one another from the shadows. If Brad hadn't known better, he might have thought they'd stumbled onto a gay cruising ground.

The trio's presence began to attract attention. What at first appeared to be a handful of individuals prowling in haphazard fashion soon banded together as a unit. The gang focused its attention on the newcomers like hyenas circling a kill.

"This could be trouble," Brad said, eyeing the gang.

"Do you think they're as mean as they look?" Jarod asked.

"I'm sure they can be if they need to be," Brad said.

Jarod pulled out a camera and snapped a picture. Several of the men stopped and posed for him. "The one with the swastika tattoo is kind of cute," he said.

Suddenly, one of the men snapped a finger and the

gang splintered, approaching on both sides as if to cut off any retreat.

"I saw that move in *West Side Story*," Jarod announced. "Jets on one side and Sharks on the other."

"Keep walking," Brad said tersely, as the circle slowly closed around them.

"Gulp!" said Jarod.

"Let's try down there," Brad said, indicating a turn in the road.

Before they could reach it, however, a second group appeared ahead of them and stood blocking their path with arms crossed over their chests.

"Can you speak enough Spanish to ask for help if we get separated?" Brad asked.

Jarod shook his head. "No, but I can say 'Fuck off, punk' in Cantonese."

"That should be useful," Brad noted.

"Should we make a run for it?" Zach asked.

"That's just what I was thinking," Brad said.

Before they could make a move, a bullet pinged off a lamppost. The gang looked around in confusion. A second shot bounced off a car. Bodies scattered as men leapt into doorways and dove behind rusted vehicles.

"*Ping! Ping!*" Jarod cried, as bullets continued to rain down on them.

Brad glanced down an alley in time to see the green-eyed Mexican taking aim from the far end. His next shot elicited an angry squawk, followed by a harangue in Spanish.

Someone called out. "Hey, man! You fuck! You killed my cat! You are one dead hombre!"

The gang suddenly drew their guns and began firing. The green-eyed man turned and ran down the alley. Taking advantage of the distraction, Brad waved Zach and Jarod across a small concrete bridge to the far side of the river. They were soon safely out of range, but Brad wouldn't let them stop.

"Keep going!" he urged, as they tore through an alley between two warehouses.

"Is it always this fun where you guys are?" Jarod called out, sleeves floating behind him.

"Oh, this is nothing!" Zach said. "You should see when Brad really gets excited."

Once they were safely away from all danger, Brad hailed a cab and herded Zach and Jarod inside. "Look after each other. I'll meet up with you as soon as I can," he said.

"Don't worry about us. We'll be fine," Zach said.

Brad tapped on the car roof. "Take them to the beach. *¡A la playa, rápido!*" he ordered.

The car shot off down the road. Brad watched it disappear around a corner before turning and heading back to the neighbourhood they'd just escaped.

11

Sirens wailed as Brad made his way back to the square. A crowd of onlookers had gathered, mostly old women and children. Brad stood at a distance watching the police do their work. The gang had vanished along with the green-eyed man. If anything, they probably regretted having a shoot-out on their own turf. It could only draw unwanted attention. Even if they bribed the police, as was often the case, the public would still demand an investigation. In all likelihood, the police would round up the usual suspects and make it look like justice was being served. Then public anger would be appeased and things return to normal, letting the gang continue whatever nefarious operations they were running behind the neighbourhood squalor.

Apart from the uniforms, Brad couldn't see much difference between the police officers and the men who'd just been shooting at one another. Still, he knew they couldn't all be bad. Corruption was as native to Mexico as tequila, but lately a growing awareness had changed public attitude from one of fearful tolerance to non-acceptance of violence on either side of the law.

Leaving the police to their investigations, Brad slipped back across the bridge and away from that neighbourhood. The one he found himself in next was just as tawdry, but here and there a burgeoning bougainvillea branch or the groping tendrils of a strangler fig accented the walls and lent the decay a hint of majesty and beauty.

A bar loomed ahead. Zach and Jarod would be safely

on the beach by now, Brad reasoned. He could afford to stop and have a quick drink. If he was lucky, he might overhear some local gossip about what was going on and pick up some worthwhile information.

Brad pushed through the saloon doors, letting them flap to a close behind him. The place was a typical family-run establishment with a handful of wooden tables, a karaoke machine, and a mirrored bar with a shelf of the usual poison arranged in front. Heads looked up briefly at his entrance and dropped down again.

"*Hola, amigo*," came the bartender's friendly voice. "Welcome to Casa Ricardo."

Brad ordered a margarita and sat perspiring at a table. He wiped his face with a shirtsleeve and stared off in the distance. The bartender placed a glass in front of him and withdrew. Brad sipped his drink and yawned loudly. Time seemed to have come to a standstill in the sleepy little tavern.

He pondered the recent events. Either the green-eyed man had very poor aim or he hadn't seriously been trying to kill anyone. His shots had gone wide enough for an army to slip between them. Brad tried to think when he'd latched onto their tail. Had he followed them across the mountaintop? Maybe he'd been waiting outside their villa that morning when they left. What was he hoping they would lead him to?

In any case, Brad knew, he'd been right in getting Zach and Jarod out of the way. Even though Zach was technically part of this operation, he was in-training and still had a lot to learn. His Vision Quest was only a few days away. At least that would get him out of town for a while. With things heating up, Brad was glad he'd be leaving. He'd feel much better tackling problems on his own for the next little while.

He was absorbed by these thoughts when he felt an insistent tugging on his sleeve. He looked down to see a boy of about four or five staring up at him. It was one of the Chiclet Chicos. Brad reached into his pocket for some coins. Instead of gum, however, the boy produced a feather. Brad grasped it and turned it in the light. It was identical to the feather Zach had found lying beside the pool.

He stared at the boy. "Who gave you this? *¿Quién te lo dio?*"

"*Un hombre,*" said the child, frightened by Brad's forceful gaze.

"*¿Que hombre?*" Brad insisted, trying not to scare him further.

The child shrugged and backed away. He slipped out the door and was gone.

Brad sprang to the window, but the boy was already out of sight. The street looked deserted in the blazing afternoon sun. He tried to settle his thoughts. *A feather!* Who else could have sent it but his former partner? But Little Wing was dead. Brad had watched him die four years earlier, his life pumping out in the blood that covered Brad's hands and the shirt he'd used as a tourniquet in a vain attempt to save his life.

But if Little Wing was dead, then somebody was doing a damn good job of impersonating him. It wasn't just the feathers. The man in the VW who'd shot at the taxi driver had looked exactly like him. Could someone imitate another human being so perfectly you thought the dead had returned?

Brad felt a hand on his shoulder. He turned with a start and found himself looking up at the taut cheekbones and dark eyes of his former—and formerly-dead—partner. Obviously, still very much alive.

"Of all the gin joints in all the towns in all the world, you walk into mine."

Brad was speechless as he gaped up at the powerful face with the long black hair tucked behind the ears.

"Relax, Red! You look like you just saw a ghost."

Brad shook his head. "I—I don't understand," was all he could manage.

Little Wing shrugged. "What's to understand? Hell, Red, you know what they say: 'Everybody comes to Ricardo's.'"

"How … how…?"

"How am I?"

"You're dead!" was all Brad could think to say.

"*Was*," Little Wing corrected. "I was dead." He winked. "These things happen, Red. Can I join you?" Without waiting for an answer, he swung a chair around and sat facing Brad. He picked up Brad's empty glass and sniffed. "Still self-medicating, I see," he said with a knowing look.

Brad sat shaking his head over and over. It was like seeing a ghost. Worse, it was like realizing you were still in love with someone you hadn't seen for years—had never stopped loving them, in fact—when a chance encounter brings you face to face again and the past springs out at you like a tiger from a bush.

Little Wing reached up and tugged on his left earlobe, a gesture Brad recalled from when they'd worked together. No doubt about it, Brad thought—unless he was staring at a clone, this was the genuine article.

Suddenly, instinctively, they lunged with arms wide in a crushing embrace that left them both breathless. Finally, Brad stepped back to look at Little Wing. Where some men barely inhabited their bodies, and others seemed only to swim awkwardly in theirs, and still others barely stepped in and out of them occasionally as though they were in a way station awaiting a bus, this man filled his body to the brim, pouring himself into it like beer in a glass. He looked incredible.

But how could this be Little Wing? The last time Bradford had seen him, he'd been a corpse. And yet, Brad thought, he'd never seen anyone who looked so vibrantly alive.

"You … you look amazing!" Brad managed.

"Ah shucks! What can I say, Red? Death becomes me. But never mind me! Look at you! You're fucking awesome! You gotta be what now—thirty-one, thirty-two…?"

"Don't say it!" Brad gasped reflexively. He still hadn't got over turning thirty.

"Why? You look fantastic? You look even better now than you did then!"

"Yeah, well, thanks, but … you may not have noticed but my eyelids are starting to droop." He made a deprecating gesture. "A bit."

Little Wing snorted. "Fuck that! You're still fucking perfect." He cocked his head. "By the way, were you part of that commotion happening down the street a while ago?"

Brad nodded. "Yes, but not willingly."

"Yeah, right!" Little Wing nudged him. "Same old Red—rushing in where demons fear to tread. You wanna watch out for them Federales. You can't trust 'em. And you can't always buy their co-operation these days either. Times are a-changing."

Brad glanced at the window. "I'm not sure they were Federales. These guys looked like full-time gringo-haters with a drug operation on the side."

Little Wing shrugged. "In this town it's the same thing, dude. Don't be fooled by appearances." He leaned back, arms clasped behind his head, stretching his body full out. He gave a hearty, comfortable laugh. "I could probably tell you a thing or two about appearances." He winked. "Anyway, I'm glad you got out of that one by yourself. I can't always be there to save your skin."

Brad cocked his head. "That was you the other day in the VW. I knew it!"

"I thought you saw me." Little Wing nodded. "You saved my skin once. Looks like we're even."

Brad shook his head. "What happened when you took off after that guy down the highway?"

Little Wing's lips curled. "Typical Mexican traffic. I nearly had him, Red, but a trailer transport ran me off the road. You've probably noticed they don't believe in passing lanes here—it's like the Indy 500, day and night. By the time I got back on the road, the other car was gone. Who was he, anyway? And why was he trying to kill you?"

"I don't think he was—at least not at that point. I think he was trying to kidnap me."

Little Wing sat back. "I see. So you're not just down here for a quickie suntan and a tequila hangover."

Brad shook his head.

"And since it's top secret, you can't tell me what it is you're doing. And I wouldn't ask you to, either. How's Grace, by the way?"

Bradford smiled half-heartedly. "What can I say? Grace is Grace. But I can tell you this much. Something big is happening in this town. An agent got killed the night before outside a bar called Garbo's..."

Little Wing whistled. "So the rumors are true," he said. "If it helps, I heard it was gang-related. I'm telling you, the Federales have really fucked this place with their little turf wars trying to gain control of the drug trade."

Brad nodded. "Maybe, but I don't think it's related

to the case I'm on. That guy was my contact. He said he thought he was being followed, so we agreed to split up and rendezvous in a more private place. By the time I got there, he was already down. I think the guy who killed him was the same guy you saw trying to kidnap me."

Little Wing smacked the table with his fist. "It makes my blood boil when these fuckers start killing good people. Just think of the ego of someone who kills by choice. It's not self-defence; it's an act of cold-blooded destruction. Someone decides you don't need to exist any more and *poof!* There goes a life, a history, a whole future that will never happen—some of which may have included raising a family or creating amazing art or inventing something that might have advanced civilization."

Little Wing slumped his chin onto his palm and looked out the window. Brad could only guess what deep personal level this was resonating on with him.

As if reading his thoughts, Little Wing turned to him and smiled. "Time to change the subject. The past is past. I don't want you on a downer now that I'm here!" He signalled to the bartender. "Dos martinis. My amigo and I are celebrating."

"Sí, señor," the man said, setting two glasses on the bar.

Little Wing looked over at Brad. "I forgot to ask. Do you prefer stirred or shaken?"

"Depends. I like my vodka bruised but my gin treated gently. I've heard it's healthier that way."

"Amen to that!" Little Wing said with a laugh. "But these are tequila martinis. Though in my humble estimation, if you're drinking for your health then you're in mucho trouble, my friend."

The martinis arrived. Little Wing raised his glass. *"Gracias a la vida."*

"*A la vida*," Brad seconded. He took a sip then put down his drink. He stared at Little Wing for a long moment. "I need to know," he said finally. "Why didn't you die in Paris?"

Little Wing nodded. "I did. But I was revived— because of you. You kept me alive long enough that the emergency workers were able to resuscitate me. It happened on the way to the hospital. Where were you, by the way? How come you didn't come along for the ride?"

Brad shook his head. "They wouldn't let me. I was taken away for debriefing immediately afterward. When it was done, they told me you'd been pronounced dead on the way to the hospital."

"Is that so?" Little Wing picked up his glass and downed it in one gulp. "Drink up, Red. Humour me." He motioned to the bartender for refills.

"I've always felt I let you down," Brad said. "Why did they tell me you died?"

Little Wing locked eyes with him. "Because I did. When I came out of my coma, they told me I'd died. In fact, they said the odds were so against my survival that none of the emergency room doctors would bet on me to come out of it. I thought that over for a while and the next day I told them I wanted to stay dead. I'd been thinking of quitting and there was the opportunity staring me in the face. I was out of the game. Kaput! Finito! I told them I was going to disappear and that they weren't to tell anybody. Are you getting the picture?"

Brad nodded. "You realized it was a miracle you were still alive and you didn't want to jeopardize your second chance at life."

"Something like that."

"I've felt like that a few times," Brad said. "When life gets really messy and something terrible happens to someone I care about, the first thing I think about is getting out—just disappearing and never coming back. I figure if I do, people will draw their own conclusions."

"As you did in my case."

"But I would have told *you*," Brad insisted. "I would never have left you wondering."

A tear welled in Little Wing's eyes. He pulled on his earlobe again. "I'm sorry," he whispered hoarsely. "I can't tell you how many nights I've spent regretting not doing exactly that, Red."

"It's okay. I understand." Brad put his hand over Little Wing's and held it there. "Where have you been all this time?"

"Here and there. I was up north for a time in a place called Skeleton Canyon. It seemed appropriate. I had a job escorting Mexicans back across the border for a while. Yeah—I was a bounty hunter. Scum of the earth, right? Hell, I couldn't believe people actually wanted into that blood-sucking country of ours, considering who was running the place. I tried to convince them to stay where they were and make things better for themselves here. I tried to convince myself I was doing the right thing, but I couldn't. What the hell do I know about it? Since then I've been down here in PV—mostly."

"And all this time no one else has known you're alive? Not even your family?"

Little Wing bit his lip. "My family's long dead."

"That's right—I nearly forgot. You're a foundling like me."

"Anyway, I'm used to it. I know I'm better off alone." He paused. "But you seem to have done well for yourself."

Brad looked up curiously.

A smile crept into Little Wing's face. "I'm talking

about that blue-haired boy you're with. Very impressive. You always knew how to pick 'em, Red."

"You saw us at the beach together?"

"There … and other places." He turned to look out the window. "It's cute how you two spoon together when you're sleeping. Nice 'toos, by the way. I couldn't quite make out what was on the boy's belly—a horse's head maybe? And of course, I remember those wings of yours. That was some flight you used to take me on."

Brad felt a tremor of fear, but he knew not to let it show. "So it was you who left that feather on our balcony."

Little Wing nodded with a big goofy smile. "I had to drop off my calling card. But of course, I couldn't leave without seeing you in the flesh. Sorry—I didn't mean to creep you out."

"How'd you get in?"

"You know me, Red. Did I ever have trouble gaining entry to any place when we worked together?"

"Fair enough," Brad said. "I secretly used to believe you were a bird, you got into the craziest places. For a while you almost had me convinced you really could fly."

Little Wing stared at him. "Almost?" He broke into a toothy grin. "Just joshing you, Red. Human beings can't fly—can they?"

"Of course not." Brad laughed self-consciously, not wanting to let on how spooked he was by all of this. "What about you? No hottie boys in your life these days? You can't be that alone with all the cuties in town."

"I tend not to get attached to anyone or anything. I had a goldfish for a while, though. I have just two rules in life these days." He smiled and lifted his boot-clad feet onto the table. One—cowboy boots are always acceptable footwear. And two—never get attached to anything you can't flush down the toilet."

Time passed. They were on their fifth martini. Brad reached out clumsily for his glass, accidentally knocking it over the table edge. Little Wing's hand shot out and caught it before it was halfway to the floor.

"You've still got your reflexes, I see," Brad said admiringly.

When they'd worked together, Little Wing had been famous for his "trick." He would extend his hand in front of him with a glass perched on top. At a signal, he would pull his hand back and, with the same hand, draw, fire and shatter the glass before it hit the ground. He'd once ranked third nationally in a quick-draw competition.

Little Wing said, "I've still got a lot of things I used to have."

Brad blushed.

Little Wing looked away. "So you're really attached to that boy of yours?"

Brad nodded. "I think this is it. He's even applied to join the agency."

Little Wing whistled. "You really know how to make a convert." He paused and looked down at the dusty floor. "I guess it would be an inappropriate time to tell you how much I missed you." He looked up. "Fuck, Red. You have no idea how much I've missed you."

Brad was struck by the vehemence in Little Wing's tone. He had no idea what to say.

"I guess I shouldn't ask if you missed me too," Little Wing said.

Brad looked away. "Every night for a long, long time."

"Do you remember—?"

"I remember," Brad cut him off.

"After you, I never wanted anyone else." Little Wing searched Brad's face. "Fuck, I've missed you. I miss you pounding into me in the middle of the night. I miss your chin stubble scraping my back raw. I especially miss waking up beside you and that iron-hard erection every morning." He laughed sadly. "You're the only guy I've slept with who never had morning breath. You're fucking perfect! Even your teeth are perfect. How is that?"

"My partner Zach says it's karma. I was good in another life and now I'm reaping the rewards."

Little Wing nodded. "Partner. Right. Lest we forget. I guess this is my karma, huh?" He leaned in suddenly and pulled Brad's face toward him. Their lips fused. Neither of them made an effort to stop it. Finally, Little Wing broke it off with a sigh.

"Fuck! I meet the most perfect man in the world and I have to lose him just because I died. Talk about fucking *karma!*"

Brad searched his face. "It's been four years, Little. Maybe it's time to get attached to someone again. Love … love's a good thing when it works."

"I've heard people say it can be like a religious experience."

Brad nodded. "You might call it that."

"I still get those in bars on a good day." Little Wing nudged Brad in the ribs. "You're still too serious, Red. Nah—marriage isn't for me. To be married requires a great deal of patience and no imagination. I have no patience and far too much imagination. Besides, I'm a happy guy. What do I wanna fuck it up for?"

A cacophony sounded from outside. They looked out the window to see a four-year old Elvis, replete with sunglasses, sequined pantsuit and pasted-on sideburns, standing on the corner playing *Love Me Tender* on marimbas.

"Look at this town!" Little Wing exclaimed. "It's dirty and dusty and tacky as hell, but I love it more than any place else on earth. I've got whales in the bay and lime and mango trees outside my door, and good old Elvis himself on the street corner." He shook his head. "Nah—I don't need anything else, Red. Thanks for reminding me."

Little Wing got to his feet and stood looking down. "*Adiós, amigo*," he said, with an ironic salute.

"Is that it?" Brad demanded. "After four years, don't I deserve more than an hour's conversation and a couple of martinis?"

"You're right—you deserve a lot more." Little Wing bent and kissed Bradford on the lips again. "And I'm real sorry I won't be the one to give it to you." He headed for the door then stopped and turned around. "But we'll always have Paris, Red."

Brad shook his head. "Excuse me, but wasn't Paris where I watched you get knifed to death?"

Little Wing shot him a lopsided grin. "Yeah, well—nothing's perfect." He stood there for a moment. "Don't try to follow me, Red. I've still got all the instincts, so I'll know you're there."

"Wait! How will I find you again?"

"Just look over your shoulder, pal. Whenever you need me, I'll be there."

Brad watched as his former-partner strode into the street, leaving the saloon doors flapping and taking with him a very large piece of his heart.

12

By the time Brad reached the street, Little Wing had vanished. It felt like eons since he'd entered the bar, but the sun had just reached the midpoint in the sky. He sat on a bench and looked up and down the deserted thoroughfare. It all seemed too incredible. In fact, he was willing to bet that if he told anyone about it they wouldn't believe him. So who better to tell than the most sceptical person he knew?

Brad pulled out his cell phone. Whether she believed him or not, Grace needed to know about this new development.

"It's getting so I can almost set my clock by your calls, Red," his boss told him. "What have you got for me today?"

"How does a real live conversation with a dead agent sound?"

"Intriguing. Go on."

Brad described his meeting with Little Wing in detail. Grace sounded no more shocked than usual, which was not at all. He was never sure if he detested or admired that quality in her.

"We wrote Agent Little Wing off as dead four years ago," she said. "It was exactly as you said. The version of events we got from the emergency workers jived precisely with your account at the time. Except for the happy ending, of course. I've never actually heard of an agent 'opting out' of the business like that. There would at least have been a decompression process, some serious attempt to deprogram him before he got sent back into the so-called 'real' world."

"But not if you thought he was dead."

This elicited silence. Brad ran a hand through his hair. Something had to make sense here. "Did you see the body? Go to the funeral, perhaps?"

"No. That would have been foolish. I have no physical contact with any of my agents except under the most dire circumstances."

What could be direr than death? Bradford wondered. Somehow she made it sound more like germ avoidance than a safety protocol.

"Has anything like this ever happened before?" he asked.

Grace paused. "I had an agent disappear once before," she said finally.

"What happened to him?"

"I never found out, though I have a theory I won't bore you with just now. In any case, I take it you're sure this was really your guy and not some carefully constructed fabrication? It's been four years, after all."

No one could imitate those kisses, Brad thought. "It was him. He knew far too much about me for it not to have been. He still tugs on his left ear when he talks. Plus he left a feather on our patio a couple of days ago."

"A feather?"

"It was his calling card whenever he went around snooping. You'd know he'd been there if you found an owl feather lying around. It was a jokey signature thing he liked to do."

"Like Zorro leaving a trail of slashed Z's everywhere he goes?"

"Kind of."

"Goodness—the things you people don't tell me. And he says he's retired now and as good as dead as far as anyone in our world knows?"

"That's what he told me."

"Hmm. I wonder…"

From the sound of her voice, Brad could tell he wasn't going to like whatever she was about to say.

"If he's really alive—and I believe you when you say he is—then that means someone arranged to extricate him from my department without telling me. Which pisses me off big time, but I'll deal with that later. Given the current state of events, however, it's likely that whoever got him out secretly had him pulled into another division and is now using him down there as an agent for his or her own reasons."

"So you think Little Wing might still be an agent— a *special* agent—within the organization."

"It happens. Once in a while, the other ops put agents on my tail to keep their eye on things. I've raised bloody hell over it before, but it hasn't stopped them yet."

"Why would they need to keep an eye on things?"

"Maybe they don't trust what I'm doing…"

"Or maybe they don't trust your current agents," Brad murmured.

This elicited another palpable silence on Grace's end. It left Bradford feeling more than a little nervous at the thought of intra-agency squabbles. If Little Wing was still an agent, what was he doing in Vallarta? Now that Grace had raised the possibility, he realized there were two things that bothered him about Little Wing's story. First, it just seemed too convenient. How likely was it that he'd turn up at the exact moment Brad was being kidnapped? Second, why would he contact Brad just to say he was no longer an agent, so long, farewell and *auf*

Wiedersehen? If he really wanted to be left alone—and knowing that Brad already believed him to be dead—then why get in touch after all this time?

Grace interrupted his internal monologue. "I'm still not sure what you should be looking for, Red, but I need you to keep your ears to the ground. You and that blue-haired boy of yours. His talents are going to do great things for us one day."

"We're doing that, but there's not much to report. We've been making the rounds while trying to appear to be tourists. There's one thing worth noting, though: a number of faces keep recurring in any gathering we've been to, starting with the night Panther was killed. On the other hand, this is a tourist resort. There's no reason to suspect any of them as yet."

"Well, I can tell you this," Grace said. "It's only a rumour, mind—but I've had word from the boys upstairs that something is going to happen soon in the Celine department, if you take my meaning. Whatever else might be going on, keep your eyes on her. If that means hanging out in bars and buying a few extra martinis for the boys you meet, I can pad your budget."

For a moment Brad thought of mentioning the Celine impersonator and Esmeralda's spirit-channelling act, but it seemed just too kooky to bring up on top of everything else. He let it pass.

"I'll do my best," Brad said.

"Good. Now get back on that beach and mingle."

All the way back to the beach, Brad wondered what to tell Zach. Or rather, how much to tell Zach. As far as anyone was concerned, Little Wing had been Brad's *work* partner—nothing more. In all the years since, he hadn't breathed a word of their affair to anyone, not even Grace. And in her books, that would be the first cardinal sin: not to disclose everything. Absolutely *everything*. Even to himself, Brad had never dared use the word "love" in relation to his former partner. If asked, he might have admitted to having a brotherly affection for Little Wing, but he now saw it had been much more. Despite his denial, love was what he'd felt. Still, as far as Brad was concerned, there would always be things no one else needed to know—certain intimate details of his personal life that deserved respect as much as circumspection. If Grace didn't get that, well, then tough.

But not telling Zach was another story. Until now, Brad had held nothing back from him. Total honesty and total commitment—wasn't that the mettle of a true relationship? On the other hand, did Zach really need to hear about every itch he'd scratched or know every detail of Bradford's past? He felt a pang of conscience as he trudged along the beach. Against all odds, Little Wing had returned to his life. All the same, their affair was definitely a thing of the past.

Or was it?

Could there be more to this than Brad dared admit? Didn't he owe it to himself to see what might still be there? He shook his head. No—that was crazy! He'd never been as content as he had since meeting Zach. More than just content, he was happy. So why question a perfect relationship just because some guy from the past showed up again? Brad had no doubts about Zach whatsoever. If anything, the doubts lay at his own doorstep. The very idea that he was even thinking this was reason enough to suspect his motives. What kind of fool would consider re-connecting with a past love when he was already in a perfect relationship in the here-and-now? Brad felt a kind of indignation on Zach's behalf for his own treachery. What was his problem, anyway? Sheesh!

He'd almost reached the Blue Parrot. Looking past the bodies crowded under the sun umbrellas, he saw Zach waving from a distance. Concern was written on the boy's face. No doubt he'd been worrying the whole time Brad was gone for—he checked his watch—holy crap!—nearly three hours! What had he been thinking?

"I was so worried!" Zach exclaimed as Brad caught up to him.

"I'm fine," Brad said.

You have to tell him what happened, Brad reminded himself. It's only fair to make a full disclosure to Zach right here and now.

"So what happened?" Zach asked excitedly. "What did you find?"

"I—uh—nothing." Brad's mouth gaped. "I mean, nothing much. It was pretty much all over by the time I got back there."

It was hardly the full confession he'd planned. He felt like kicking himself.

"I meditated on you while you were gone," Zach said. "All I kept getting were feathers."

"Feathers?" Brad gulped.

Zach shrugged. "Sometimes it's hard to understand the symbols. Maybe I've got birds on the brain today. It must be because of that dream where I saw you flying."

"Don't worry—all's well. I stopped for a drink then put in a call to Grace." He could always tell Zach about Little Wing later, he rationalized. There was no sense worrying him further at this point. "Where's Jarod?"

Zach smiled. "You know Jarod. He couldn't keep still long enough to wait for you to come back. But don't worry—I impressed on him the need for secrecy. I told him he'd need more than a facelift to disguise himself if anyone came after him to stop him from talking."

"Good thinking!"

Brad ordered a beer and tried to relax. The crowd began to thin as the afternoon wore on. The surf was pounding. Gulls screeched and children screamed as waves overran the sand to tickle their toes.

"By the way," Zach said. "Angie came by. I bought you this." He held up one of her trademark burgundy bags with the horizontal white strip.

"Wow—thanks!" Brad held it up to admire it. It was the size of a small duffle bag and handsomely made—perfect for socks and a change of gym clothes. Brad looked around the beach and saw a half dozen others just like it. "She's been busy, I see."

"Ten dollars—special for me!" Zach winked. "Oh, and before I forget, we've been invited to Sebastian's ship this evening. I accepted for us. I thought it would be a nice way to spend our last night together before I go on my Vision Quest."

Brad looked remorseful. "Right—you're going away. I should be the one buying you the gift."

"No worries." Zach grinned. "You can make it up to me in other ways tonight."

"I can certainly do that." He stopped and a frown came over his face. "You still haven't told me much about it. I need to know how much to worry while you're gone."

"It's perfectly safe. You don't need to worry at all."

"Believe me, it comes with the territory," Brad replied.

"Then I'll tell you so you can put your mind at ease. For a Vision Quest, you isolate yourself in a place with powerful vibrations. Some people choose a monastery. Others choose remote mountain locations. I chose the desert. I've heard there's a native village nearby. If they have a *bruja*, I might take a little peyote to help open my chakras."

"*Bruja*? Peyote? And you're telling me not to worry?"

"A *bruja* is a witch, in colloquial terms. She's really the village wise-woman. She'll know exactly which type of peyote plant is safe and how much to administer. They even place it on your tongue for you. It's pretty standard territory for this sort of thing. The place I'm going to has long been the scene of native power ceremonies."

"Magic?"

"In a sense," Zach nodded.

"What does that entail?"

"Nothing too mysterious. Basically, I'm going out there to fast and connect with my spirit so I can claim the destiny I need to follow in this lifetime."

"Won't it just come to you anyway?"

Zach shook his head. "The opportunity is there, but you have to actualize it. For instance, I knew the moment you and I met that we had a strong connection, but there was no guarantee things would work out. They nearly didn't, as you may recall."

Brad looked down. His own skittishness and self-doubt had almost kept them apart, as he recalled.

Zach smiled. "Anyway, that's why I persisted. But I know I don't need to worry about that any more."

Let's hope not, Brad thought guiltily. "Will we have any contact while you're gone?"

"I've got my cell phone in case of emergencies, but I probably won't have a chance to call you much from the desert. I'll try to connect with you on a non-physical plane. I'll send you vibrational messages along with a text or two. It's a good time to brush up on your telepathic receptivity."

"And how do I do that?" Brad asked, pushing at the sand with his toes.

"Just be open to it. Interpret the symbols you see around you. It might be something unusual that catches your attention. I'll do my best to send you clear signals."

"How will you know where to send them? I mean, it's not like they'll have an e-mail address for me. How do you know they won't get lost in the ether?"

Zach grinned. "You've got to stop thinking in material terms. The vibrations I'm talking about aren't limited by a time and space continuum just because most humans are caught up in the physical world."

At that moment, a giant wave lifted a dozen body-surfers high up before pummelling them mercilessly against the shore. A few of the less fortunate ones hobbled out of the surf and crawled across the sand to recover on their beach towels.

"What was it you just said about ignoring the physical world?" Bradford asked.

"I said don't be bound by that kind of thinking—we ignore the physical world at our peril. In fact," Zach said, looking out at the ocean, "waves are a perfect explanation of what I'm talking about. When you look at a wave, what do you see?"

Brad put his hand over his brow and stared out at the water. "A crest at the top and a trough below where the wave rolls forward."

"Exactly. But what most people don't realize is that it's not the water that moves forward."

"It's not?" Brad said.

"No—it's the energy moving through it. A wave is energy in motion, pushing forward as it moves from one group of molecules to the next, energizing and releasing each in turn. The water you see at the top of the crest now isn't the same water that was there a few seconds before. The energy pulses through it and moves on."

"That makes sense," Brad said, wondering why he'd never thought of that before.

"It's the same with etheric vibrations," Zach continued. "That's what people call telepathy. The mind literally forms an energy wave and sends it out as a thought. It's extremely subtle, though a receptive person can pick up on it. But regardless of whether you're receptive or not, you can be affected by it. An emotion is energy in its purest form. If you stay in a room full of depressed people long enough, you'll start to get depressed as well. Or love." He reached for Brad's hand. "If you're around someone who truly loves you, you'll pick that up too."

"I see."

Brad looked down at his hand clasped in Zach's and thought guiltily of Little Wing. Perhaps he should have told Zach about their encounter after all. On the other hand, why worry him over nothing? He turned his gaze out to the sea. The waves seemed to crash on shore with a relentlessness that was almost beyond anything he'd seen.

13

The evening wind was warm and sultry as the water taxi ferried Brad and Zach across to Sebastian's boat. A trio of dolphins accompanied them across the harbour like comical cheerleaders, diving and resurfacing with playful snorts. They stayed with the taxi all the way to the ship, then turned and swam off as though satisfied the pair had been delivered into good hands.

Brad and Zach were among the last to arrive. The jolly captain greeted them personally, reaching a hand down to pull them aboard. "Welcome to the *Rainbow Warrior*. I've invited every beautiful man I could find, and you two are the cream of the crop."

"If you flatter us too much, you may never get rid of us," Brad said.

Sebastian grinned. "Now that you mention it, I could use a couple of good deck hands. Have you ever been to sea, Billy?"

Sebastian left them with an admonishment to enjoy the party as he went off to get the trip underway. A waiter waltzed by, offering the newcomers champagne. Brad and Zach clinked glasses and kissed.

One by one, the sails were hoisted and quickly strained against the wind. They were already heading north when a final taxi roared up alongside and delivered Jarod on deck, his shirtsleeves competing with the sails for wind.

"Catch!" he yelled to Brad as he flung his burgundy bag upwards.

Brad caught it in both hands, surprised by its heft.

"Moisturizers," Jarod explained. "That bag is a godsend. I never go anywhere without it now. I may not kill that little sideshow huckster after all."

Once the ship was under way, Sebastian resurfaced with the look-a-like lovers, one on either arm. This was the furthest apart Brad had seen the pair yet. Funny he hadn't spotted them on board earlier. It was almost as if they'd appeared from nowhere. They wore matching colour-coordinated shorts and skin-tight sleeveless T-shirts. Every visible inch of their bodies was tanned.

"Have you met our Brazilian friends, Moses and Joshua?" Sebastian asked, adding in a loud aside, "Their mothers had high hopes for them, I gather. I'm just glad they didn't call them Noah and Jesus. No floating arks or water-walking tricks for this sailor, thanks."

The pair exuded the arrogance of the extraordinarily beautiful. They declined to shake hands, nodding sullenly at Brad and Zach instead.

Their host steered them along. "Not the best-mannered boys you'll meet, but very pretty to look at," he said over his shoulder. "And fortunately, they don't understand a word of English."

Sebastian was right in saying he'd invited only the best-looking among the beach crowd. The deck resembled an infomercial for an exclusive line of men's skin care products. Everywhere, beauty twisted and gyrated to a loud beat as the boat sailed merrily along.

Waiters appeared with trays of canapés. Grilled crab legs vied for attention with smoked oysters, fresh caviar, mouth-watering slabs of sashimi, and a variety of exotic hors d'oeuvres arrayed in a swirl of colours and textures. It looked as though the Naked Chef had been doing a sultry tango with Martha Stewart in the galley.

As they rounded the northern arm of Banderas Bay, Brad thought he'd never seen a more beautiful sunset than the one unfolding over Sayulita at that moment. It was as if the sky had been daubed in the most delicate shades of violet and hung out to dry. Closer to shore, the colours seemed to flee along the sand, mirrored in the shallow water. Headlights flashed by on the coastal highway above, while bonfires flared below. Here and there the black outline of fishing trawlers crawled homeward with the day's catch. The sea and shore were alight.

With a start, Brad recognized a set of sails dead ahead. For the second time in two days the *Rainbow Warrior* was about to overtake Celine Dion's boat. How was it, he wondered, that wherever Sebastian Mathers sailed the *Libre* turned up?

Brad looked at Zach and shook his head. "This can't be a coincidence," he said.

They watched carefully, but once again failed to see anybody on the *Libre*'s deck. It was a ghost ship. What exactly was the point of sailing if you didn't surface to take in the beauty around you once in a while? Was Ms. Dion so oblivious to the allure of the physical world that she just ignored it? Or was she being cautious because of the kidnapping threats?

Their silver-haired captain returned suddenly. "Looks like a good place to have a party!" he announced with gusto.

The boat slowed and stopped. An anchor slid beneath the waves. The music blared and the guests danced on, while the waiters made their rounds. One by one, stars turned the sky into a gigantic twinkling canopy. Brad looked over to where Zach stood talking with Jarod. He snagged a champagne flute and headed to the foredeck, struggling to keep steady while the ship rocked beneath him. With his legs dangling over the bow, he sat and looked across the water. From here he had a good view of the *Libre,* not fifty yards away. Lights softly illumined its sides and reflected in the waves.

At least he was following Grace's orders in keeping an eye on the singer's boat. He wondered yet again what he was really doing in Puerto Vallarta. As far as Brad was concerned, Celine Dion needed a bodyguard, not a top-secret agent to follow her around and prevent her from being kidnapped.

A swell hit broadside and he reached out to steady himself. The champagne was affecting him. He was getting drunk. He looked over his shoulder where the dancing went madly on. A shadow crept up behind him.

"Something told me I'd find you here," Zach said. "Bored with the party already?"

"Not at all. I was just convening with the stars." Brad looked up, pointing out a constellation. "Not long before he died, my father said that if anything ever happened to him, I could just look up and know he was in Orion's Belt. He said my mother was up there waiting for him to join her one day."

"Did he know he was going to die?"

Brad shook his head. "Not that I know of. He died in a freak car accident. Maybe he had a premonition."

"People sometimes say things without really knowing why," Zach said. "It's the subconscious talking. Maybe intuitively he knew he was going to be leaving and he was already missing you."

"Well, I sure miss him," Brad said, as a falling star flashed across the sky.

"It must have been hard losing both parents so young," Zach replied.

Brad remembered his father and could even recall

the sound of his voice, but his mother always eluded him. He knew her mostly from photographs and stories passed down to him by his father.

"When I was young, it just seemed unfair. You're given these people who are supposed to look after you and show you how to exist in the world, and suddenly they're gone. I don't remember my mother very well, but my father and I bonded in the years following her death. I think he was trying to be two parents for me."

Zach leaned his head on Brad's shoulder.

"Despite the sadness I felt on losing him," Brad continued, "I don't think there could have been a better choice of father for me. He taught me the values I live by. He was a man of total integrity—honest, compassionate, loyal."

"That's pretty much how I see you," Zach said. "If it's any consolation."

Brad's arm snaked around Zach. "I hope he's looking down at us right now. Because I want him to know how proud I am to be with you."

Zach squeezed Brad's hand. "According to Buddhist thinking, the circumstances we're born into aren't an accident. That goes for our families too. Everyone comes into our life for a purpose, to teach us something."

"I wonder what Grace is supposed to teach us," Brad said.

Zach sat up suddenly. "Do you want to know what I think?"

"Sure."

"I've spent a lot of time meditating on her. It's what helped me decide to join Box 77. I think Grace was part of a similar group in Atlantis. The same people were in charge—people like President Bush and Vice-President Chaney. They screwed things up royally then too and were responsible for the blasts that sank the island."

"Blasts?"

"Yes, it wasn't an accident that Atlantis vanished. It was destroyed by the abuses of power. That's why there's almost nothing left of it. Grace was one of the ones who tried to stop them. It makes perfect sense that she's in charge of an organization striving to maintain world peace now."

"Cheers to that," Brad said, lifting his glass to the absent Grace. "If reincarnation is a fact, does that mean we're doomed to repeat everything?"

"Not if we can get it right this time around."

"Karma," Brad said.

"Karma," Zach said, "is simply the meeting of self. It's an ironic form of justice, but it's always fair. Do something good and it returns to you. Do something bad, and you get to clean up your mess. It's always in a subsequent lifetime however. There's really no such thing as instant karma. That's just a guilty conscience working overtime. But it's a good bet that anybody significant in our lives this time around is someone we've known before."

"So it's probably a good bet that we both knew Grace in another lifetime."

"Definitely. She's had a number of lifetimes where she was responsible for the well being of others. Not all of them ended happily, however. I had a vision of her the other day by the pool. In that life, she was a mother who poisoned her children during wartime to keep them from falling into enemy hands. To her, death was preferable to that."

"Sounds pretty extreme," Brad said, shaking his head. "Were we in that lifetime?"

Zach lifted his gaze to the stars. "Actually," he said softly, "we were the children."

"Oh, terrific!"

"Don't worry! Because of that, she's going to be incredibly protective of us in this lifetime. She doesn't realize any of this, of course."

"And we won't tell her?"

Zach shook his head. "I don't think it's a good idea."

A silence crept around them, broken only by the slapping of waves against the bow. Brad pulled Zach closer. He was about to suggest they rejoin the party when he saw movement at the front of the boat. A hatch opened, barely visible in the darkness, as a figure in scuba gear emerged.

"Look!" Brad said quietly.

Before they could do anything, the figure slipped over the side into the water. Brad had no doubt he was headed for the Dion boat. Now he knew why the *Rainbow Warrior* had anchored here. He looked at Zach. What could they possibly do to prevent it from happening?

"I know!" Brad said. He stood and walked over to the mid-deck. "Hey, Jarod!" he called out.

Jarod looked up, a cocktail in either hand. Brad pointed out the *Libre*. "Have you seen who followed us here tonight?"

Jarod's scream carried clearly across the water. "*Aaaack!* She's right here! We've got to do something!"

He scampered away and was soon heard calling to the other guests. Within seconds, the deck was swarming with drunken partyers, each professing to be Celine's biggest fan ever. Without further ado, Jarod broke into the opening of *My Heart Will Go On*. The sound reverberated over the waves far into the night.

Surprise, surprise! Jarod was actually a decent singer with a sweet, silvery tenor. He took up Celine's watery anthem with an infectious gusto as the others joined him in their homage to the diva.

Only at a gay gathering, Brad noted, would everyone know all the words to every Oscar-winning tune and be able to sing in perfect four-part harmony without a rehearsal. By the final chorus, the entire party had joined in. All except one, Brad reminded himself. But who was missing? He looked around the crowd of faces, trying to recall who had been on the ship earlier. Jarod was there, of course. As was Sebastian and his unruly gang of knockabouts. Then it struck him: the dark-haired Brazilian boy was missing.

Brad looked across to see the anchors of the *Libre* being hoisted, its invisible crew motoring away to a more solitary berth. He nudged Zach. "Mission accomplished," he said quietly.

"Hey—they're leaving!" someone shouted, offended that their beloved diva would return their compliment with a nose-thumbing run.

"I don't think they appreciated having their cover blown," Brad called out with a laugh.

Sebastian turned to them, looking agitated. "Wherever we go, that boat shows up!" he griped. "You may find it hard to believe, but I think that captain is following us."

Following us! Had he not known better, Brad might have believed him.

Three hours later, the *Rainbow Warrior* returned to Puerto Vallarta. The evening was nearly at an end, but it wouldn't finish without one final unpleasantness to mark it's passing. As they reached the pier, an angry shouting came from below deck. The Brazilian bombshells, united again, stormed upstairs clutching their burgundy bag between them. Brad hadn't actually seen the dark one return in his scuba gear, but he thought he could make a pretty good case for it if he had to. Perhaps the wet suit was packed inside the bag they were holding onto so dearly.

The pair pushed through the disembarking partyers, nearly forcing Brad over into the water as they barged past.

"Hey! What's your rush?" Brad shouted after them.

Jarod had come up behind them. "I don't think I like those boys very much," he declared with a sniff, stepping onto the pier. "They may be sexy as hell, but they're not very friendly, let me tell you!"

"I'll say," Brad said.

Jarod threw them a baleful glance. "I mean, when all you do is *touch* someone's bag and they point a gun in your face…"

Brad and Zach whirled around at the same time. "What?"

"That's what *I* said. 'What's the big deal?' I mean, sheesh! It's only a beach bag."

"Tell us what happened," Brad said.

"I went down below deck to grab my bag of moisturizers, which just happens to look exactly like the bag those two carry everywhere with them." He shook the bag on his shoulder as if to prove his claim. "When I got their bag instead of mine, out came the gun. It was like, 'No more Miss Nice Guy!' Well, I'm sorry, but having two guns pointed at me in one day is just one too many. I mean, what could they possibly have in that bag that's so darned special?"

Which was exactly the question Brad had been asking himself. "I can't believe they threatened you because you accidentally grabbed their beach bag!"

Jarod appeared to be contemplating this. After a moment, he said, "I don't know if they were actually *threatening* me"—he blinked in his confusion—"but they definitely pointed a gun in my face."

Brad resisted the urge to roll his eyes. "And the difference is?"

"Well," Jarod replied, "no one actually said, 'Get your hands off that effing bag or I'll shoot you in the face, you little faggot.'"

"Probably because they don't speak English," Zach reasoned.

"But I speak Portuguese!" Jarod declared indignantly. Then he slumped. "Of course, they don't know that." He shrugged. "Okay, so yes—they threatened me in a non-verbal sort of way."

"I'll say," Brad said, wondering what it would take to get a look inside that beach bag.

They escorted Jarod to the Blue Parrot in time to see the ill-mannered pair of lovers barge into the elevator past a waiting crowd.

"Are they staying here, too?" Brad asked, as the Brazilians disappeared behind the closing doors.

Brad looked around at the faces gathered to await the next elevator. A number of them had been guests on Sebastian's boat that evening.

"We're *all* staying here," Jarod said blithely. "Everyone but you two!"

Everyone but you two! Now that, thought Bradford, is a most interesting fact.

They bid Jarod good night and headed to their villa. For the most part, they walked in silence, holding hands. It was already past midnight by the time they reached their mountaintop retreat, let themselves in and re-armed the security system.

Once Zach had gone to bed, Brad stepped onto the patio and stood staring out over the magical city below. His thoughts crept around to the incredible events of the past few days: a fellow agent knifed to death, a Mayan princess who channelled the spirits of dead movie stars, and a man returned from the dead who had just walked straight back into Brad's life. And he still had no idea what he was going to do about it.

For a moment, Brad thought he heard a silent heartbeat reaching to him across the twinkling lights. Somewhere out there, his former partner—and former lover—lay sleeping. Or maybe Little Wing too was staring up at the night sky and thinking about Bradford Fairfax, a.k.a. Agent Red of Box 77.

14

For the first time ever, Brad woke without a spontaneous erection pressing up against the back of his blue-haired lover. The unthinkable had finally happened. It was the guilt, he realized. If he'd only come clean about meeting Little Wing yesterday he wouldn't be suffering these pangs of remorse now. Amazing how little it took to render a guy impotent!

To make up for it, Brad cooked a gourmet breakfast of scrambled eggs, chorizo sausage and refried beans, and then refused to let Zach help with the dishes. Afterwards, sitting by the pool, he thought Zach had never looked so beautiful. His hair had curled in the humidity, framing his face in grapevine ringlets. His skin held a blush of sun. His eyes sparkled like the ocean in the far distance, almost as if Brad was looking through two windows in his skull to the water beyond. It was the last they would see of each other for the next few days. Brad wanted to savour the moment as much as possible. The approaching separation was necessary, but he felt nervous about it, especially given the unexpected reappearance of his former lover.

At half past nine, they headed for the bus station. A wind had scoured the city overnight and the ground was dusted with fallen bougainvillea petals and the miniature finger-like blossoms of the trumpet flower. This was how Mexican winter made its exit, Brad noted, with a gentle shower of purple and orange covering the streets and sidewalks.

Brad waited as Zach boarded the bus with his knapsack and took a seat by the window. His heart felt heavy. The bus lurched onto the roadway and Brad waved till it drove out of sight. "Wait!" he wanted to call out. "Have you got everything you need? Money, clothing, cell phone…?" He felt like a worried father watching his only child leaving for university, far away and out of reach should he be required to help or give words of advice.

Brad turned and made his way back through town, feeling bereft. With Zach gone, he was determined to make headway finding Panther's killer. He would focus his attention on work and push all other thoughts aside. It would be awkward knowing Little Wing was somewhere in the city and not attempt to meet up with him. There was so much he needed to ask, so many questions that only Little Wing could answer. Was it love he felt for his former partner or was it merely regret? Either way, he needed to rein in his emotions. A little temptation could be a dangerous thing.

His gaze took in the dusty streets. Of course, there were the usual distractions he could join in if he got bored, but the thought of yet another jungle tour with tourists "cutting loose" for the afternoon gave him pause. The idea of zip-lining through the trees similarly filled him with dread. Why a rational human being would want to hang suspended far above the earth for any purpose other than air travel was beyond him. (And even that was only to be done at times of the direst of needs.) The beach, too, held little appeal. Who knew which part of his anatomy might droop next if he spent any more time in the sun? The thought of his wing tattoos sagging on his abdomen one day nearly brought on a bout of despair. No—it was best if he stuck to the villa for the time being.

Up there on the patio, surrounded by jungle, he had all the height he needed. He could easily watch the harbour through his binoculars while he stayed safe under his sun umbrella.

Brad was back at his cliff-top villa before noon. He spent the afternoon keeping a lookout for Dion's boat, but it was nowhere to be seen. Most of the usual boats were present, including Sebastian's, but the *Libre*'s prominent sails had vanished. Where had Celine gone? Had she spent the night somewhere? He felt like an obsessive fan. When he checked the itinerary on her CD, there was a blank until the following evening. It was a mystery then.

The day passed without incident. Brad thought of Zach, hoping he had reached his destination safely and wondering what he was doing at that very moment. He also tried unsuccessfully a number of times *not* to think of Little Wing, but that was harder to do.

Evening arrived. He ate supper alone on the patio and watched the sun set as he emptied a bottle of Viognier, a crisply complex little wine he'd recently made the acquaintance of. Unfortunately, the combination of sunset and alcohol made him utterly melancholy.

Brad began to feel uncharacteristically sorry for himself. He felt an aching loss at being alone on such a beautiful evening in one of the world's most enchanting cities. Still, he told himself, it was only temporary. It was a very different kind of loss he'd felt on leaving Paris four years ago. Little Wing had just been wrenched from his life violently and without warning. There'd been no time to prepare for the initial shock or the months of depressing speculation afterwards, waking at 3, 4 or 5 a.m. night after night to wonder what he might have done differently to save his partner. Only to discover four years later that he had, indeed, saved his partner.

So why had Little Wing left him thinking he was dead? How could you do that to someone you cared for? Maybe he too hadn't fully understood the intense feelings they shared, convincing himself like Brad that it was only sex, one man's touch given to appease another man's need. In all fairness, Brad had only come to understand the depths of his own emotions in the aftermath of the attack, once he'd had time to contemplate how much his partner truly meant to him.

The evening wind blew cool against Brad's skin as the stars crept into the sky. He told himself not to get wrapped up in his emotions, but it was no use. The wine had let loose a flood of feeling and he would follow it to its conclusion, as he always did: Bradford Fairfax, the sensitive man's secret agent.

When he woke again it was past 2 a.m. His head was slumped onto his chest where he lay sprawled in the deck chair. When had he opened that third bottle of wine? He crawled off to bed, only to wake again a few hours later. He went to the window and looked out. The city was blanketed in fog, while his mind was blanketed in deep despair. He felt he couldn't stay in the villa another second. Unlatching the front door, he stepped onto the walkway. For some reason, the fog was so thick he couldn't see the ground below.

Brad unlocked the gate and strode boldly along the dirt road running past the villa. He hadn't gone far when he came to a cemetery. Odd—in all this time he'd never noticed it. Beyond its walls, a faint glimmer moved slowly along one side of the path. Mexican fireflies? Brad leapt effortlessly over the fence and followed the light beckoning him onward, past gigantic tombs housing the remains of families who'd lived in Vallarta for generations. The glimmer picked up speed. He was barely able to keep up with it. He tripped and found himself face to face with a fresh gravesite covered by a mound of earth. Someone had recently been buried here. Brad looked for the light, but it had disappeared, leaving him alone in the darkness.

This must be my destination, he told himself.

He sat and began to dig at the earth with his hands, feeling the cool damp between his fingers. A fat grey rat waddled by on the path, shooting Brad a contemptuous look, while a foot-long centipede wriggled free of the dirt in his hands.

Brad turned back to the grave. He'd dug down just a few inches when he felt the coffin lid. It was surprising to find it so close to the surface. Weren't they supposed to bury these things much deeper? His heart pounded so violently he feared it might burst. He wanted to yell for help, but he knew no one could hear him up here on the mountain. Besides, he'd been disloyal to Zach, so no one would come to his aid.

Brad brushed the dirt from the coffin. He felt revolted yet fascinated at the same time. Who was buried here? Had a final judgment been passed on whoever lay inside the casket? You might hide your sins from other people, he knew, but not from a Higher Power. Everything you did and said and thought was being judged somewhere high above you. That was karma, he reminded himself.

His fingers grasped the coffin's handle. A clock struck twelve as Brad yanked the lid open. There lay Zach, wreathed in flowers, his skin as blue as his hair. I've killed him! Brad thought in horror. I should never have let him go off alone. As he watched, the boy's eyes flickered open. Zach sat up.

"When did you die?" Brad demanded hoarsely.

"I didn't," Zach declared. "You did!"

Zach reached up and clasped him in a passionate embrace. Brad wanted to scream, but all he could do was moan as his boyfriend's fingers groped between his legs. Despite his revulsion at being groped by a corpse, he was unable to resist his growing desire. Suddenly Zach bit Brad's neck, drawing blood.

Brad drew back in shock. "Why did you do that?" he demanded.

"I'll never tell," Zach cried. "Go on and beat me. You know you want to!"

"So you want to play with the big boys, do you?" Brad said, raising a fist.

"Hit me!" Zach cried, laughing in his face. "What are you waiting for?"

Brad dropped his hand. "I can't," he protested. "It's only supposed to be a game!"

"A game?" Zach screamed. "Are you just playing with me?"

Overhead, something shrieked. Brad twisted to look past his shoulder. Celine Dion was perched like a harpy in a tree, black hair trailing to the ground. She shrieked again and Brad covered his ears.

"You're not Maria Callas!" he shouted.

"*Aack! Aack!*" a voice cried. Jarod came running along the path, flapping his sleeves like the wings of a bird.

"Save me, Jarod!" Brad cried.

"Too late!" Jarod replied, as he went tearing past. "You should never have dug up the past. Such cruel worms!"

Brad gasped. Everywhere he looked, little white worms twisted and wriggled in the dirt. A hand grasped his hair, pulling him around to face the coffin. A pair of lips brushed his. The kiss tasted like melted toffee.

"I'm leaving for Paris tonight. Are you coming?" a voice whispered in his ear. Only this time it wasn't Zach, but Little Wing, lying splendidly butt-naked beneath him.

"Love me, big boy!" Little Wing cried, yanking Brad down into the coffin. He hoisted his legs overhead and planted his ankles on Brad's shoulders. "Let's do the old heave-ho, the old one-two!" he shrieked in Brad's ear. "Let's do the old stuck-together-like-crazy-glue!"

Brad suddenly found himself naked as well. He tried to resist, but he felt his erection slip deep inside Little Wing's ass. The pleasure was indescribable. "Ah, yes—this is what it was like!" He moaned and felt himself shooting wildly as streamers of fireworks went spurting in the air around them. Spent, he collapsed in the coffin beside Little Wing.

"Now you're mine forever," Little Wing cried, holding him tightly.

Brad panicked. If he didn't escape, he was going to be shut in here for all eternity. He pushed Little Wing aside and leapt from the coffin in time to see the city going up in flames. "Wow!" he thought. "That was some hot sex. Talk about setting the world on fire!"

"Save me!" Little Wing yelled. "Don't let me die!"

Brad turned to look. He was shaken by the helpless expression on Little Wing's face as the lid slammed down and the coffin sank back into the earth.

Brad woke shivering with his sheets drenched in sweat. The memory of Little Wing's kiss and their passionate embrace still clung to him like ghostly fingers. He closed his eyes and shook his head to clear the cobwebs from his mind. He felt a burning shame. Shouldn't he have tried harder to resist Little Wing's advances, even on the other side of consciousness? His impotency problem had transformed into one of being attracted to the wrong person. Even worse—that person was a dead guy.

He got up to wash his face at the bathroom sink, staring at himself in the mirror. Zach had said he should interpret the symbols, but these hardly needed interpreting. He was feeling a case of repressed guilt over having abandoned Little Wing.

His cell beeped. It was a few minutes past 4 a.m. The phone yielded a single text message: *Arrived safely. Looks like I've got Wi-Fi out here under this starry sky so will be in touch periodically. PS. I love you, super cool agent dude—Zach.*

The irony of the timing could not be denied.

Brad went out on the balcony and sat beside the pool. It was still dark, though the stars were already fading. A lone rooster let out a remorseful cry. Brad thought again of that rainy night in Paris four years ago. Was he really still in love with Little Wing or was he simply in love with the idea of a dead man returned to life, a man Brad had admired and whose death he still felt guilty about? If he had gone around that corner first, he reminded himself, it would have been him who died and not Little Wing. If he had to do it again, he knew, he would gladly have died in his former partner's place. Or rather, *not* died, as it turned out. There was the rub.

The scene replayed in his head: the ill-advised tail through the rainy streets, a shadowy figure lurking in the doorway, a silver flash in the air and *pfftt!* A life suddenly over, the light fading in Little Wing's eyes just as the coffin lid had closed down on him in his dream. But to what purpose? Why sacrifice your life to the greater good if it all ended up on the shit-heap of time, as Esmeralda's channelled evocation of the Near-Immediate Future of Mankind had suggested? Why not take a run at having a few good years of pleasure instead? Food, wine, world travel … a few tasty love affairs and plenty of great sex. What else was there, when all was said and done?

"Well," a voice inside his head answered, "there's your own sense of integrity, for one." True enough, Brad thought. There was also the knowledge that you'd used your time well and done something worthwhile—not just for yourself, but for others too. You couldn't take pleasure to the grave with you, but you could take the satisfaction of a life well lived. After all, what remained of sex once it was over? Not much. Love mattered, of course. It was something to say you'd truly loved someone and been loved in return. Of course, loving implied duty, commitment, sacrifice—because in some way, on some level, if you truly loved someone, you would sacrifice your life for them.

Brad tended to agree with the voice in his head. But where did that leave him? Like a man in the real world who experiences an otherworldly vision and finds he can't turn his back on it, he thought. Because he'd just encountered the ghost of his past, and he couldn't go on denying it, if he valued his sanity. Which he mostly believed he did.

It was nearly dawn. A glow hung on the horizon. The binoculars lay on the table where he'd left them the evening before. He picked them up and scanned the harbour. The *Libre* was still missing. And so was the *Rainbow Warrior*, though it had been there last night. Was there more trouble afoot between the two boats? If so, then he should be there for it, though he had no idea where *there* was. He felt a stab of panic. Panicking wouldn't help, he reminded himself. There was nothing to do but wait till the ships returned.

In the meantime, he couldn't continue to deny what he was feeling. Though he loved Zach with every inch of his being, and had every intention of being loyal to him, something was eating away at Brad's soul. A nagging feeling of unfinished business lay between him and Little Wing. It had dogged his waking hours and was now invading his sleep. He needed to confront those feelings and discover what lay beneath them.

He recalled what Zach had said about karma: it was "the meeting of self." Surely that was another name for "unfinished business." If ever he'd had a karmic connection, then it was with Little Wing. Now *that* was a pull he found hard to resist.

It would be tricky, but he needed to see Little Wing again.

15

Brad couldn't shake the dream warning about digging up the cruel worms of memory. If he persisted, would he risk endangering his future? Was he even now dismantling the pillars that supported and made possible his present existence with Zach? A happy and contented existence, he reminded himself yet again. Perhaps one day he would look back on this moment as the beginning of the end of all that was good about his life.

Was it possible to love two people, each of whom represented different aspects of his love, both pulling him in opposite directions? With Little Wing he'd been like a best friend, but with Zach his role at times seemed more like that of a father or older brother. Lying there by the pool, he felt like a religious devotee trying to balance the strictures of the spirit with the longings of the flesh. He could embrace the contradictions of both spirit and flesh, but could he embrace two lovers at the same time?

He was nauseated by all the wine he'd drunk, though it seemed more than just a case of indigestion and the beginnings of a hangover. Heartache or heartburn—who could tell the difference? He found himself walking along the dusty road past the villa, just as he had in the dream. Only this time the fog was in his head, not hovering over the ground. The day dawned clear and bright. At the bend in the road where the nightmarish cemetery had stood, there was nothing more than an overgrown lot brimming with cactus rather than the oversized tombstones he'd

137

dreamed of. His wanderings took him down the mountain, through the back streets to the Río Cuale where the dry gulch that passed for a river offered scarcely enough for a dog to lick itself clean under the searing sun.

Halfway across the bridge, he stopped and looked down into the thin grey waters. His reflection appeared to be standing not on a bridge but on the edge of a vast sea. He saw himself holding his breath, one foot in the water and the other on shore, waiting.

He could resist no longer. For the second time in two days, Brad entered the hushed interior of the little family saloon and deposited himself at the table by the window where he'd sat with Little Wing. There was a new bartender on duty. This one was shorter and meaner looking, with a bristling moustache that said *¡Viva Zapata!* and *Fuck all gringos!* in strident tones. He might have been one of the gang who'd threatened him yesterday before the green-eyed Mexican came along and ruined their party. He sauntered over and nodded as Brad ordered a lemonade.

"*¿Limonada?*"

"*Sí.*"

The bartender looked down at him with narrowed eyes, his jaws working a toothpick held between his lips. For a moment, Brad wondered if he'd offended the man. Maybe ordering lemonade was considered an insult to the bartending trade in Mexico.

The man slowly returned to his bar. A minute later, he returned carrying a big pitcher of lemonade with a jolly tropical fruit selection skewered on a colourful pick. He set it down on the table and turned to leave without a word.

Brad considered him for a moment. "*¿Amigo, conoces a un hombre muy grande? ¿Con músculos y pelo largo?*" Brad asked. Right—a big muscle dude with long hair. How many people could that be in this town?

The bartender turned back and studied him gravely. He worked the toothpick. Again, Brad felt he might have asked the wrong question. He was prepared for anything.

"You mean the Indian dude?" the bartender said thoughtfully.

"Yeah. You know him?"

"Sure," the bartender said. "He comes in quite a bit."

"Really? What does he call himself?"

The bartender shook his head. "Nothing. He calls himself Nothing."

"OK," Brad said, feeling idiotic. "Will you let him know Red's here, if you see him?"

"No worries, mate. I'll tell him. Cheers!"

While Brad sipped his lemonade, his thoughts returned to the night Little Wing had been stabbed. By the time the ambulance arrived, his own people had rushed Brad away before the police could question him. They'd kept him isolated for twenty-four hours before letting him go. He'd anxiously searched the papers the next day for news of the stabbing, but there was no mention of it. Nor the day after that. That should have told him something.

Of course, the folks at Box 77 hadn't known that Brad had an intimate personal connection with his partner as well as a professional one. Otherwise they might have treated him differently. They'd simply done their best to wipe the incident from his mind and hope that time would deal with the rest.

Afterwards they left him alone, telling him only to rest and not think about what happened. *Not think*. As if he could. When he opened his fridge and pulled out a steak, he thought of Little Wing lying bleeding in the rain. Even the sight of a butter knife might make him ruminate on the murder for hours. Vegetarian pizza and salads became a staple for a while. A rainy night could still bring him right back there.

The worst thing had been the lack of contact. Suddenly, he belonged nowhere once again. With the death of his father, Brad had found himself without any family. When he joined Box 77 he abandoned the rest of his life, including whatever support system he'd had. From then on, his only contacts were his colleagues at Box 77. After Little Wing's death, he checked his in-box each day with a growing dread. No news followed more of the same. Every day he asked himself the same questions: would they take him back? Suspend him? Tell him to go fuck himself and toss him out on the street like so much garbage?

It was the same each day. Nothing and more nothing. Little Wing's murder had been completely hushed up. A month went by and then another. Finally, just when he thought they must have forgot about him, a note in his e-mail box carried one word in the subject line: *Grace*. It seemed ironic, as though she were offering him a reprieve. He wasn't sure he wanted one.

Until then, Grace had only been a voice at the end of the phone line. After Paris, she became the emblem of everything that his life had now become. On some level, he knew it was all deception, cover-ups and lies. Yet on another level, it was something far greater. She reached inside him to convince him of that and bring him out of himself. She reassured him that what he was going through was normal and, above all, that he had to go on. Not just for himself, but for his dead partner as well. Otherwise, she said, Little Wing's death would mean nothing. Or less than nothing, if Brad insisted on paying for it with his future as an agent.

She talked him into coming back to himself. She said all the right things that worked on him in just the right way. After his father died, he'd heard much the same from people he'd never met before and who were suddenly experts on the impact death was having on his life. But he'd listened to them and it had helped. Once more, similar words pulled him from the abyss he'd fallen into.

Maybe that was why he was drawn to Little Wing now. With his father's death, fifteen-year-old Brad had been thrown into a world of grief unlike anything he'd ever known. With Little Wing's death, it had happened all over again, only for Bradford to discover that it hadn't really happened at all. Maybe on some subconscious level Little Wing represented the hope that his father too would be returned to Brad whole and reborn.

Brad set his empty glass down with a crack. The whole notion was crazy. Whatever possessed him to return to this bar? He looked to the window where a bright morning sun peeked into the bar's dim interior. Then he felt the hand on his back. It rested between his shoulder blades, right where a wing might sprout, if humans had wings. He turned.

"Hey."

"I'm sorry," Brad said. "I know you said to stay away, but I couldn't stop thinking about you—"

"I know," said Little Wing. "I felt it too!"

Their embrace came close to violence, knocking over chairs and making the cats scurry for cover.

"I knew you'd come … I knew you'd come…" Little Wing kept whispering into his shoulder.

"Just hold me," Brad said.

He felt the massive chest, the powerful arms surrounding him. He had no doubt that Little Wing was real and not a ghost. An electric current radiated through his entire body. Last night he'd dreamed of Little Wing's passionate kisses, of being wrapped in his arms. Now that he was really here, the rest of the world could go to hell.

But not Zach, Brad reminded himself. Not Zach.

An hour passed and then another. Lemonade turned to beer, and the beer turned to tequila. Brad still hadn't managed to say half the things he wanted to say, but he knew he couldn't stay there all day. Instinct told him he needed to get back to business and watch for the return of Celine's boat.

"I've got to go," he said, rousing himself from the stupor he'd drunk himself into. "A greater power calls."

"Grace?"

Brad nodded, but he wasn't able completely to leave Little Wing behind yet again or wait one more day to continue this conversation. It had to happen. "I'd like to meet you later tonight." He smiled hopefully. "How about a good old-fashioned date?"

Something flashed across Little Wing's face. Fear? Concern? He shook his head. "I wish ... I wish we could go somewhere to be alone, but I can't invite you back to my place, Red. I'm not ready for that."

And I don't trust myself alone with you, Brad thought, feeling the tingle where his fingers lay nestled in the hairs on Little Wing's forearm.

"No worries," Brad said. "But maybe we could have a drink and grab a bite at a *Pollo Loco* outlet afterwards? What do you say?"

"A glass of wine, some Crazy Chicken and thou?" Little Wing broke into a smile. "Sounds great!"

In his drunkenness, Brad suddenly recalled Esmeralda's invitation to return to the Blue Parrot that evening to see if she could channel Agent Panther. Would that be mixing business with pleasure? Then so be it. He could still check in with Esmeralda to see if Panther put in an appearance without involving Little Wing directly. He needn't even know what was going on. And after that? Well, after that he would see what he would see.

"I know," Brad said, as if the idea had just occurred to him. "Why don't we meet at the Blue Parrot around eight?"

"Sounds perfect!"

And relatively safe, Brad thought. After all, it was just another nightclub.

Little Wing stood and gave an ironic salute. Brad watched him go out the door and head up the street. For a moment he considered following, if only to find out where he lived. But that would make me a stalker, Brad thought. I'm already breaking enough rules as it is.

He swayed as he got to his feet. I need to sober up, he told himself. He headed back up the mountain, sweating in the afternoon sun. Yesterday's litter of blossoms had turned brown and lined the gutters on the sides of the road. He wondered if he'd made a mistake by asking Little Wing out. But what could it hurt? It was just a friendly gesture to satisfy himself that he hadn't lost his mind. That he wasn't about to lose his grip on reality. One date and that would be all, he told himself, as his feet fairly flew along the dusty road back up to the villa.

He was crossing the walkway when his phone rang. It was Grace, making an uncharacteristic and unexpected call. His guilt flared. Had she known where he'd been? Of course not, he told himself.

"I've just received some vital information. Red, you've got to get yourself over to a place called the Blue Parrot tonight," she said, to Brad's surprise.

Coincidence? he wondered.

"Do you know it?" she asked.

"Erm, yes, as a matter of fact."

"I've just had word that something is happening there tonight. It might be the break we need."

"That's it? Just that 'something is happening'?"

"That's all I know. Use your wits," she told him.

If I have any left, Brad thought. "I'll be there," he said.

The call clicked off. Brad pocketed his cell phone. This could complicate things considerably if whatever might happen proved dangerous. Still, he had no way to cancel his date with Little Wing now. This would happen, one way or another.

16

The wheels were turning. Brad was concerned by Grace's assertion that she had "vital information." What or who was the source? It almost sounded as though there was another Box 77 operative at work in Puerto Vallarta. If anyone could say for certain that important events were about to unfold at the Blue Parrot tonight, then that person had to be far more knowledgeable about Brad's environs than he was. He didn't care to entertain the possibility.

He lifted his binoculars and scanned the harbour. There was the *Libre*, sails gleaming in the sun, looking as if it had never left port. Where had it been the previous evening? He wished he'd been on the ball to see what direction Celine's ship had returned from, but it was too late.

His mind turned to the collection of oddballs he'd met in PV over the past few days. In particular, he could think of two sexy Brazilians who merited a closer look. He recalled Jarod's story of how he'd accidentally picked up their bag while on board the *Rainbow Warrior* the night of the cocktail party. Whatever the bag contained, it must have been something important. Maybe it had held explosives intended to scuttle the *Libre* and flush out the reclusive Dion when Jarod's singing scuttled their plan instead. It was possible.

Brad had a few hours before his date with Little Wing. Make that his *joint* date, he reminded himself. He

145

also had a rendezvous with Agent Panther in the Otherworld. In the meantime, it might be worthwhile to pay a visit to the Blue Parrot where, according to Jarod, "Everyone but you two!" was staying.

His new present from Zach sat propped on a chair. He picked up the bag and fingered the zipper. If he could distract the Brazilians for a few moments, he might be able to switch their case for his and see what it contained. It just might work, he thought, as he began to fill the burgundy bag with the binoculars, suntan lotion and the rest of his mini-pharmacy. At the last second, he added a beach towel and a clean pair of socks for good measure.

Brad threw a glance up and down the beach. All the regulars were there. He quickly located Sebastian and his unruly band. The *Rainbow Warrior* must have returned around the same time as the *Libre. Quel coincidence!* Sebastian was happily ensconced at the centre of his group, telling tales and ordering drinks to keep his boys happy. They'd probably keep him busy for quite some time.

Not far off, he saw Jarod looking over a blanket that Angie was holding up for him. Even Esmeralda had come out to lie in the sun, her bald head gleaming like an unhatched ostrich egg. The Siamese lovers were there too, entwined in each other's arms with their burgundy satchel tucked between them. Brad watched them kissing from a distance. Clearly, they had no intention of unlocking tongues and leaving anytime soon. There'd be little chance of switching bags under their noses. In the meantime, however, it might prove interesting to see what their room contained. He'd have to be quick to make the most of things while they were all on the playa.

In the hotel lobby, one of the spectacular blonde,

blue-eyed SS guards was busy doling out abuse to any guests who approached his desk. Two butch lesbians requesting a wake-up call were quickly reduced to tears. Brad got in line for a flaying while piecing his cover story together.

An English accent was often useful in situations like these, he knew. For some reason, its fusty syllables implied authority and self-assurance. And apart from France, where English accents were loathed, it usually garnered respect wherever it was heard. He might be asking for the crown jewels of Russia, but with the right accent he could always find someone to take him seriously.

The line parted. An older man with a cane limped away cringing.

"Next!"

The clerk's abrasive tone hung in the air. Brad stepped forward to be eyed with a supercilious regard. Whatever he hoped for, it suggested, he needn't bother asking.

"Yes?" the clerk demanded, impatiently tapping a pencil on the desk.

"I beg your pardon, my good man. I'm in a frightful spot. Might I ask you to be discreet?"

The pencil left off its tapping. The man's demeanour suddenly changed. He was no longer addressing a potential annoyance, but an attractive man with an English accent.

"Why, certainly, sir. How may I be of assistance?"

"I was here last night with some, erm"—here Brad raised his eyes and lowered his voice—"friends."

"Friends?" the man repeated, as though enchanted by the sound of the word.

"You know … *fri-e-e-e-ends*," Brad said, drawing out the syllables and ending with a shy grin.

"Ah! I see," the man replied. "In that case, sir, you needn't worry. Discretion is my middle name." He batted his eyelashes in an attempt to convey a sympathetic mien.

"I'm afraid I left something behind in their, erm, suite." Brad did his best to look as sheepish as possible. "Accidentally, of course. You wouldn't by chance be holding anything for a Jonathan Witherspoon, would you?"

The man stood staring at him. Brad continued to smile.

"Sir?" the man said with an expectant look.

"Yes?"

"What room did you say?"

"Oh, dear!" Brad made another lavish display of embarrassment. "Let me see—I think it was…" He made a pantomime of trying to remember, but finally shook his head. "How silly of me. I can't recall. It was all a bit of a blur, you see."

The clerk nodded as though he did indeed see.

Brad scratched his nose. "Moses and Joshua?"

"Ah! The Brazilians. Oh, yes—I see!" The clerk smiled conspiratorially and seemed to regard Brad in a new light. "And how … er … big would this object be?"

Brad mimed something zucchini-like. "Possibly just a little longer in real life. Battery-operated, of course." He sheepishly pointed to the shelf behind the reception desk. "It might just fit in one of those pigeon-holey things on the wall."

The clerk looked carefully through the slot for room 404. He turned back to Brad. "I'm sorry, sir, but there's nothing there for anyone by that name."

Brad looked chagrined. "Oh, dear! Then perhaps it wasn't Moses and Joshua after all. Let me see … what about Jarod Scythes—like the Grim Reaper?"

The clerk gave Brad another appraising stare. "Let

me see what I can do about that." This time he sifted through the slot for room 406.

They were next-door neighbours! Jarod hadn't mentioned that.

The clerk turned back to Brad. "Sorry, sir. Nothing there either. Anyone else?"

Brad knit his brow. "Sebastian Mathers?"

The clerk's eyebrows shot up. "My, my! You certainly had a busy evening," he murmured approvingly as he went through the slot for room 402.

One on either side, Brad noted. It gets curiouser and curiouser.

The clerk turned back again. "Regretfully, sir, nothing to report there either. Shall I inquire of anyone else?"

Brad thought of Esmeralda then thought better of it. Some things were just not believable, English accent notwithstanding. He shook his head. "Not that I can recall, but perhaps it will come to me," he replied. "Oh, dear! What beastly luck! I don't know what to tell Harry about his missing, erm … watch?"

The clerk brightened. "Oh, that's easy," he said. "Just tell him it broke, and then do your best to look like a sad puppy. He'll buy you a new one. Guaranteed! Works like a charm every time."

Like this accent, Brad thought. "Brilliant!" he exclaimed. "Cheers! Thanks ever so!"

He wandered across the lobby and busied himself looking into a potted fern. When the clerk was busy haranguing the next guest, Brad slipped into the elevator. (Or rather, into the *lift*, his accent corrected.)

Up on the fourth floor, he looked around as the elevator doors closed behind him. The hallway was deserted, but the distant strains of Abba came from one of the far rooms. Abba made the short list of music Brad would never take with him to a desert island. That list included anything by Frank Sinatra, Olivia Newton-John, Enrico Caruso, Johnny Cash and Madonna, as well as a former childhood neighbour named Carmine, a dope-smoking hipster who wore red sunglasses and sang pla-giarized Paul McCartney tunes off-key. For some reason, the experience had made Brad realize early on that he wanted to be gay when he grew up.

As for his desert island anti-hit list, he realized there wasn't much rhyme or reason to it, but then the same might be said of those singers. ("I'm not a snob," he once reassured Zach. "I just don't like a lot of things.") There were, of course, far worse singers, but few annoyed him as much as those. Still, he couldn't deny the strange power music exerted over him. Hearing Johnny Cash's gravely dump-truck growl made him want to grow bushy sideburns and drink Arkansas moonshine. On the other hand, Abba's cloying harmonies, belted full-force, gave him an urge to don pantyhose and shimmy in the moon-light. Either that or gargle with warm salt water. At present, he was feeling conflicted. Perhaps a midnight swim in the ocean later that evening would satisfy both urges.

Brad had just reached room 404 when the elevator dinged its return. To avoid being seen, he slipped into an adjacent doorway. To his surprise, Jarod exited the eleva-tor with a burgundy bag slung over his shoulder.

Brad watched as Jarod strode down the hall to room 404, glancing nervously around. But according to the desk clerk, Jarod was staying in room 406. Had the clerk made a mistake? Not likely, given his Aryan efficiency. Then maybe Jarod had gone to the wrong door, but that didn't seem likely either. Just then, the tall thin man looked fur-tively around him. Brad pondered his tale about the inci-dent on the boat. Accidentally picked up their bag, my eye! he thought. You know what's in that bag and you want it for yourself.

Jarod retrieved an entry card from his pocket. He was about to insert it when the elevator returned. He looked up, panic written all over his face. "Ding!" he cried, and raced down the hall to his own room.

The elevator opened and the condor-like profile of Esmeralda emerged, carrying yet another burgundy bag. The Mayan princess looked carefully around before stealthily approaching the door to room 404. Brad watched as she too reached into her pocket and withdrew a pass card. Before she could try it, however, the elevator dinged yet again. Esmeralda raced down the corridor and into a room farther along the hall.

A dumpy looking chambermaid emerged pushing a trolley. Brad felt sorry for these poor women who were forced to perform menial labour just to survive. He pictured them struggling their entire lives to raise children and support boozy husbands and then, youth gone and strength fading, heroically starting all over again in time to help raise the grandchildren. This one looked oddly familiar, however. Not to mention peculiar. She was well over six feet tall—unusual for a Mexican peasant—and quite lumpy, as though she'd donned her outfit over street clothes. Tucked beneath her maid's cap was a silvery mane. Stranger still, she too had a burgundy bag tossed over one shoulder.

Wa-a-a-it a minute! Brad thought. That chambermaid looked suspiciously like ... Sebastian!

The elevator dinged yet again. It was worse than a runway at a busy airport. This time the door opened on the officious desk clerk. He took one look at Sebastian and stepped back inside.

"*Buenos días,*" the clerk said, nervously punching

several buttons without bothering to look at the numbers.

"*Heil Hitler!*" Sebastian exclaimed, to the confusion of both himself and the clerk as the elevator closed again.

As soon as the door closed, Sebastian made a dash for room 404. At the same moment, both Jarod and Esmeralda stepped forward into the hallway. All three did a double take on seeing the others, retreating to their respective rooms and slamming the doors behind them.

Taking advantage of the momentary diversion, Brad rushed over to room 404. He slipped a card-sized object designed to break codes into the key reader. A series of numbers flashed by like a Las Vegas slot machine. Three cherries? Four lemons? Whatever. Something whirred and the lock flashed green. Three cheers for modern spy technology! He grasped the handle and turned.

The room was dim. The interior carried the air-conditioned hush characteristic of hotels worldwide. The bed was unmade. White jockey shorts and sleeveless T-shirts lay strewn about. Brad pulled open a dresser drawer: more jockies. Another contained only sleeveless T-shirts. So much for a versatile wardrobe.

Brad quickly went through the entire room, but found no contraband of any sort. In fact, there was nothing so dangerous as a set of common nipple clamps. He was making one final check under the bed when he heard voices coming down the hall. Footsteps stopped outside the door. The lock clicked and the door opened just as Brad slid under the bed, hoping no one would sit on it and squash his face against the tiles, which he found attractive but rather cold.

He heard a series of squat syllables that sounded like Spanish, but weren't. In fact, it sounded pretty much like gibberish. It was the Brazilians. The words sounded familiar but none of their conversation made sense to him. He tried to recall if he'd ever had a Brazilian boyfriend. None came to mind, though there was that dentist who'd spent a month in São Paolo and come back with a skin rash he claimed he'd picked up from some capuchin monkeys.

The ultra-hot lovers stopped talking. Bradford listened carefully for clues as to what they were up to. All he could hear was breathing. He peeked from under the bed to see the pair engaged in what could only be called a full-body kiss. The burgundy bag slid to the floor as hands groped at crotches. Brad nearly cried out as he watched their shorts swell dangerously close to the breaking point.

The lustful murmuring increased as clothing was shredded and tossed aside until the pair stood dressed only in their jockies. Then even these were shredded. Obviously that was why they had drawers of them, Brad realized, because they clearly needed a healthy supply. He gasped as a pair of monster phalluses sprang free from the restraining fabric. Surely some law of physics was being transgressed here. Was what he was seeing even biologically possible?

The dark-haired one pulled his blonde companion toward the bed. Uh-oh! Brad thought. This could be disastrous in more ways than one. He pictured his squashed face and saw himself trying to make a getaway with a boner straining his pants. Two pairs of feet stood dangerously close to where Brad lay hidden. One of the lovers had a crooked baby toe while the other obviously never cleaned under his toenails. So there were differences between them after all.

Just as Brad prepared to have his face sat on, one of the twins grunted and dragged the other off. Brad watched their splendidly hairy butts strutting to the bathroom. He waited till the shower started up before crawling out from under the bed, torn between creeping over to the bathroom for a peep show and getting his hands on the bag.

After all, what's more important? he asked himself.

I know, I know, came the reply—but I've got to get a look inside that satchel.

He had just reached out to grab it when he heard a click at the door and dove back under the bed. Furtive footsteps stole over to the bag. Just then, Brad heard the shower curtain pulled back and bare feet slapping across the bathroom floor. The intruder quickly grasped the bag and plopped an identical bag down in its place. Brad watched as he fled to an armoire, jumped inside and pulled the door closed behind him. At that moment, a pair of muscular legs emerged from the bathroom and walked dripping over to the dresser. Hands yanked open a drawer and retrieved an economy-size container of lube. The legs stomped back to the bathroom.

Now what?

Before Brad could decide, the intruder stepped from the armoire just as the hall door opened again. The thief jumped back inside the armoire. Brad held his breath as yet another pair of legs crept stealthily over to the bag.

The latest newcomer hastily grabbed the bag and dropped another in its place as the door opened again. The legs rushed over and hid behind a set of heavy curtains. Moments later, the next person picked up the newest bag, dropped off another in its place and left as swiftly as he'd arrived. Before Brad could move, the first intruder fled, followed quickly by the second, both clutching variations on the same bag. Brad couldn't see any of them above the knees.

Damn!

He'd just crawled out and crossed the room when the shower stopped. There was no time to duck back under the bed. He grabbed hold of a curtain and stepped onto a balcony overlooking the beach. It was little more than a ledge.

Brad sucked in air. He felt himself swooning over the dizzying heights as he clung to the wall behind him. He turned and peered into the room. The Brazilians had emerged from the bathroom, still as hard as rock. Wow! Brad thought, momentarily distracted from his dilemma. Whoever had nicknamed it "Land of the Giant Purple Phallus" was right! He watched in wonder as they proceeded to make out. Apparently the shower had merely been foreplay. By the looks of it, they were in no hurry.

Brad glanced over to the next balcony. If he could reach it, he might escape through the adjoining suite. But wait! Hadn't he done this number already? He grasped the railing and looked down. His stomach reeled and his heart palpitated. Whatever Zach might tell him, it was a good deal more than twenty feet down this time. That was what came of making fun of parasailers. Okay, calm down, he told himself. There's only six inches separating the two railings. You can do this if you try.

He had just reached out to grasp the neighbouring rail when a seagull splatted on his head. Never mind that now, he reasoned. Anyway, it was supposed to be good luck. Not that a corpse needed luck. With a quick thrust, he swung over and onto the next balcony. He drew a breath and looked up. Clouds sailed gracefully past. His heart pounded, but he was safe for the time being.

He tried to recall whose room this was. If it was Jarod's, perhaps he could ask to borrow some moisturizer. He peered in. It was empty. He tried the door. Locked. So now what? Another balcony lay just around the corner. This one was farther off, but an open window lay between them. Maybe he could grab onto the window and gently swing over to the next balcony.

You're nuts! he chided himself. You could slip and fall, and where would that get you? On a one-way trip to the beach. He shook his head. It looked like this was going to turn into another long-winded conversation with himself. Enough! Just be brave. Yeah, right! he told himself. You try it.

He grabbed the open window and felt the frame swing forward while he held on. Try as he might, he couldn't get close enough to the adjacent balcony to reach it. So far, no one had bothered to look up and see the cat burglar climbing from balcony to balcony. On the other hand, if anyone noticed him they might take him for an amorous lover. All in a day's fun!

That was when he realized he was dangling between balconies four floors up. He turned and spotted a group of sun worshippers on the beach. Someone pointed at him. A hand waved, then another. What the hell, he thought, and waved back.

Clearly, he wasn't going anywhere in a hurry. He gave up and swung back till he found himself on the balcony outside the look-a-like lovers' room again. He peered in. They were still at it.

How long could this go on?

For the next forty-five minutes he watched the equivalent of a Chi Chi LaRue video marathon. He could scarcely believe the pair's stamina as they traded thrusts and positions, pleasuring one another audibly and forcefully. Impressive, Brad kept telling himself. But that's gotta hurt!

He was just beginning to wonder if he'd be stuck on the balcony all night when at length the pair reached some sort of mutually agreed on climax. They collapsed in a heap on the floor, right beside the look-a-like burgundy bag that had been substituted for their own by one of the intruders who trekked in and out of the room while Brad hid beneath the bed. Too late now to find out what was in the original bag.

Brad waited a few minutes till the Brazilians' telltale snoring told him he was safe. He gently pushed open the window and crept past the sleeping beauties, remembering to grab his own bag as he headed for the door. The sun was setting by the time he left the hotel.

17

It was just past eight when he returned and the elevator opened to admit Brad onto the rooftop of the Blue Parrot. He flashed a bill at the doorman—no waiting around this time. Brad could see Little Wing seated near the stage just up ahead. His heart began to pound. What a beautiful man, Brad thought. His former-partner had slicked his hair back and put on a black T-shirt that neatly framed his torso. His physical appeal had only increased since they'd first met.

Brad made his way through the crowd and plopped down in the seat next to him. He'd just had time to make it home and shower and stuff his bag with a change of clothes. In case the weather turned, he told himself. Because of course there was no reason to believe he would be staying overnight anywhere. Still, you never knew. It didn't hurt to be prepared.

"Sorry I'm late," he said. "I had to, uh, hang around a bit and take care of some things."

"No worries," Little Wing replied. "I knew you'd come. I thought I should grab some seats before they were all gone."

He leaned across the table for a kiss. As their lips connected, Brad felt a tingling that left him breathless. He broke off the kiss, reminding himself he was here largely on business. Pleasure—whatever pleasure there might be—had to come second.

"Good to see you, Little."

"Good to see you too."

Brad scanned the rooftop. After the earlier shenanigans, it would be interesting to see who turned up tonight. He wished he knew which of the three intruders had got to the Brazilians' bag first. Esmeralda, no doubt, was downstairs preparing for the show. Brad wondered if he could sneak into her dressing room while she was onstage and see what her bag contained. Jarod sat in a far corner looking highly moisturized. His own bag sat on the table in plain view. Watching him, you'd think nothing out of the ordinary had occurred. Clearly, Brad's ditzy new friend was anything but what he seemed.

Behind them, the elevator opened with a whoosh of laughter. Brad didn't have to turn to know it was Sebastian and his gang. They commandeered a table on the far side of the stage. The only ones missing were the look-a-like muscle boys. Had they realized yet that their bag had been switched? Maybe they were still engaged in their post-coital power nap.

The lights dimmed and the opening act began. Brad felt Little Wing's hand steal into his own as Britney, Whitney and Liza lined up to be shot, scolded and panty-whipped by a fire-breathing Latina prom queen who looked like Jennifer Lopez crossed with Cruella de Ville.

Next came Celine in a flaming red robe. She stood centre stage, head bowed—just a simple diva and her dress alone before God. Brad heard the opening strains of *Tell Him*, Dion's celebrated duel with the even-more legendary Barbra Streisand. Babs, however, was nowhere to be seen.

The music died after a few bars. Celine looked around. She peaked behind the curtain. Where was her arch rival-slash-singing partner? The MC stepped on stage, looking equally concerned over Barbra's absence. He conferred privately with Celine, who shook her head in consternation.

The MC turned to the audience. "We're having a little trouble locating Barbra," he said. "Has anybody seen her? Maybe she's hiding under someone's seat. Could you have a look for us?"

The audience laughed.

Suddenly a voice cut through the air. "What are you looking under your seats for? You should be looking up! I'm the biggest star ever!"

The audience looked overheard. Cheers and gasps broke out in the evening air as Barbra swooped in by parasail, landing neatly on-stage.

"She'll do anything for attention," Celine confided to the MC, her remarks picked up by his microphone and boomed over the speakers.

Barbra, still wrapped in her parasail, looked coolly over at Celine. "Sweetheart, I don't need to *do* things to be noticed…"

Celine and the MC waited as Barbra adjusted her straps.

"What are you looking at?" she demanded. "This is my dress!"

"I didn't think you'd make it," Celine replied politely.

"My dress or the engagement?"

"Both, actually."

"*Hoped* I wouldn't, you mean. Did you think you'd just sing the entire song by yourself?"

"No—of course not. I would never do that to you, Barbra!" Celine looked aghast.

"Admit it—you're just waiting for me to die so you can take over the world," Barbra crowed.

"That's not true!" Celine protested. "Anyway, I

already own Las Vegas."

"Only because we let you," Barbra chided, tossing the parasail aside and stepping to the front of the stage.

The music returned in earnest as the duo began a torrid rendition of their hit, followed by an amusing version of *Bang Bang (My Baby Shot Me Down)*. Halfway through, an outraged Cher barged onstage in a dressing gown to claim the number.

It was during the melee that Brad noted the arrival of the Salsa Machado twins. The pair slipped scowling to their seats, clutching their bag. Had they looked inside it yet? Brad wondered. He was bursting with curiosity.

Barbra and Celine soon vanished, trailed by a grumbling Cher. The MC returned.

"I know what you've all come to see, so let's not keep you waiting." He extended a hand to the side of the stage. "Please welcome the one and only ... Esmeralda, True Mayan Princess!"

The crowd cheered and stomped as Esmeralda schlepped out, looking as ungainly and unattractive as the first time Brad had seen her. Once again, she stood there as if awaiting her music cue. After a minute of silence, her body started its telltale twitching. Finally, a girly-boy voice broke through. "Yeah—cool! JT here. Justin Timberlake, that is."

The MC stepped up. "Well, this is one spirit we don't have ask to introduce himself," he said.

"Nah! You can leave the stage now, dude. I'm in charge," Justin said.

Brad felt Little Wing grab his arm. "Pretty weird drag, Red, but I'm still glad to be here with you."

Esmeralda seemed to have paused for station identification. After a few moments, a second voice came through, this one only slightly less effeminate than Justin's.

"Oh—so you're in charge. Is that so?" came the voice.

"Yeah—it's so, baby," Justin assured the other personality.

A loud crack resounded from the stage. Esmeralda's head swivelled as though she'd been struck.

"Cheat on me, will you?" screamed the second voice.

Esmeralda swayed back and forth, struggling to orient herself as the voices battled for prime time supremacy.

"Yo—bitch!" came Justin's voice. "I told you! I didn't give you them crabs, Britney! No way! I love you, baby!"

The next slap threw JT off balance as a bewildered Esmeralda staggered and tried to regain her composure.

"Britney, baby! Don't slash your wrists!" Justin screamed. "You gotta stop that drinking!"

"Yeah, right!" Britney snarled. "Just wait and see what else I'm gonna slash, wonder boy!"

A third slap sent Esmeralda reeling and clutching her headpiece. "Whoa!" cried Justin. "Wardrobe malfunction! Don't hit me, Brit! I gotta be beautiful for my people!"

By the fourth blow, Esmeralda was practically off the stage. "Go back to your pussy Eminem, motherfucker!" Britney screamed as a battered and bewildered Esmeralda retreated behind the curtain.

The MC rushed up front. "How delightful! We'll just take a little break, folks. I'm sure Esmeralda will be right back," he assured them. "After those two lovebirds get things settled, that is."

This was certainly a festive diversion, Brad thought, but he couldn't afford to neglect his mission. "Excuse me," he said to Little Wing. "I just need to visit the little boy's room."

Brad slipped backstage and down one flight. He found himself gliding along the ghostly hallway past the dressing rooms. Esmeralda's was unlocked. He let himself in and looked around. There was the bag. He picked it up and opened it to find—moisturizers! Dozens and dozens of skin care products filled the pouch.

Brad smacked his forehead. This was Jarod's bag. Then who had the original? Brad slipped out in time to see a ghostly Celine heading toward him dressed in a nightgown, clearly having finished her act for the night. There was no way to avoid her. She smiled as she passed.

"*Bonjour, là!*" she said.

"Hi there! I'm just, uh, looking for thc washroom," Brad said.

She pointed over his shoulder. "*Mais oui. C'est là-bas,*" she said in exquisite French. "It's just down there."

How clever of them to hire an impersonator who spoke French, Brad thought. No wonder her lip-synching was so perfect. Jarod was right: you almost would think this was the real Celine. Brad thanked her as he crept back upstairs to rejoin Little Wing.

When he returned, Little Wing was paying the waiter for another round. Esmeralda was back onstage, her wig slightly lopsided and her make-up a little slapdash after the mistreatment she'd endured as Justin-versus-Britney. Brad had just slipped back into his seat when her reptilian eyes seemed to spy him. She stopped and stared at him without speaking. Suddenly she began to clutch the air, gasping for breath. A murmuring arose from the audience.

"Do not be alarmed!" the MC commanded the audience. "Whatever happens, remember it's only an apparition!" He turned back to Esmeralda. "Spirit, say who you are!" he commanded.

"Ayuh!" came a familiar Tennessee twang. "Y'all can call me Panther," the voice drawled between gasps.

Brad was startled. For a second, he could've sworn he heard a banjo playing in the background. But more important, he realized he hadn't told Esmeralda Panther's name.

"Spirit, why are you here?" the MC demanded.

Panther's eyes narrowed. "Ah got a message," he said.

"For whom?"

Esmeralda fixed her eyes on Brad. She raised a finger and pointed at him. "Fer that man over there."

Little Wing looked at Brad. "What's going on?" he whispered.

"Just a little exercise in faith," Brad said. He stood up. "Panther, do you know me?"

Esmeralda craned her neck to look Brad over. "Ah sure do! How y'all doin', Red?" Panther's spirit croaked out like some bayou Carrie. Esmeralda couldn't have known about Panther's accent or Brad's code name, either.

"What the hell is going on?" Little Wing demanded.

"Bear with me," Brad pleaded. He turned to the stage. "Panther—who stabbed you?"

Suddenly, Esmeralda seemed to shift personalities again. The voice that replied sounded like something from a low-low-low-budget horror flick. "Bewa-a-are!" came a demonic sounding growl.

"Panther—come back! Who stabbed you?"

"He walks among you!" the gravelly voice pronounced.

"Who? Tell me who killed you!" Brad demanded.

Esmeralda raised a finger. It wavered, pointing first

at the Brazilians, then at Jarod, and then Sebastian, before finally turning and pointing directly in Brad's face.

"You—!"

Brad felt a shiver in his veins. All heads turned to watch him.

"—are doomed!"

Brad felt a hand grab him.

"Duck!" Little Wing yelled.

At that very second, a shot rang out. Esmeralda fell to the stage. People screamed and leapt from their seats. Brad whirled to see the green-eyed man aiming a gun right behind him. He hit the floor hard as the second shot exploded in his ears. By the time he got to his feet again, the green-eyed man was already running for the exit. Brad was torn—should he follow the gunman or help Esmeralda?

He leapt onto the stage and knelt beside Esmeralda. It was as though he was looking into Panther's eyes again.

"Ahm dyin', Red!"

"Stay with me, Panther!" Brad shouted. "Don't die on me again!"

A crowd had formed around them. Brad felt Esmeralda's body go limp and her head droop forward. Behind him, he heard shouting. Hitler's elite had arrived. Hotel security had reached the scene and were busy barking commands at the panicked crowd.

Brad turned to Little Wing. "Wait here for me!" he yelled.

He raced to the exit and tore down the stairs to Celine's dressing room. It was empty. He turned at the sound of footsteps. Little Wing had followed him.

"What's going on?" Little Wing demanded.

A scream came from outside in the corridor. Brad raced back into the hall where the green-eyed man had hold of Celine by her hair. Had it been a wig, Brad noted, it would have come flying off. But this was real hair. Brad was surer than ever that this was also the real Celine.

The green-eyed man aimed his gun at Brad. "Don't try anything stupid!" he snarled. "Or the bitch dies!"

Brad had no doubt he meant it. He backed off with Little Wing at his side. They watched as the green-eyed man dragged Celine down the hallway and into the stairwell. The door slammed.

"What are we waiting for?" Little Wing stared at Brad.

Brad shook his head. "We have to let him go. He'll kill her!"

Little Wing grabbed Brad's arm. "There are two of us. We can head him off!"

Brad had only seconds to decide. Should he involve Little Wing in this? Hell—he already was involved. "All right," he said. "I'm going up to the roof. You head downstairs and cover the front door. Whatever happens, don't do anything rash!"

Little Wing dashed for the elevator. As Brad raced to the stairs, he felt a surge of joy. It was just like old times, working with his partner again and loving it!

Halfway up the stairs, he was confronted by a strange scene. Barbra Streisand stood, shoe in hand, looking down at the green-eyed man sprawled on the floor.

Barbra looked up. "I clobbered him, honey!" she barked. "Nobody upstages Barbra!"

Brad looked around. "Where's Celine?"

The DQ shrugged. "Who cares? Maybe she's having a singing lesson."

A muffled cry came from above. Brad looked up to see Celine struggling with a second figure in the dimly lit stairwell. The green-eyed man had an accomplice! Brad sprinted up the stairs as the door slammed in his face. It was barred. He retraced his steps down the hallway to the elevator and rode it to the top. The door opened and Brad stepped cautiously onto the empty rooftop. He surveyed the overturned tables and chairs. Security was busy herding the last guests down the stairs. Where had Celine and her captor gone?

Brad's eyes travelled to the stage. Something rippled behind the curtain. He crept silently forward. What to do? If he pulled the curtain back too fast, he risked startling the kidnapper and his victim. He'd have a double tragedy on his hands if they fell. On the other hand, if he pulled it back too slowly, the kidnapper would have time to get a clear shot at him. Then he saw the curtain raiser.

He pressed the button and the curtain began to rise. If he was quick, he could snatch Celine from the kidnapper's grasp before he realized what was happening. The curtain lifted off the floor. Brad waited three seconds then charged, wrenching the fabric aside.

Night breezes brushed his cheek. There was no one there. Whoever was behind the curtain had vanished. He looked down, fearful of seeing two bodies lying at the base of the hotel. Nothing. They'd eluded him. How was it possible?

Brad ran across the rooftop and yanked open the stage door. He tore down the stairs, past the spot where the green-eyed man had lain. Gone! Brad felt like kicking himself, but there'd been no time to tie him up. Then he heard shots from the beach.

One-two-three.

He raced down seven flights and through the lobby. The beach was shrouded in darkness as he tried to make out shapes moving over the sand. He dashed toward the ghostly rows of chairs and umbrellas, hoping he wasn't running right into an ambush. Ignoring his fears, he rushed past and down the beach. He was relieved to see Little Wing silhouetted by the light reflecting off the sea.

"I was so worried…" Brad began, as Little Wing stumbled and collapsed.

Brad knelt beside him. Little Wing's eyes opened.

"Did you get them?" he gasped.

Brad shook his head. "What happened?"

"There were two of them. They came down from the roof by parasail."

Brad smacked his forehead. Of course—Barbra's dress!

"I chased them along the beach," Little Wing continued. "I took a few warning shots, but I couldn't risk aiming at them while they had the girl. Just as they were leaving, one of them turned and winged me."

"We'll get you to a hospital," Brad said.

Little Wing grimaced. "I'll be all right. You go after them."

"I'm not leaving you!" Brad shouted.

"Red, you've got to go after them. Stop them from getting away!"

At that moment, a powerful boat motor started up somewhere down the beach. No doubt the kidnappers were in it with Celine. Brad could just make out the V-formation of waves whiting offshore in the moonlight.

"Too late," he said.

18

Brad wrestled Little Wing to his feet. It was like lifting solid brass. With his former partner leaning heavily on his arm, they stumbled out to the street and flagged a cab. The driver looked at them with trepidation. Brad flashed a twenty and told him to ignore the blood dripping from his companion's arm and down his leg.

Many things in Mexico ceased to be problems once you'd paid enough for them, Brad realized. Sure enough, the man's expression shifted to a happier gear. "Ees not a problem, señor," he assured them, handing back a box of tissues he no doubt kept on hand for such occasions.

The driver dropped them off at a hospital emergency room where they sat on a narrow bench in the waiting area. It was a light night for emergencies, and Little Wing's dripping blood guaranteed quick admittance.

"What happen to you?" the nurse asked, carefully turning his arm to examine it.

"Motorcycle accident," Little Wing replied. "No big deal."

She rubbed her finger lightly over a powder burn. "Hmm," she murmured. "The boolet is gone, but thees need to be clean and require manny stitches," she said.

"*Hable español,*" he commanded her.

She switched to Spanish, telling him she was going to give him a local anaesthetic.

He shrugged. "*No importa,*" he said. It doesn't matter.

"*Eres muy macho*," she said sarcastically.

"*Soy un hombre macho y sincero.*"

"*¿Macho y sincero?*" She giggled. "*Ese hombre no existe*," she said. No such thing.

She shrugged and began cleaning the wound. The bullet had gone through the fleshy part of his underarm and out the other side, narrowly missing a bulging vein. Little Wing caught Brad's eye.

"I know what you're thinking—I bleed a lot when I'm around you."

"Close. What I'm actually thinking is, 'Please don't die on me again.'"

Little Wing grunted. "I'm not planning on going anywhere now that I've found you again, Red."

He didn't even wince as the nurse began to sew up the wound.

It was nearly 2 a.m. by the time the stitching was finished. The nurse had won her argument that Little Wing wait at least fifteen minutes before leaving, as he clearly had no plans to stay in the hospital overnight. Brad didn't try hard to convince him either. The last thing they needed was for the police to come snooping around.

The nurse warned him his blood pressure could drop dangerously the moment he walked out the door.

"*Estaré bien*," he told her. I'll be okay. "Thanks to you."

She blushed. "*Gracias*," she said, quickly gathering up her surgical tools.

The night air hit them with relief after the stuffiness of the examination room. Little Wing draped his good arm over Brad's shoulders as they walked through the hospital parking lot. The dressing on his wound gleamed in the darkness.

"Eerie how you were nearly killed just by being near

me again," Brad said with a shiver. "I never forgave myself last time for what happened. I don't know what I'd do if I lost you a second time. And this time it really would have been my fault for getting you involved."

The street was deserted in the early morning. The bright lights of a gas station up ahead were the only sign of life.

"Now what?" Brad asked.

Little Wing shot him an ironic look. "It's been a fun date so far, but I think it's a bit late for *Pollo Loco*."

"I think we should get you back to your place," Brad said. "Let's find another cab."

"No," said Little Wing. "I can walk. It's not far."

"In your condition?"

Little Wing snorted. "*Yo soy un hombre macho y sincero*," he said.

"Yeah, well, there's macho and then there's just plain stupid."

"I'll be fine with you holding me up, Red."

Twenty minutes later found them in front of a tenement complex a block from the Río Cuale. Cats skittered away at their approach. Spanish moss hung from branches of trees enwrapped in the murderous tentacles of strangler figs. Roots erupted through cracks in the sidewalks, making walking perilous. Little Wing looked up at a darkened second-storey window as if deciding whether he had the right place or perhaps wishing for the thousandth time that he hadn't. Hardly the lap of luxury, Brad noted, thinking guiltily of his own palatial circumstances.

Little Wing unlatched the door and they stepped into darkness. "Watch your step," he warned. "There's no light. Power company's cut me off again. I haven't paid my bill in months."

Brad thought of Grace's admonitions that Little Wing might actually still be an agent, but on a different payroll. She'd laugh if she saw him now, but the laugh would be on her. Brad promised himself he'd do something to help out his former partner financially. Maybe he could pull a few strings and get him a job anonymously.

They picked their way up a flight of stairs. At the top, a door creaked open. It wasn't even locked. By the light of the street lamp shining through the window, Brad could make out a small cramped kitchen with a sink and stove shoved up against one wall. A fridge sat off-kilter at the far end, leaving just enough room to manoeuvre past it.

Brad glanced around. Something scurried away from what looked like a half-eaten plate of nachos on the counter. Yeesh! Did rats really grow that big outside of New York City? He felt a growing sense of disgust. The sound of a dripping tap completed the scene.

Little Wing opened the fridge. It emitted a rush of warm, foul-smelling air that seeped through the room. "Welcome to my humble abode," he said, reaching for a bottle of Dewar's. He fished two shot glasses from a cupboard, filled them and handed one to Brad. "To your health," he said. "And mine too, while we're at it."

"Amen to that," Brad said.

They clinked glasses. Little Wing turned and parted a beaded curtain. "Let me show you around," he said, walking through the shimmering portal.

Even in the dark, the room redefined the word "squalor." Refuse filled the interior with an assortment of oddments like some demented junkyard filing system. A sofa hunkered against one wall like a cornered beast, its cushions threadbare. Little Wing sat on it, motioning Brad to a chair across the room.

Through a window at the far end, the outline of the city presented itself like a painting, pristine and beautiful in contrast to the room's interior. Lights twinkled in the distance like a Christmas pageant. It was a stark reminder that somewhere, life could be beautiful.

"I haven't been a huge success since I went solo," Little Wing said. "Does it show?"

"I've seen worse," Brad said unconvincingly.

They drank in silence, peering at one another through the darkness.

At last, Little Wing spoke. "You know, I tried hard to forget you these past few years," he said. "But it was impossible. You've haunted me every night, Red. I lost my faith in life when I lost you. I never got it back."

Brad studied him, trying to make out his face. He recalled the bartender's forlorn words: *He calls himself Nothing.*

Little Wing poured another glass. "This stuff works better than the hospital anaesthetic," he said, downing it in one gulp. "So tell me what happened earlier. For the record, my guess is that it has something to do with why you're here in Vallarta."

Brad hesitated. Would he break protocol and tell Little Wing about his mission? On the other hand, Little Wing had been an agent once too. He was saved the bother of deciding.

"I figure it has something to do with that kidnapping we witnessed. Was that the real Celine Dion, by any chance?"

"I think so. But I've pretty much been kept in the dark so far. I was never told what I'm supposed to be doing here, except keeping her out of danger."

Little Wing grunted ironically. "So now you're a bodyguard for celebrities."

"And not a very good one, it seems."

Little Wing nodded. "That's one of the problems down here. It doesn't pay to get ahead. If you're rich, you become a target. Here's a statistic for you: someone is kidnapped in Mexico every six hours. One in eight is murdered." He shook his head. "Add police corruption on top of that and you can understand why nearly everyone wants out. They don't really want to go to the States—they just want to be anywhere but here. If they could walk straight across the border into New Zealand or Thailand, you can bet they'd do that instead."

As he sat there listening, Brad was aware of the sound of their breathing, the far-off scream of a cat, a trickle of sweat on his skin. A fan sat motionless in one corner, like a useless reprimand against the heat.

"So who's Panther?"

"Panther was the agent who got killed trying to hand me the information I needed."

"I don't follow. Why was a drag queen impersonating him?"

"Well—it's a little hard to explain, but I'll do my best. That drag queen—Esmeralda—is what's called a channel. The dead speak through her. Are you with me so far?"

Little Wing grunted, whether in agreement or disbelief, Brad couldn't tell.

"Anyway, after her show the other night I asked if she could channel anyone she wanted. She said usually all she needed was a name. She told me to come by tonight and see what happened."

"So you gave her Panther's name and a so-called spook came through."

Brad shook his head. "No. That's the freaky part. She told me to come by tonight and tell her the name then. I never said who I wanted to talk to, but Panther came through all right—right down to his Tennessee twang. He even called me by my code name."

"I noticed that." Little Wing was silent for a moment. "So I guess you were two-timing me on our little date," he said.

"Or three-timing you. I actually forgot about it till after we'd made plans for tonight. Thanks for the warning about the gun, by the way. It was that cab driver from the other day. You saved my life—again," Brad said. "I only wish I could've done the same for Panther and Esmeralda. My score is pretty downright rotten these days."

Little Wing nodded thoughtfully. "Don't sweat it, Red. You never know when your time is up. Once you come close to dying, you start to wonder when the real thing will come along. I can't tell you how much time I spend thinking about how I'm going to die. Or at whose hands. I still have nightmares…"

"I don't blame you for having nightmares," Brad said. "Not after what happened to you."

Little Wing shook his head. "Except these nightmares aren't about dying, Red. That's the funny part. They're about living. Night after night, I suffer terrible dreams telling me I've wasted my chances, that I'm not doing anything worthwhile with the time I've been given. I had a therapist for a while. She said I have latent fears of dying again, so instead I dream that my life is a failure." He shrugged and glanced around the darkened room. "Maybe she's right."

"Therapy, huh?" Brad said. "Sometimes I think I should try it, but I know I never will. I have that in-born WASP conviction that wanting to see a psychiatrist is proof you're insane."

Little Wing laughed. "That's my Red." He struggled unsteadily to his feet. "The funny thing about dying is how it makes you realize how little we truly live. That's why I knew I couldn't die without seeing you again. I've spent a lot of time thinking of ways to bring you back into my life."

"You should rest," Brad said, looking up at the figure towering over him.

"Rest? I don't want to waste another second with you. I want to live every moment from now in full colour. No more shadow life for me."

Little Wing knelt and put his hand on Brad's thigh, running his fingers along the muscles. Brad felt a tingling in his groin.

"No underwear?" Little Wing slid his hands up the leg of Brad's shorts and grasped his balls.

Brad shrugged. "Still don't wear any."

Little Wing laughed. "Same old Red," he said, stroking him. "Fuck—I've missed you! You are still the most beautiful guy I've ever met." He nodded sharply. His eyes rolled backwards and were already closed as his head hit Brad's lap. A snore escaped him.

Brad sat unmoving till Little Wing's breathing lapsed into something like peacefulness. He turned to the window where the moon outlined the silhouettes of branches heavy with Spanish moss. So much of life was lived in shadows, he mused. The vague outlines of things you could barely make out.

Brad lifted Little Wing onto the couch and slipped a pillow beneath his head. He crouched beside him, stroking his sleeping face.

"I could never cry when you were taken from me," Brad said softly. "Not once in all these years. Maybe this is why—because I knew one day you'd come back to me."

He stood at the window, looking down into the

courtyard, watching to see if anyone had followed them from the hospital. Nothing moved but the restless cats that combed the city every night. An hour passed as he stood guarding his former-partner. His body felt numb, but he stayed a while longer, as though he could make up now for what he'd failed to do in the past. Once he thought he saw something moving in the shadows and was instantly on the alert. He waited without breathing for nearly a minute, but nothing further ensued. Perhaps it had only been a cloud passing over the moon.

At last, he knew he needed to leave. He went back to the couch where Little Wing lay spread-eagled across the cushions. His skin glistened in the moonlight, his snores rending the air. Brad leaned down and kissed the sleeping lips and smoothed the hair from his brow. "I'm sorry I have to leave you again,' he said softly.

He took a pencil from his pocket, searching among the debris for a scrap of paper. He scribbled his cell number on it, curling the sleeping fingers around the note. Then he slipped down the stairs and back into the night, cursing the strangeness of fate.

19

The streets were silent in the pre-dawn darkness. On the far side of the river, Brad got his bearings and headed back. The likelihood of finding a cab in that end of town at that hour of the morning was nil. He set off at a jog, his footfalls echoing through the empty thoroughfares. His shadow grew long on the outer walls of houses and then shrank again with each street lamp he passed. He was back outside the Blue Parrot in ten minutes.

The beach was carved up by moon shadows and light thrown from an occasional hotel window. The relentless roar of the waves sounded in the distance. Brad combed over the sand, but it was impossible to distinguish one set of footprints from another and he quickly realized he was doing more damage by walking around. He would come back and search again by the light of day. He might find something he'd overlooked.

Inside the hotel lobby, a sleepy-looking receptionist chatted with a police officer who fit the description of "bumbling" to a T. The cop told the clerk not to let anyone go up to the rooftop while he went off to find a burrito. He would be back in five minutes.

The officer left. Brad strode confidently through the lobby as though he were a guest there. The receptionist regarded him with sleepy eyes.

"Still here?" Brad asked. "You deserve a medal, my friend."

The receptionist nodded half-heartedly. Brad entered the elevator and rode it up to the roof. Yellow police tape surrounded the nightclub entrance, cordoning it off to anyone who paid attention to such things. Brad ducked underneath and began to look around.

The scene looked the same as when he'd last been there: the curtain slightly raised, tables and chairs overturned when people fled. Apart from that, there was nothing to indicate a kidnapping and shooting had taken place here a few hours previously. But in fact they had. An international recording star had been kidnapped and a Mexican entertainer shot dead. Some hotshot peacekeeper I am, Brad thought. Why the hell hadn't Grace warned him he was in over his head? All she'd said was that she had "vital information." Had she not realized he needed a backup? He was glad at least that Zach had been safely out of the way.

Brad felt a surge of relief followed by a pang of guilt as he looked over at the table where he'd been sitting with Little Wing. The table where Little Wing had kissed him and held his hand. There was his bag, safe and sound, sitting right where he'd left it. The white stripe gleamed in the moonlight. In the commotion, he'd forgot all about it.

He tossed it over his shoulder and was about to leave when he heard voices. Two shadowy figures entered the club. They were talking under their breaths, but it was clear they were arguing. Brad ducked behind the bar. The words were unintelligible, but whoever it was was speaking Portuguese.

The look-a-likes!

Brad watched them from the shadows. They walked stealthily, lifting things up and peering underneath. Only this time, they'd come without their bag. Then it dawned on him—that's what they were looking for! With the shooting and the resulting pandemonium, they must have lost it. Maybe they were unaware it wasn't even the same bag. They continued their search, stopping occasionally to bicker amongst themselves. Brad wished he could understand what they were saying.

From behind him came a loud whirring as the elevator dial began to climb. The policeman was coming back. The door whooshed open with a *ding!* as the porn twins ducked through the stage exit. The burly, bumbling officer emerged chomping on a burrito. He belched loudly and gave a half-hearted look around the site he'd no doubt been under strict orders not to leave. Satisfied all was well, he sat and continued his feast.

Allowing the twins plenty of time to leave, Brad sneaked past the cop and down the stairs. He nodded to the sleepy-eyed receptionist on his way back through the lobby.

He was dead tired. By the time he reached the villa, there was a massive pain constricting the flow of blood in his head. It had been an exceptionally long and worrisome day, even for a secret agent. He pulled out his cell phone, pacing the room. The dresser clock said 5:27 a.m. What time was it where he heard the phone ringing? Grace could be anywhere in the world. All Brad knew was that she lived with five afghan hounds. She might even be up already exercising her furry friends.

The voice that answered was clear and alert, as though she'd been at her desk for hours, breakfast behind her after that brisk morning run, and a third coffee already in the works.

"Hard luck, Red," she said. "I've already heard."

For a moment, he thought she was talking about

his guilty feelings over Little Wing. But of course, that was absurd—she'd heard what had happened at the hotel earlier that evening.

"Why wasn't I informed that was the real Celine Dion?" he demanded.

There was a notable pause. Then, "Who says I know any more about what's happening than you, Red?"

He ignored the question, certain she was telling him a good deal less than she knew. "How can I do my job if I don't know what's going on?" he demanded.

"And just how the hell do you think I feel?" she snapped. "Do you think I enjoy finding out these things after everyone else? You're the one who's down there. You should be feeding me information. Don't wait for me to tell you what's going on!"

Brad stopped pacing and sank into a chair. "I suppose the kidnapping will be all over the media in a few hours," he said.

"On the contrary," Grace said. "Our people are keeping things as quiet as possible. We can't afford to have the kidnappers panic. Once we get Dion back"—she left a pause big enough for him to crawl through—"we'll let the media have a heyday with whatever they decide did or did not happen. Not that the facts will have any bearing on what they report, of course."

"So now what?" he asked.

"Now you're going to do what my best agent always does: keep your eyes open and your ears to the ground. The kidnappers will contact us with their demands in their own sweet time. Meanwhile, I have complete faith that you're going to do a splendid job in getting everything back to normal."

"Exactly how am I supposed to do that?" he said testily. He didn't like how she was painting him into a corner.

"When you figure that out, I'll be delighted to know."

The call ended. Brad snapped the phone shut and looked in the mirror. He felt an uncharacteristic wave of panic. Surely this was the biggest disaster Agent Red had ever been part of. What weird, screwed-up tangent was life throwing at him now?

Since joining Box 77, he had tried to do the impossible: to give life on earth a fighting chance. No—to give it a *peaceful* chance. He'd wanted only to let good flourish and prosper. And from time to time, he even felt mildly successful at doing just that. Even if no one ever knew what he did or what horrors he'd prevented, it helped him knowing the world was a safer place because of it.

So what did life want from him now?

He'd failed in his bid to keep a much-loved singer safe from harm. Somewhat closer to home, a fellow agent had been killed, a former agent maimed, and a Mexican drag queen shot dead. On top of everything else, he'd hardly been the faithful lover Zach believed him to be. Who would trust him again? Everything he was confronting seemed to be a reprimand against him. How was he going to face such utter contradictions: a former partner returned from the dead to test his faith, and a young man who loved him more than anyone he'd met until now?

Until now.

What a great divide lay between yesterday and today. How was he going to get across the chasm and redeem himself? Frankly, he hadn't a clue.

20

Brad woke with a start. He lay sprawled on his bed, still dressed in last night's clothes. He glanced at the clock: just past eight. He'd managed to get in two hours' sleep. He grabbed his bag and ran out of the villa, down the hill.

Playa de los Muertos was a mess of surly waves and disgruntled tourists when he arrived. Clouds raced overhead and gulls jeered at the humans gambolling in the surf despite the obvious threat to their safety. Or perhaps the birds thought the humans were stealing the fish again. In either case, it was an ugly scene.

Brad circled the sands for a quarter hour, but the beach was a parade ground of footprints. It was impossible to tell this morning's footprint's from yesterday's or to discern anything that had gone on the night before. Curiously, it almost seemed that none of it had happened. Brad stopped and looked around. Last night a murder and a kidnapping with international ramifications had occurred within a block of this strip of beach, yet life just went on as always. Waiters made their drink rounds, vendors displayed their wares, and the Chiclet Chicos braved the early morning crowds, smiling their baby-faced smiles as pure as the newborn day. Had Icarus fallen from the sky, wings aflame, Brad bet none of them would bat an eyelash. But then, why would they? What had happened was Brad's fault, not theirs. To them, it was just another glorious day in PV.

From the far end of the beach, Jarod greeted him

with flowing sleeves. He waved his arms about as though semaphoring across the playa: *DQ Shot Dead, Famous Singer Kidnapped Due to Ineptitude of Secret Agent Bradford Fairfax.* That was ridiculous, Brad knew, but even if Box 77 managed to hide Dion's kidnapping from the media, surely someone from last night's audience would spill the beans before long. If it hadn't been made public already. The rumour mill was ripe for the picking.

"That was quite the spectacle last night, wasn't it?" Jarod enthused, his over-moisturized skin shining at a distance.

"Yes," Brad said guiltily, thinking of the recently departed Esmeralda. "It certainly was."

"How do they stage something like that?" Jarod asked.

"Stage?" Brad cried. "Surely you don't think…?" He stopped and did a double take: off to the right he saw Esmeralda's condor-like profile where she lay prone on a beach towel, sipping a margarita through a curved straw. "I thought she was dead!" Brad cried.

Jarod squinted at him in the sunlight. "I know. It looked so real!" he said. "Of course, Esmeralda was on another plane the whole time. She says she can't remember a thing!"

Brad's mind was racing. What was going on here? Was this yet another Box 77 cover-up? Wipe off the bloodstains and hush up the kill? Maybe Grace was right in saying there'd be no kidnapping scandal bandied about on the front pages of international newspapers. Not for the time being, at least. It looked like nothing had happened.

"I thought it was sheer brilliance how they staged that mock-kidnapping in the middle of the show," Jarod went on. "It was postmodern theatre at its best!"

Surely not, Brad told himself. It couldn't all have been a charade. Had the events of the evening fooled everyone or was Jarod simply feigning ignorance? Even now, the kidnappers were probably sending out ransom messages, while Celine Dion lay tied up in some dingy, rat-infested hellhole.

Brad glanced around for Jarod's bag. There was no sign of it. Had he been the one to enter the Brazilian's room first and deprive them of their precious cargo or had someone else got there before him?

"Say, Jarod," Bradford said. "I forgot my suntan lotion. Might you have any extra I could use?"

Jarod looked over. "Not today. I left my bag behind. I was too exhausted to drag it along."

Of course he'd come without it, Brad reasoned. If Jarod had the Brazilians' bag, he wouldn't be foolish enough to be seen running around with it in public. He'd hide it somewhere safe. Even so, that didn't solve the mystery of what happened on the Blue Parrot rooftop last night.

Sebastian hailed Brad and headed over to him. "Quite the show last night, wasn't it?" he exclaimed. "Imagine, staging a shooting like that. Those drag queens sure are outrageous!"

So Sebastian too thought the events of the previous evening a brilliantly staged ruse. It was unbelievable. Had the entire audience been duped? Brad was beginning to think some sort of mass hypnosis was at work. If so, it was probably the result of too much television. It warped the mind. After decades of TV watching, people had lost touch with reality. They no longer experienced day-to-day events as something real. Instead, they viewed things as though they were watching them on TV. Entire generations had grown up wearing TV-coloured glasses. When something happened to them in real life, its meaning eluded them because they thought they were still at home watching television. TV was no doubt accruing a very large karmic debt for how it had contributed to warping the human perspective.

Just then, Esmeralda stood and strolled down the beach, as imperturbable as a real Mayan princess. Of course everyone thought it was staged! No one seemed to have been hurt. For a split second, Brad wondered if he'd dreamed the whole thing. Maybe he hadn't even been here last night. Maybe he was dreaming now, suffering the after-effects of too much sun and a tequila hangover. Was it possible he'd hallucinated the entire episode?

Sebastian turned to Brad. "Where's that winsome young man of yours? Should I be worried on his behalf that you were out gallivanting with a veritable stud last night?"

Well, someone had seen him after all. He hadn't hallucinated that part.

"Thank you for worrying about Zach's honour— and mine by default—but there's nothing to fear. He went inland for a few days. That was just an old friend of mine you saw me with last night."

That much was true, at least.

A bout of snarling arrested everyone's attention. Heads swivelled trying to locate the source, hopeful for a bit of entertainment. The source, in fact, was the look-a-like lovers, enjoined in look-a-like snarls as surely as their kisses and embraces had happily mirrored them on previous days. They were still arguing, only much more loudly than last night. And they were still bag-less as well. Brad hadn't dreamed that either.

He was surprised to see them. If they were mixed up in the kidnapping then they should have been anywhere but here, wandering the beach in broad daylight. Yet here they were, griping and lounging like common tourists. Could those two beauties really be murderers and kidnappers? At the moment, it seemed hard to believe. In Puerto Vallarta it might look like all was sunshine and margaritas, but Brad knew that hardened criminals were at work in this town. He couldn't afford to get sloppy now.

"Well, that's interesting," Jarod said, glancing at Brad. "It's good to know even the perfect couple isn't perfect."

"Can you understand what they're saying?" Brad asked.

"My Portuguese is a bit rusty," Jarod said, "but from what I can make out, they're accusing each other of sleeping with another boy, and both denying it, of course."

Sebastian grinned. "Lover's spat," he said.

"There's more," Jarod continued. "They think whoever the other one slept with stole their precious bag!"

Now that, thought Bradford, was news. They hadn't realized the real bag had been stolen from their hotel room right under their, uh, noses.

"I hope they don't threaten me again like they did on the *Rainbow Warrior*," Jarod exclaimed. He looked up to see Sebastian staring at him. "Oops! I didn't say that. Nobody pointed a gun at me on your boat."

Sebastian looked perplexed.

Brad shrugged. "The night of your party, Jarod mistakenly picked up their bag and they threatened him with a gun."

Sebastian glanced back and forth between them. "You two seem to get yourselves mixed up in some very questionable situations. Is that intentional?"

"Just lucky, I guess," Brad said.

Sebastian looked past him out to the bay. "Speaking of, I should probably make a trek out to my boat sometime today."

Brad followed his glance to the *Rainbow Warrior*. The *Libre* had vanished again.

"Looks like that three-master disappeared sometime in the middle of the night," Sebastian said. "They must have pulled up anchor and gone off to another port."

"You didn't see them leave?" Brad asked.

"Nah! But good riddance to them." Sebastian's gaze swept the shoreline. "Lot of good-looking bodies here today. I should do another party round."

Sebastian wandered off to audition for his next sailing expedition. Brad stayed on the beach, questioning people who had been in the audience the previous evening. The general consensus seemed to be that last night's occurrences had all been part of the show and that there was nothing to be concerned about.

For now, at least, Brad's terrible secret was safe.

21

The day wore on. Nothing much appeared to be happening at the beach. Meanwhile, Panther's murderer was still at large. Brad knew he wouldn't redeem himself one bit by lying in the sun.

He slung the bag over his shoulder and made his way back up to the villa, his mind in a whirl. What had really gone on at the Blue Parrot last night? Had there been a kidnapping or hadn't there? Clearly there'd been a shooting, because Little Wing had been shot. That was no illusion. But what of the rest of it—the green-eyed man, the shooting of Esmeralda, and the supposed kidnapping of Celine? Was he going nuts? Maybe it was the strain of his job. That wouldn't be hard to believe. He might have breached an invisible gap between the everyday and the fantastic, ending up in some altered state. Maybe his chakras were doing strange things, emitting the wrong vibes. Zach would know, except Zach wasn't around to tell him. Whatever it was, something mighty peculiar was going on. He was going to have to figure it out all by himself.

Funny, but he hadn't heard from Zach since the message sent on his arrival. Perhaps he was too caught up in his Vision Quest, engaged in whatever rituals it entailed. Brad wished now that he'd asked a few more questions about it. Still, the silence was worrisome.

By chance, he looked over his shoulder as he trudged up the hill. It might have been coincidence, but he thought he saw someone duck behind a tree. He moved along a few more steps and glanced back again. Yes, he was sure of it now. Someone was following him. But it wasn't the green-eyed man. Rather, it was the dark half of the Brazilian meatball sandwich. Brad ducked behind a gate and waited. The dark beauty soon passed by, heading up the road. A minute later, he stopped and looked around in bewilderment to see where his quarry had disappeared. Brad stayed out of sight. The boy shrugged and turned in the direction of Brad's villa. That was bad news. It meant the boy knew where he was staying.

Brad had just emerged from hiding when a second figure appeared, looking very grim and determined. It was the blonde SS clerk from the Blue Parrot. Was he on the tail of the Brazilian or was he too following Bradford Fairfax, a.k.a. Jonathan Witherspoon, a.k.a. Agent Red? The boy's head snapped in Brad's direction. His eyes lit on the burgundy bag slung over his shoulder.

"Halt!" he cried, raising a hand like a zealous border guard.

Whoops! Brad thought. His British accent wouldn't save him now. He dashed around a corner and slipped between two small villas. The SS clerk followed him to the top of the hill, but then seemed to lose sight of him. The boy waited a few seconds. Brad watched him peer around a wall, keeping a sharp lookout. A moment later, he turned and strode away in the same direction as the Brazilian.

Well, well, well, thought Brad. Who's next? He didn't have to wait long to find out. A few seconds later, a third figure came huffing and puffing up the hill. It was Sebastian. The silver-haired captain seemed intent on the blonde and the dark-haired beauty ahead of him. Something told Brad he wasn't "casting" another party on his yacht. He too turned and followed the trail uphill.

This was getting kooky. Who would be next to show up for this impromptu tea party? It occurred to Brad that if one of the look-a-likes was on his tail, the other might be nearby. If so, the pair may have concluded that he had their bag. They'd been quick to point a gun in Jarod's face for merely touching it. What would they do if they thought that he'd actually taken it? He couldn't afford to be careless for a second.

Brad high-tailed it up to his villa, slowing as he came within sight of it. Sure enough, he saw the dark-haired Brazilian loitering around the next corner. No doubt the others were there somewhere waiting for Brad's return. But why were they all after him?

Brad knew there was no chance he could get inside without being seen. For now, he'd have to find a place to wait it out. The most important thing was to let Grace know that he'd been the object of a fairly intensive manhunt by some of the more questionable suspects in Celine Dion's kidnapping. Maybe she would have a suggestion.

He pulled out his cell. On dialling the agency, however, he learned that Grace was unavailable. She sure picked a dicey time to disappear. The operator told him to stay put and wait for her call.

No can do, Brad thought. Staying put was not an option right now.

With his bag tucked under one arm, he slipped unobtrusively down the hill and headed for town. Only now did it strike him how alone he was. Had Zach been there, they would have hashed out the recent events together, compiling various hypotheses about one thing or another. This time he'd have to ponder them on his own.

His thoughts were restless. He was plagued by the reappearance of Little Wing. The near-tragic events of last night had awakened Brad's deepest fears, bringing out his true feelings for Little Wing. Was it a sign they were destined to be rejoined and spend the rest of their lives together making up for the lost years? He had no idea what to think.

Zach would tell him to meditate to try to find the answers to his dilemmas, but Brad wasn't much of one for sitting and pondering things. He preferred action. He could barely lie on a beach for five minutes without getting bored, let alone sit and contemplate his internal workings for hours on end.

Until he heard back from Grace, there wasn't much he could do. The sun bore down on him, forcing him to slow his pace. Maybe he could find a nice little café and go in and have a beer and relax. "Relax" had always been a dirty word to him. It implied laziness, indolence, and a whole lot of other undesirable qualities. Yet oddly, he realized, to most of the human race it meant something good. Maybe there was a reason he felt different from nearly everyone else he knew.

A *zócalo* bisected the road just up ahead. Brad stopped in the square and sat on a bench under the shade of a lime tree. He needed to formulate a plan that did not involve staring at his phone and waiting for it to ring. He recalled the posture Zach used in his meditations: legs tucked under and crossed at the ankle, hands resting on his knees. The lotus. He tried to replicate it, making himself comfortable on the bench while raising his palms upward.

Uneasy thoughts floated through his mind. Why was everyone tailing him? How much longer before Grace returned his call? Didn't she realize he might have news of the kidnapping? Surely she would take him seriously after everything he'd been through in the last few days.

Too much thinking, he reminded himself. Zach had said the object of meditation was to free yourself from thinking and let the universe float freely through. But how could you stop thinking?

Well, a voice replied, you just stop and let it happen!

Let what happen? Who was talking here?

Just turn off your conscious mind, said the voice.

Hmmm—was there an off-switch somewhere?

Brad tried to relax, but his thoughts drifted to Little Wing and the electric jolt that surged through his body when they touched. He recalled all the years of despair that lay between the night of Little Wing's supposed murder and now. Then he thought of Zach and the happy home they'd made together. Panic crept in. Was it all about to come crashing down?

Hey! the other voice shouted. Stop thinking!

Okay, Brad told himself. I've stopped.

Clearly you haven't, replied the voice. Or you wouldn't be answering me.

Oh, right.

Just try to think of nothing!

Impossible! a new voice interjected. How can you think of nothing?

Yeesh! There were too many voices in his head. Was this what Esmeralda experienced when she channelled?

Brad sighed and took a deep breath, all the while being conscious of not thinking. He envisioned a white wall. Was that the same as not thinking? Gawd, I'm bored, he thought. How long has this been going on? It feels like hours. He checked his watch. In fact, less than two minutes had elapsed. How long would he continue to sit here doing nothing?

He tried to concentrate on his breathing. In and out. In and out. In and o-o-o-o-o-o-u-u-t… Before long, his mind relaxed and the chatter receded to a dull buzz at the back of his brain. He sank into what he might have described as "a place where there was nothing," had he been thinking about it.

But in fact, Brad was not thinking now. He was experiencing some sort of vision, except it seemed to him that he was really there. His father was there too. They were standing in the middle of a large field, carrying bows and arrows. At first Brad thought his father was teaching him to hunt, but he soon realized there was something else going on.

His father raised his bow and pulled back, stretching the string. He concentrated, closing one eye while keeping the other on the target. Then he released the arrow. Bullseye! He repeated the feat as Brad watched in amazement. He'd never known his father to be such an expert marksman.

They were talking about love. In a quiet moment, between taking aim and releasing, Brad asked his father about his mother. How had he known she was the one for him?

"Love's arrow flies straight and true," said his father, as he released yet another shaft with a soft snap. It too flew to the target's centre. "You may not recognize it right away, Bradford, but you know when it hits you."

The vision faded. Brad opened his eyes. The sun was still directly overhead, though it felt as though he'd been sitting there for hours. He checked his watch. Scant minutes had passed. Was it a memory? He couldn't recall practicing archery with his father at any time in their fifteen years together. Then what was it? He hadn't even been thinking about his father when he sat down. Nor had he consciously tried to imagine him. But suddenly, as he pondered his life and love, the vision had simply come to him. Was that meditation?

"Love's arrow flies straight and true," his father had said. It made sense. Of course, that didn't account for neurotic, obsessive personalities like Brad who swerved and turned and made one effort after another to avoid love, as he'd done when he first met Zach. He'd trotted out every argument in the book not to take Zach seriously, but fate had thrown them together in a way even Brad couldn't deny had been fortuitous. Love's arrow had hit home.

Then what did that say about what he felt for Little Wing? He'd denied his feelings all through their training and their working partnership. It only struck him after Little Wing vanished—was stolen from him—that he'd loved him. Did that somehow mean that what he felt was wrong or misguided? Perhaps it wasn't meant to last. The path it had taken was certainly anything but straight. You couldn't tell him that a person who died and came back to life four years later had made a direct and unbroken connection to his heart. No, that was about as crooked and disjointed a path as Brad could imagine.

Still, what he felt for Little Wing was definitely powerful. When he thought of his former partner, Brad's hands shook, his palms got sweaty, and his face flushed. He felt lit up, incandescent. Wasn't that love? When Little Wing touched him, he got an instant erection. Didn't that mean anything? Even in sleep, when his cock slid into Little Wing, he'd swooned and had a wet dream.

And then what happened? asked one of those pesky chattering voices in his head.

Then I woke up, Brad thought.

Before that.

Oh, yeah! Brad suddenly recalled. Then the coffin lid closed down on him. He'd already forgot that part of the picture.

Brad considered this. Maybe he'd made a mistake. Little Wing had said he didn't get attached to things he couldn't flush down the toilet. That was a sure way of saying he wasn't interested in a lasting relationship, but then last night he'd confessed his torment on losing Brad and his desire to bring him back into his life. Still, any future with Little Wing promised to be uncertain and unstable at best. Not just because of the dream. One look around that filthy apartment had turned Brad's compassion to pity. How could you love someone as your equal if you felt sorry for him? Love and pity weren't amiable bed-mates.

Perhaps so, Brad admitted, but in the meantime he had things to do. He stood and looked down the street, scouring the road ahead and behind him. Somewhere out there was a pair of kidnappers and killers. He had to put aside his personal problems and find them before they did any more damage.

Brad's cell phone rang. Finally, it was action time. "Red here."

He heard someone breathing hard. "Red, it's Little." His voice sounded desperate. "I *need* you, buddy!"

22

Little Wing's words were still ringing in Brad's ears as he tossed his cell phone in his bag and raced down the street in the direction of the Río Cuale. At the same time, he kept his eyes open for signs of Sebastian or the SS clerk or the Brazilian look-a-likes, though he had little time to worry about them as he headed for Little Wing's apartment.

The front door of the tenement was unlocked when he arrived. He let himself in and took the stairs two at a time. Upstairs, Little Wing was splayed on the ratty old sofa where Brad had put him to bed a few hours ago. He was dressed in his boxers, with a sleeveless T-shirt and a pair of cowboy boots propped on the table before him. Even in this ridiculous guise, he was glorious to behold. A half-finished bottle of Dewar's Special Reserve stuck up from between his legs. He grabbed the bottle and held it out to Brad.

"Care for a drink?"

His gaze seemed steady, but Brad got the impression he was completely drunk. "I rushed right over," he said. "What's up?"

"Ah, Red! You always ask such leading questions." Little Wing winked. "I could certainly show you what's up, if you'd let me."

"Little, I, uh—" Brad began.

"I'm just glad you're here," Little Wing interrupted. He held out his arms. "I missed you, baby." He patted the

197

seat beside him.

"You sounded desperate on the phone," Brad said from the doorway. "I was worried something had happened."

Little Wing opened a pack of cigarettes, tapped one out with his finger and lit it. "It's all cool, Red. Everything's under control now. Nothing to worry about."

"Good. I'm glad to hear." Brad cast a worried glance around. Despite the assurances, his senses said something wasn't right. "What exactly is under control? Are you sure everything's okay?"

"Now that you're here, I meant. Yeah—it's all good." Little Wing blew a ring of smoke then raised the bottle and took a pull. He smacked his lips with a satisfied sigh. "So fine."

"Maybe you should put the bottle down now, Little." Brad poked his head through the beaded curtains and looked around the kitchen. The note with his cell phone number lay on the kitchen counter. Everything looked just as it had the night before, but something definitely felt wrong.

Little Wing set the bottle on the floor beside him. "You know what they say, Red. I'd rather have a bottle in front of me than a frontal lobotomy." He waited a beat then shook his head. "You're supposed to laugh here."

"Right. Funny. How's your arm?" Brad asked, coming back from the kitchen.

"Just fine," Little Wing replied, waving the bandaged limb. "Getting better all the time."

Brad peered into a back room—a mattress lay on the floor alongside a scattering of magazines, food cartons and empty whiskey bottles. Flies buzzed around the room. By the light of day, the place looked far worse. It seemed a portrait of neglect and despair.

He was about to turn back when something caught his eye. Through a crack in the bathroom door, he saw a spray of red dripping down the shower curtain. He walked cautiously in and pulled aside the curtain. The green-eyed man lay sprawled—and dead—inside the tub. Brad drew a breath. When he turned around he nearly jumped out of his skin. Little Wing stood right behind him.

"Nothing to worry about," Little Wing said. "I had a small problem. But as I said, it's all under control."

"What happened here?"

Little Wing shrugged. "He was looking for you, I think."

"For me?"

"Yeah." Little Wing took a drag on his cigarette. "That's what he said. Seems he thought you had something he wanted. He showed up this morning not long after you left. Do you know him?"

"Of course I know him," Brad said, trying to keep his voice calm. His heart was pounding. "I mean, I don't know him, but…" His words trailed off. "This is the guy with the gun from last night. The same one who tried to poison me at Garbo's and who you chased down the highway the day you stopped to rescue me."

Little Wing peered at the face. "Now that you mention it, I think you might be right. Yeah—I think it is the same guy."

"Tell me what happened," Brad said, dreading whatever he was about to hear.

Little Wing took another drag and exhaled loudly. "He came here waving a gun in the air and looking for you. He threatened to shoot me unless I told him where you were. I told him you were in my bathroom taking a leak. When he walked in, I grabbed my gun and popped him."

Brad looked over at the tub. "You shot him? Just like that?"

"What the fuck, Red? It was him or me. I'm still a pretty good shot, remember? Even totally pissed, I can still do the glass trick." He held out his hand—it was completely steady.

Brad shook his head. If Love's arrow flew straight and true, this path was getting crookeder and crookeder by the second.

Little Wing sighed. "You're so damned beautiful, Red. You're so fucking perfect."

"Little…" Brad held up a hand. "Fuck! I don't know what to say. There's a dead man in your bathroom and you're making a pass at me."

"Just say you love me! That's all I want to hear…"

Brad's eyes darted back and forth between his former partner and the body in the bathtub.

"Because I love you, Red. And you feel the same for me. Surely you know that, don't you?"

Brad nodded dumbly.

"Do you have any doubts about me you'd like to air?" Little Wing asked. "Because if you do, I'd like to get them out in the open now before things start to get crazy."

"No," Bradford said. "I have no doubts about you, it's just…" He looked at the red stains oozing down the curtain. "What about this?"

"You know what they say, Red. A friend will help you move, but a good friend will help you move a body." He winked.

Brad stared at him. "Are you asking me to ignore this? We can't do that. We have to report it. *I* have to report it. You won't get in trouble—as you said, you were protecting yourself from someone who was hunting for me…"

Little Wing pressed forward, crushing Brad against the sink. His breath was thick with alcohol. "Let's do it right here…"

"Little!"

"…then afterwards we'll just disappear. Vanish into thin air."

Brad stared at him. "Why? Why would we do that?"

"We'll take the money and get the fuck out of here forever. No more worries, no more cares…"

"What money?"

"Red…"

"What money? What are you talking about?"

Little Wing dropped his butt on the floor and ground it out with his boot. "It's okay, Red. I know all about it."

Brad pushed him roughly against the far wall. "What the fuck are you talking about?"

Little Wing smiled his big, goofy grin. "I love it when you treat me rough, baby. Go on—hit me, big boy."

"Little, I swear if you don't tell me what's going on I'll…"

"You'll what? Shoot me?" Little Wing looked away for a moment. His face was dead serious when he turned back. "Last chance, Red. We could take it all and just disappear. I'll be with you a hundred percent. Unless you want it all for yourself, that is."

Brad looked at him as though he'd just said he came from Mars. He spoke very slowly and quietly. "What are you talking about?"

"I'm talking about the money in your bag. I know you've got it."

Brad shoved him aside and stormed into the front room. He picked up the burgundy bag and turned to Little Wing. "Here," he said, holding it out. "It's a change of clothes from last night. It's socks and sunblock…"

"Open it."

"What?"

"You heard me—open the bag."

Brad's fingers felt like ice as he unzipped his bag. He plunged his hands inside and tossed out a T-shirt. Next came his binoculars followed by a tube of suntan lotion and a packet of paper bills. "You see—it's just…"

"Just what, Red?"

Brad felt his breath coming in shallow gasps. "Just … erm…money? It's…fuck…a lot of money." How was this possible? He looked up. "I … I … swear I didn't know I had this." His mind raced as he tried to piece together the events of the last twenty-four hours. He'd had the bag when he left the Brazilians sleeping at the Blue Parrot. Then he went home, showered and grabbed a change of clothes before returning to the hotel to meet with Little Wing. And then… "It was at the club last night. I left my bag behind when you got shot…"

"So where did the money come from?"

Brad shook his head, feeling dazed. "…and after I left your apartment I went back to the club. When I got there, I realized I'd left my bag behind. I'd forgot all about it." He shook his head again. "I swear, Little! The bag was on the table right where I left it last night. I just went over and … and…"

"…picked up a bag with a lot of money in it. A cool five million, to be precise."

Brad whirled on him. "Five million? How would you know that?"

"They were testing you, Red. And you fell right into their trap." Little Wing shook his head. "I thought you were smarter than that."

"What? Who? No! I didn't know!" He smashed the

wall with his fist. "I don't know anything about this."

"Why do you think this guy came sniffing around here?" Little Wing said, poking at the body in the tub with the toe of his boot.

"Are you saying he was after me for the money?" Brad flashed on the trail of people following him up the hill to his villa. Was that why Sebastian and the others had followed him home? Had they all known what he was carrying?

"That's my guess. He must have known you had it."

"But how? How did he know I had it? I didn't even know I had it!"

"There's a tracker in the bag, Red. We're not stupid."

"Who the hell is 'we'?" Brad demanded. "A tracker for what? What the fuck is going on here?" Something dawned on Brad. He recalled Grace's words of warning about Little Wing's disappearance. "You're still an agent, aren't you?"

Little Wing cocked his head. "Why didn't I die in Paris, Red?"

"You did die. You said you did!"

Little Wing shook his head. "I was never wounded." Suddenly he didn't sound drunk at all.

"But...!"

"I was never wounded." He held up a hand. "Sometimes you can be incredibly naïve for someone in your position. You've got to start trusting your instincts, Red, not your logic. At some point, logic fails everyone. Remember that, if you want to survive."

"What are you talking about? I saw the knife! I saw the wound!"

Little Wing shook his head impatiently. "Wrong!

Your eyes told you I had blood spilling from my chest. Did you even examine the cut?"

Brad stared at him. "What?"

"Did you?"

"N-no…" Brad shook his head. "I just put my shirt over it to stop the bleeding."

Little Wing's hand reached up to the collar of his T-shirt and yanked at the fabric. The cotton strained and ripped down the front, exposing his chest. "Show me," he demanded. "Show me where I was wounded."

Brad's eyes played over the rock solid muscles, looking for a scar or some trace of the wound that should have been there. He reached out and touched Little Wing's chest. The skin was smooth and unblemished.

"But that's impossible…"

"It was all a fake, Red. A fake—for you and anybody else watching."

"What? Then how…?"

"Watch my lips: it never happened."

Brad shook his head. "But I saw you! I saw it happen with my own fucking eyes!" His voice was panicked.

"Listen to me, Red," Little Wing said gently and patiently. "I was never wounded. I was *disappeared*. And you and Grace and everyone else bought it." Little Wing's black eyes bore into Brad. "You asked why I never let you know that I was still alive. So now I'll tell you. Because I knew that if I fooled you, then I'd fooled everyone … because you were right there." He drummed his finger into Brad's chest. "You were right fucking there, Red! And that's why I could never tell you."

Bradford just shook his head. "Then what are you?" he asked weakly. "What the hell is going on?"

Little Wing looked away a long moment. When he looked back, he said, "I'm End Ops."

Brad was suddenly filled with a profound dread. If he'd had trouble with Little Wing's earlier explanation, this one was much harder to accept. End Ops were the grey zone guys, the ones only rumoured to exist. The ones you were never sure you could trust even if they did exist. No one even knew whose side they were on. End Ops was the shadow within the shadow. It was said when an agent was forcefully retired he'd actually been taken out by End Ops. End Operations. The final exit.

Brad shook his head again. "And last night? You *were* shot, right? That was real, wasn't it?"

Little Wing nodded gruffly. "Last night was real. I was shot. It still burns like hell," he said.

"Then what's going on?" Brad barely got out.

"You're what's going on, Red."

Brad's head reeled. "What? What do you mean?"

"They don't trust you, Red. Ask yourself—what are you doing in Puerto Vallarta?"

"I don't know. Yes, I do know! I'm protecting Celine—"

"Celine Dion has a troop of bodyguards. Why would she need you?"

"I ... I..."

"You're not here to protect anybody. They were testing you. What reason do you have to be considered unworthy?"

"None!"

"Think again, Red."

"None! I'm telling you the truth!" Brad took a deep breath.

Little Wing reached out a hand and placed it consolingly on Brad's shoulder. "It's okay, Red," he said softly.

"Does Grace know what's going on here?" Brad managed at last.

Little Wing shook his head like a teacher despairing of a slow child. "Of course she knows. She knows precisely why I'm here. I'm following *you*, for fuck sakes! Who do you think gave those orders?"

Brad thought this over. Was it possible? Was that the reason she hadn't told him why he was in Vallarta? Brad shook his head. "I don't believe you," he said.

Little Wing shrugged. "Go ahead—call her."

Brad fished around in the bag for his cell phone. His fingers fumbled as he dialled the number that would connect him with his boss. It rang once. An operator answered.

"This is Agent Red. I need to speak with Grace now," he said.

"This call is unscheduled…" the operator began.

"Put her on now!"

"Yes, Red?" Grace's voice came on the line as though she'd been listening in the whole time. He pushed the phone toward Little Wing. "Talk to her," he commanded.

Little Wing reached out and took the phone. "Hello, Grace. This is Little Wing."

Brad couldn't believe this was happening. Little Wing listened for a moment, then grunted and handed the phone back to Brad.

Brad put the phone to his ear. "This is … Agent Red," he said.

"It's out of my hands, Red," he heard Grace's gruff bark. "Do whatever Little tells you to do. And don't fuck up this time."

The call clicked off. He put the phone down and looked up. "What about Zach?" he asked woodenly.

"The kid'll be fine." Little Wing smiled gently. "You still haven't figured it out yet? He's your replacement."

Brad's mouth fell open, but nothing came out.

"Had any messages from your lover boy lately, Red?"

Brad shook his head.

"No? Why is that? I wonder. Well, let me tell you, there won't be any. Didn't you think it a little convenient how he was given permission to go off on that Vision Quest? I mean really, Red. Didn't you smell something fishy? Peyote? A trek in the desert? How naïve are you, for fuck's sakes?"

Brad felt like crying. His entire life had just exploded in front of his eyes. "Now what?" he said softly. "What are you going to do with me?"

"You could change your mind. We could still take the money and run, Red."

Brad shook his head. No matter what happened, that wasn't an option. "I can't do that," he said.

"So be it." Little Wing took Brad's hand and placed the palm flat against his chest over his heart, right where there should have been a scar. "You risked your life to save me once. I'll give you a chance to run."

"What?"

"It's time for you to vanish, Agent Red."

"You're letting me go?"

Little Wing nodded. "You overcame me in the heat of the moment…" He kept nodding, as if to force Brad into agreeing with him.

"You're stronger than me. They know that," Brad said.

Little Wing pulled out a gun and held it over his head. The shot went into the roof, sending sand and dust down around them. He lowered his hand. "But you were always faster. I couldn't stop you, Red."

"But…!"

The next shot went into the floorboards inches

from Bradford's feet. "Get the fuck out of here. Now!"

Before he knew what he was doing, Agent Red, a.k.a. Bradford Fairfax, turned and ran down the steps of Little Wing's tenement, clutching the bag of cash under his arm.

More than anything, he needed to get away and think. How the hell could this be happening? Fake deaths, fake kidnappings, and now this? The money was a plant. Surely they would know that. Agent Red was as diligent and honest as they came. Sure, he'd broken a rule or two. And maybe he'd screwed up once or twice. After all, hadn't they taught him to be insubordinate and double-crossing and sneaky right from the beginning? They'd taught him to use his brain, not just be a tool following orders. But this was…!

This was way too much for him to think his way through. He wished Zach were here, but then Zach was double-crossing him and had agreed to replace him. In which case, Brad was glad he wasn't here. He couldn't face Zach right now. What a colossal mess. He'd been in some tight spots before, but he hadn't a clue how he was going to get out of this one.

23

As if by instinct, Brad found himself heading up the same mountain path he and Zach had climbed a few days earlier, back when life had been sweetly idyllic and relatively uncomplicated. This is what comes of letting a dead man back in your life, he reminded himself.

He recalled his dream—or rather, his nightmare—about the cemetery. It had clearly been warning him about unearthing the past. How prescient. He could kick himself for not heeding it, but it was too late for that. In the meantime, he had to figure out what he was going to do about this mess. Not only was he going to have to go into hiding from everyone on his trail (minus a certain green-eyed Mexican, he noted grimly), but also from his own colleagues at Box 77, including Grace and Zach, who now thought him the enemy.

Shadowy things. That's what Grace had said when he demanded to know what was really going on in Puerto Vallarta. He'd had no idea how shadowy till now. But, oh, the betrayal! To think that Grace had set Little Wing on him while conspiring with Zach behind his back to replace him. How had this happened?

As he climbed he looked continually over his shoulder, convinced he was being targeted by everyone in sight. Was that old lady hiding an Uzi behind the laundry flapping listlessly from the balcony of her cinder block house? Was that young mother harbouring a handgun in her child's carriage? Probably not, but it wouldn't pay to get reckless now. Just keep climbing, he told himself.

After twenty minutes, he was winded. The sun was at its height and exposure was painful. Bradford sat in the shade of a crabbed old cactus and looked down over the city. A small dog came trotting over the hilltop and sniffed him. It was probably the closest he might come to having a friend right now.

"Sorry, boy. No handouts today. I have nothing to give you," he said. I don't have much of anything to give myself either, he thought. Still, it wasn't a good time to start feeling sorry for himself.

Empty-handed or not, the dog decided Brad was good company and curled up beside him. Brad gave his ears a good scratch. He was just about to move on when something caught his eye. Far below, he saw people climbing the hill. He took out his binoculars and looked. First in line came the SS desk clerk, looking grimly efficient. Behind him, Brad saw the dark-haired Brazilian. Not far behind him was Sebastian. And then, to top it all off, there came Jarod, sleeves unfurling like sails in the wind. How had they all found him?

The tracking device!

He smacked his forehead. How could he have been so stupid? Little Wing told him he was being tracked. The sun must be getting to him, because he was throwing protocol out the window. *Don't fuck up this time*, Grace had said. She might as well have saved her breath. He fished around in the bag and found the tiny, bug-like device and unclipped it. He was about to throw it over a ridge when a thought came to him.

"Hey, boy," Brad called out. "Maybe I do have something for you after all."

The dog looked up expectantly as Brad held out the device. The dog sniffed it. Curious, he licked it then, deciding it was worth a try, swallowed it whole. Satisfied this was the best Brad could do for him, he turned and trotted off down the far side of the hill.

"*Adiós, amigo,*" Brad said, resetting the bag on his shoulders before scuttling off in another direction.

A minute later, he looked back to see that the others had continued along the path the dog had taken. He was rid of them for now.

A bell sounded in the clear air. He looked up. Before him rose a stone tower. He'd found his way back to the Franciscan abbey where he and Zach had stopped for water. In fact, the same old man was brushing the same burro's tail in the very same courtyard.

Brad started to turn away. Wait a minute! How long could he keep running? Maybe this was what he was seeking. He ducked under the arch and made his way inside. The old man waved him over with an offer of water. Brad accepted gratefully, asking if the abbey rented out rooms to strangers. The man nodded and went off.

Brad heard barking in the distance. Looking down the hill, he saw that the dog had returned with Sebastian and the others in tow. He withdrew into the shadowy interior of a manger where he exchanged bewildered glances with a goat. He watched the progress of his pursuers from a slit in the wall as they approached and then bypassed the abbey in their zeal to keep up with the dog.

He was safe for a little longer. Still, even if they didn't find him, it wouldn't be long before Box 77 tracked him down. He didn't have much time to prove his innocence. Worse, he still had no idea how he was going to do that.

The old monk returned. Brad was delivered into the hands of a younger brother, one who was quite attractive and physically fit. But there was no time for that now. And best of all, this one spoke. The young monk told Brad he was welcome to stay with the brethren, if he had need of refuge. Oh yeah! Brad thought. I definitely have need.

He followed the man to a small room at the back of the abbey. Over in one corner, a narrow wooden pallet squatted on a rough stone floor. A straw mattress that might have passed for a lumpy bag stuffed with potatoes lay on top. Not five-star, Brad told himself, but it would do. He reached into his bag and pulled out a handful of bills, offering them to the monk. They were refused.

Compassionate eyes searched Brad's face. "You are in trouble, my brother?" the monk asked.

Brad nodded.

The monk smiled. "Stay with us, then. And have faith. God will help you sort out your troubles."

Bradford wasn't sure God could help him much at present, but he wasn't about to turn down any support he could get. His eyes roamed the tiny compartment. Apart from a few cracks and a wooden cross, the walls were bare and unadorned. As hotels went, this was about as simple as it got. If he ever got out of there, he promised himself a week at the Paris Hilton.

The monk bowed and left. He returned in a few minutes with a loaf of bread and a jug of water. Brad sat up and accepted them gratefully.

"Don't you want to know why I'm here?" he asked, tearing hungrily into the bread. It was the first thing he'd eaten since yesterday.

The monk shook his head. "I already know why you are here—God sent you to us."

"And you don't care why?"

The monk shook his head again. "We do not judge."

Hmmm ... must be an unusual sect, Brad thought.

"You and your brethren are very kind," he said.

"We must help all of God's creatures in their hour of need." The monk smiled and went out again.

Brad lay on the pallet and stuffed the bag of cash under his head. At least it would do for a pillow. He had no other use for it at the moment.

He kept watch at the window all afternoon, but neither the dog nor his pursuers returned. Brad laughed softly to himself, wondering where the pooch had led them. At dusk, the brethren summoned him to a sparsely furnished dining room. The soft crackling of a fire greeted him. The air was rich with the aroma of cooking as they bid him sit and share their simple meal. They ate in silence. Afterwards, the monks retired one by one until he was left alone with the younger brother who'd shown him to his room.

The young man spoke softly and without urgency— of the weather, of the struggles of the Mexican people for a better life, of the sorry state of world affairs. Despite his youthfulness, the monk exuded a calmness and sense of contentment that Brad envied at that moment. Not once did he allude to Brad's reasons for being there. Eventually, he stood and wished him a good night.

Through the window of his one-room cell, Brad looked out onto a vast sea of stars. His room was directly facing Orion's Belt. He looked up at the constellation and thought of his father's promise to be there for him. Maybe he was there now, looking down.

If you're up there, Dad, he thought, please help me.

Brad considered everything he'd discovered that day, including the revelation that Little Wing was a secreterthan-thou secret agent and that he, Bradford Fairfax, was now a wanted man on both sides of the law.

Of course, his instincts had been right all along. Little Wing had showed up so conveniently at just the right moment to save him from the green-eyed man. It should have been a dead give-away, but Brad had been fooled by appearances yet again.

Harsh lessons. He'd drunk from the cup of betrayal and found the dregs to be bitter, but not poisonous enough to kill him. Eventually, he knew, he would get over all this. A profound weariness would set in then he would find the strength to begin again—provided he lived to see the day. He was ill merely, not mortally wounded. He thought of Zach's kisses. They were lost to him. How bitter was love?

Brad felt a moment of contrition: he couldn't blame anyone. He'd made his own choices. Whatever happened, Bradford wouldn't hold it against Zach. After all, it was he who had brought this on by daring to look the past in the face.

That night he slept a troubled sleep, tossing and turning on the thin pallet. Clearly, he wasn't suited to a life of austerity, even with five million dollars under his head. If he ended up on the lam for the rest of his life, he'd have to find more suitable places to hide. Somewhere with chocolate-soy lattes and coconut cream moisturizers. Maybe Brazil.

The morning sun was just hitting the window when he woke. The rays sent a beam across his face. For a moment, he didn't recognize his sparse surroundings. Had he signed on for another really bad all-inclusive cruise? What was it this time, twelve islands in twenty-four hours? Then it returned to him in a flash—he was in a monk's cell on the run from any number of enemy agents. Not to mention his own organization. And he still hadn't a clue what he was going to do about any of it.

His cell phone beeped. The screen yielded a single text message: *Bring the money to the Blue Parrot by 7 a.m. or the skinny chick sings for the last time!*

The ransom! Brad glanced over to ensure that his impromptu pillow was still there. It was, and his sore neck was the proof.

He couldn't even guess how the kidnappers had managed to get hold of his cell phone number, but he wasn't going to stop and worry about it. On the other hand, what if this was merely Box 77's ruse to flush him out from hiding? That seemed far more likely. He checked his watch. It was nearly seven now. He didn't have much time to decide. If the message was real, Celine Dion's life could soon be snuffed out like a match.

Brad watched as something fluttered outside his window. It flashed like metal, turning before him in the air. A Blue Morpho! The butterfly trembled and floated into the room. It landed on Brad's arm, making itself at home among the light dusting of hair. He remembered the vivid colour of the wings—the same blue as Zach's hair. He recalled Zach's words: *There's a legend among the Amazonians that when you see a Blue Morpho you're near your true love.* Brad watched the wings beating gently. Surely if anything was a sign, this was.

A shadow passed over the window. Brad looked up in time to see the dark-haired Brazilian skirting the courtyard. No doubt about it, that was a gun he was holding. Brad shrank against the wall and watched as his pursuer turned a corner and disappeared.

A few seconds later, a knock sounded gently on his door. Before Brad could move, the door opened and the young monk entered. The man held a finger to his lips.

"There are men at the gate!" he said. "They have guns. I think they are looking for you."

The butterfly gently lifted off from Brad's arm. It fluttered past his face and out the window.

"Hurry!" the man urged.

Brad knew he could trust him. These were men of humility, men who didn't judge and who unthinkingly put their own lives at risk in order to help others. That was nearly unbelievable in the twenty-first century. He recalled Bernard Shaw's epithet: "It's not that Christianity has been tried and found wanting," he'd declared. "It's never really been tried." Maybe there was something to it after all.

Brad grabbed his bag and followed the monk through a break in the abbey wall. He kept pace as the man's brown robe turned and swayed along the road leading through the courtyard and away from the monastery. Even through that thick cassock, Brad could tell he had firm thighs and a well-rounded butt. From climbing all those mountain trails, no doubt. He sighed. Life at that altitude certainly had its advantages.

The monk stopped and pointed to a small house just ahead. Nearby, some boys were playing on a cliff top. Two of them held a parasail prepped for take off.

"There," the monk said, pointing.

Oh, no, Brad thought. No way in hell am I getting into that thing! But he had little choice. The Brazilian would waste no time in tearing up the abbey. If he didn't find Brad there, he and the others would keep searching. They could be closing in on him right now. Besides, he had a mission to accomplish.

They reached the cliff. Brad looked down at the thousand-foot drop and felt his stomach reel. For a second, his heart stopped. He was breathless. The monk looked at him with concern.

"Have faith, amigo," he counselled.

Easy for you to say, thought Brad.

"Ees ready, señor," one of the boys told him.

Brad reached into his bag. The boys' eyes popped when they saw the number 1000 printed on the bill he gave each of them. He offered ten more bills to the young monk.

"Light some candles," he said. "Pray for me, brother."

The boys had him strapped into the contraption in less than a minute. Then it dawned on him: there was no pilot's seat. He was on his own.

"Wait! What do I do?" he croaked out in a panic-stricken voice.

"It's simple," the monk told him. "Just use your weight to steer."

The boys explained how the rows of pockets sewn into the sail would fill with air as he moved forward, lifting him higher as he went along.

"Has this been scientifically proven?" Brad asked.

"*Claro.*" Of course.

"Many persons do this all the time," one of the boys said with a disapproving look.

Not this person, Brad thought.

Before he could give it another thought, the breeze buoyed him up. His feet left the ground. In another few seconds, he was hovering over the city, the wind blowing through his hair. For a moment, he was paralyzed with fear. Then it passed, and all he could think was that the world had never looked so beautiful.

24

Brad's feet hit the roof of the Blue Parrot with a resounding thud. Whew! This must be how Barbra felt. He checked his watch: two minutes to spare. Now what? He glanced around. Things had pretty much been returned to their original condition since his last visit: chairs and tables righted, and the stage cleaned and set. But for what?

He wasn't alone.

Brad looked at the foursome gathered there: Jarod, Little Wing, the SS clerk, and the blonde Brazilian stood watching him intently. Presumably, the Brazilian boy's dark counterpart was still somewhere up on the mountain searching through the abbey. Brad wasn't worried about the monks. They would know how to handle him. This was no casual social gathering, however. The blonde scowled at Brad, while keeping a gun trained on the others. A trio of identical burgundy bags lay at his feet.

Little Wing hailed him. "Right on time, Red! I knew you'd come."

"Hello, Little. What's going on?" Brad asked, nodding to the others.

"Ransom pick-up," Little Wing said, with a nod toward the bags. "It's a good thing you arrived with the cash, because our friend here"—he nodded at the blonde—"isn't too crazy about what we've shown him so far."

The Brazilian snarled and motioned with his gun to indicate that he wanted the bag on Brad's shoulder.

Brad removed it and slid it gently across the roof. It stopped right at the blonde boy's feet. Keeping his gun trained on the others, he leaned down and grasped it. Before he could open it, however, a voice barked a command.

"Hands up!"

They turned to see Sebastian holding an even bigger gun. "Put that thing down and slide it over here," the silver-haired captain instructed.

Apparently there was no need for translation. The Brazilian lowered his gun and slid it across to Sebastian, who picked it up and pocketed the weapon. He looked at Brad. "Over there with the rest of them, handsome," he said.

He waited till Brad had joined the others.

"Now isn't this an attractive little gathering? Maybe I should throw a party," Sebastian said, grinning like the Cheshire Cat. "Which bag is it, I wonder? Eeny, meeny, miny, homo."

Brad looked down at the four bags on the deck. He no longer knew which one held the money.

Sebastian pointed at the bag to the right of the blonde. "That one first," he said, aiming his gun at the blonde's head. "I know you don't speak English, but I'm sure you know what I want." The Brazilian scowled and kicked the bag over. Sebastian opened it and pulled out a bottle of skin cream.

"What's this crap?" he exclaimed.

"That *crap* is extremely high-quality moisturizer," Jarod answered, sounding stung. "You can't even buy that stuff back home, you know."

Sebastian dropped the bag with a clatter. "That one!" he said, pointing to the bag on the left. Brad deftly kicked it over.

Sebastian yanked it open. It contained a welter of colourful looking fabric.

"So," said the SS desk clerk, eyes narrowing. "Now we know who's been stealing the hotel hand towels. And I can assure you, action will be taken…"

"Shut up," Sebastian told him. "Let's have a look behind door number three."

A third bag was tossed to him. He caught it and yanked it open without even trying the zipper.

"And what's this—salad?" he demanded.

It did indeed look like some very unappetizing vegetarian entrée, the kind that gets pushed to the far end of the buffet table and sits there wilting all night long while the guests eat everything else in sight and conspire to avoid mentioning it not to embarrass the host.

"Salad my ass!" someone declaimed loudly.

They all turned to see Esmeralda wielding an even bigger gun on all of them.

"What the hell…?" Sebastian began, but stopped as Esmeralda swung the gun toward him.

"Put your hands up, motherfucker!" she commanded. "And don't try any of that bad-ass shit on me. I've seen *Jackie Brown* about a million times."

"Gush! I love that movie," Jarod gushed.

Sebastian slowly raised his arms while Esmeralda watched him intently.

"That's good. Now just kick it over to me with your feet."

Sebastian gave the bag a good kick. It slid over to Esmeralda as smoothly as a curling stone across clean ice.

They watched as Esmeralda slipped the bag over her shoulder. "This, you motherfuckers, is genuine, one-hundred percent Mexican peyote." She pointed at the Brazilian. "But just for kicks, let's see what's behind door number four."

The final bag slid over and stopped at her feet. Esmeralda bent down and slipped her hand beneath Brad's T-shirt, pulling out a wad of cash.

"Well, hello, Jackpot!" she said, as a sudden *whuff-whuffing* filled the air.

They all looked up as the shadow of a helicopter swooped down on them. A shot hit the roof right at Esmeralda's feet. She dropped her gun. The blonde was on it in a second. He raised it toward the group.

"Damn. I should've been satisfied with one bag," Esmeralda lamented. "Oh, well. Easy come, easy go."

The helicopter dropped onto the roof with the dark-haired Brazilian at the controls. They all watched as the bag of cash was loaded into the helicopter and the blonde half of the equation clambered aboard. The chopper lifted off, the blonde keeping his gun trained on the rooftop till they were out of reach.

"Nobody move!"

They turned to see Sebastian aiming a revolver at them. They'd forgot about the second gun. Without warning, Jarod flew through the air and tackled the burly ship's captain. The gun went flying. Within seconds, the skinny man had Sebastian's hands neatly cuffed behind his back. Brad was thoroughly confused. Jarod looked up and smiled.

"Agent Silver, at your service, Red."

"What?" Brad exclaimed.

Jarod winked. "Fooled ya!" He paused and looked at his watch. "Boy, we wrapped this one up just in time. My surgery's in a couple of hours." He handed Brad the gun and nodded at Little Wing. "Keep your eye on this one. He's the one we're really after."

Brad looked at Little Wing. Little Wing shrugged.

Behind them, Esmeralda shouldered the bag of peyote. "In that case, gentlemen, seeing how I'm no longer needed, I'll be off."

All eyes turned to the bald-headed channeller.

"What? Did you think I'd just leave it behind?" She patted the bag. "No way, José. Art costs money! I'm no charity. This girl doesn't work for free. Nuh-uh, baby! Besides, I'm a genuine Mayan princess. These plants be-*long* to my people."

No one challenged her as she entered the elevator. The door whooshed behind her and Esmeralda was gone. Next, Brad watched as Jarod, a.k.a. Agent Silver, marched Sebastian off the rooftop with his bag of moisturizers secured over his shoulder.

The SS clerk stooped and picked up the bag with the missing hotel towels. "And I am taking possession of this," he said curtly, before heading back inside the hotel.

When the others had gone, Brad turned, gun in hand, and looked at Little Wing. "Say it ain't so, Joe," he said softly.

Little Wing shrugged. "You always were gullible, Red."

"What did you think you'd accomplish?"

Little Wing snarled. "What did I think I'd accomplish? Everything, you dumb fuck." He shook his head. "We could've had it all, Red. You, me and the money. It was all in our hands!"

"What are you talking about?"

Little Wing's face contorted. "I thought that after I let you go, you'd see the light. I thought you'd realize how much you loved me and we'd walk into the sunset with the ransom money and live happily ever after."

"Now who's being naïve? What are you really—a double agent? Triple? Who are you really working for?"

Little Wing shrugged. "Myself. Who are you working for?"

"I'm working for peace."

"Ah, you're still a cheerleader for peace. How touching." Little Wing looked scornfully at him. "Ask yourself this: what's the difference between us and the CIA or the FBI?"

"A lot," Bradford said. "They fight to make the world a safer place for corporations and corrupt heads of state. We fight to make the world a safer place for everyone else."

"C'mon, Red! There are no good guys and bad guys any more. Admit it! There's just us and them. You gotta live for yourself."

Brad remembered his daydreams of living life for endless pleasures: good food, expensive wine, cheap sex. They dissolved. "So you thought that you and I would just say *adiós* to the world and disappear with the ransom money and let everyone else fend for themselves?"

"C'mon! We owe it to ourselves. Aren't we the little guys who are always getting screwed?"

"I thought we were the ones who stopped the little guys from getting screwed."

Little Wing watched him for a moment. He tugged on his ear lobe. "Mind if I have a smoke?"

Brad nodded. "Go ahead."

He pulled out a cigarette and lit it, blowing smoke into the air overhead.

"Talk," Brad said. "Where's Celine?"

"Where's Celine?" Little Wing laughed. "You're such a dope! There's no Celine." He took another drag and stepped away from Brad.

"Stay where you are, Little."

Little Wing turned to look at him. "What are you

going to do, Red? Shoot me?"

"Maybe. Were you going to shoot *me* if I said no to your scheme?"

"Nah! I was just going to maim you a bit. You're far too pretty to kill."

Brad watched him edge closer to the lip of the roof.

"You know, it was so easy sailing down from the roof the other night." He peered over the edge. "It doesn't look so easy now."

"You were the second kidnapper?"

"Of course. Just because you told me to wait downstairs doesn't mean I did what you said."

"You weren't really down on the beach all that time?"

Little Wing shook his head. "Afraid not. Instead of going downstairs like you told me, I turned around and came right back up here. Appearances, Red. It was me who jumped off with the parasail. It was a little scary trying to shoot my own arm in the dark. I could barely see where the veins were. But I knew you'd save me. Good old Agent Red. I could always count on you. Of course, back then I thought there really was a Celine, too. And I still needed you to believe that I'd done it for the team. We soon found out differently, of course."

"We?"

"Me and that green-eyed guy. He was my partner. Professional partner, I mean. Not my lover. You're still the only one for me, Red." Little Wing looked down at the beach. The waves sparkled in the distance. "You know it's funny, but I never knew your real name."

"Brad. It's Bradford Fairfax," Brad said, trying to hold Little Wing's gaze, begging him silently not to look away.

Little Wing considered this. "Bradford. That's nice.

It rolls off the tongue well. Balanced, sensible. Not like some of these fag names you hear: Halston and Fenwick and Crispin."

"And yours?" Brad asked hopefully.

Little Wing smiled. "Swooping Owl. I guess that's not so sensible either."

Brad nodded. "That explains all the feathers."

Little Wing raised a foot and placed it on the roof edge. "Natives are supposed to name their kids after the first thing they see when the baby's born. I think mine was a bit of a stretch, though. After all, I was born in a Seattle hospital." He cocked his head. "I suppose it beats Catheter or Stethoscope. I think my mother thought if she gave me that name I might be able to fly."

"Your mother was a smart woman," Brad said. "I always believed you could."

Little Wing looked down again. "Maybe," he said. "I'm not so sure any more." He looked up at the sky and then back at Brad. "Wanna take a walk into the sunset with me, lover boy?"

Brad shook his head. "Please don't," he said.

Little Wing placed his other foot on the ledge and stood erect. "At least now I know how I die," he said. "No more terrible dreams. No more nightmares about how I'm living my life." He looked at Brad for a moment and raised his hand in salute. "God, I loved you."

Brad lunged a second too late. His hands grasped empty air. A part of him almost hoped that Little Wing, a.k.a. Swooping Owl, would defy reality and fly off into the distance. He might even be willing to let him get away if he did, but the broken shape at the base of the hotel told him it wouldn't happen.

He took the stairs two at a time. By the time he reached the bottom a crowd had formed around Little

Wing's body. Brad broke through the gathering and knelt beside his ex-lover and former partner, who was at last undoubtedly and undeniably dead. There would be no miraculous resurrection this time.

It seemed like déjà vu, even though this was no Paris street corner. Somehow, Little Wing looked almost peaceful despite the dark stain seeping from beneath his body and running along the pavement. He might have been asleep or playing a joke. For a second, Brad would have sworn he saw the puddle form in the shape of a pair of wings.

The crowd parted and a familiar figure came through. Brad glanced up as Angie placed a hand on his shoulder.

She looked at the broken figure that had until recently been Little Wing. She shook her head. "Too much party-party," she said softly, laying a sarong over the body.

At last, Brad shook with the tears that had been denied him for the last four years.

25

Brad stood, cell phone in hand, looking down over the city from the balcony of their villa. The view was exquisite. The pool rippled at his feet. Zach was at his side.

"What about Celine?" Brad asked.

"I hate to break it to you, Red, but Little Wing was telling the truth. The real Celine Dion was never in danger. In fact, she was never even in Vallarta. Last I heard, she was in Vegas for the opening of her newest show."

"But ... weren't they all after her?"

Grace hemmed and hawed. Her Texas accent had returned. "We-e-e-el, that's a tough call there. Little Wing was supposed to be doing what you were doing—looking after the little lady. I guess he thought he saw an opportunity to make some cash if he and his partner nabbed her. Though deep down I suspect it wasn't Celine he really wanted."

Brad felt a tingle. "Then who was it?"

"I think you know the answer to that."

He paused to take this in. "You mean Celine Dion was really my decoy?"

"In a way."

"Wow!" was all he could manage.

"We knew we had a rogue agent on our hands. We sent out the fake kidnapping threat to lure him out. It was only a matter of time before Little Wing took the bait."

"What made you suspect Little Wing?"

"We'd had a couple of ops go wrong before and

figured we had a weak link somewhere. We just couldn't be sure till now. By the way, that green-eyed man was the missing operator I told you I lost a few years back. So now we know what happened to him, too."

"And he recruited Little Wing?"

"Looks like it."

Brad thought it over. "You didn't ever suspect me, did you?"

Grace paused just long enough. "Na-a-ah. Why would I do a thing like that?"

"Just a thought. Maybe it was something Little Wing said," Brad replied, wondering if he'd ever trust her again.

She seemed to read his mind. "Believe me, Red," she said. "I trust you as if you were my own child. I probably shouldn't say this, but some days I feel like a mother to you and that blue-haired boy of yours."

Brad shivered and thought of the vision Zach had confided to him on the boat about Grace's past life as the sacrificing parent. He sighed. "I don't think I'll ever understand what happened to Little Wing. That's not the partner I knew. What would make someone turn like that?"

"Greed, bitterness, anger, revenge, frustration, years of resentment turned inward—take your pick. I've seen it happen before and it'll happen again."

Brad sighed. "True enough."

"You said he told you there was little difference between the bad guys and the good guys. Maybe at the end of the day he's right," Grace said. "Maybe we're all just doomed to act out our little karmic destinies without much choice in the matter. Some of us have the comfort of knowing we've done good deeds, but is that really enough?"

Did she just say "karmic"? Brad thought.

Grace continued. "I think what it really boils down

to, when all is said and done, is that you and I can go to sleep at night and not worry that we'll have nightmares about how we've lived our lives."

"Right," agreed Brad. Hey, wait a minute! he thought. I do have nightmares.

"I'm certainly glad to see I was right about our blue-haired boy," Grace said. "He was very useful to us."

Brad looked up at Zach's smiling face. "Yes. That text message sure fooled me."

"And everyone else, apparently. It's amazing how he broke into everyone's cell phone systems, contacted them all and got them onto that rooftop."

"Speaking of being fooled," Brad said. "Never in a million years would I have pegged Jarod for one of us."

"Agent Silver," Grace said. "He sure is, though. One of the best." She paused. "I guess he won't need his CD now."

"His CD?" Brad asked.

"The one Panther tried to pass along to you. Apparently he and Silver were big time Celine fans."

"Wait! You mean that wasn't secret data he was trying to pass along?"

"Not at all. Panther was hoping Silver would track down Celine so he could get an autograph for him. They just happened to be working on the same case."

Brad shook his head. "It's a shame such a young guy had to die."

"Hmm … yes," Grace murmured. "It's too bad when these things happen."

Brad thought about this for a moment. "He did die, didn't he? I mean, he wasn't *disappeared* too, by any chance."

"Who can say?"

Brad just rolled his eyes. "What about the ransom

money?"

"There wasn't any. We never intended to pay for Celine's release. That money was stolen by those Brazilian boys. Those two had nothing to do with any of this. They're just common bank robbers."

Brad nearly choked, thinking of Jarod's declaration about the look-a-likes being escaped bank robbers on the beach that morning they'd been introduced. "But how did it end up in my bag?"

"I gather that green-eyed man broke into their hotel room and stole it one afternoon while they were otherwise occupied."

Brad groaned.

"Then Little Wing put it in your bag, hoping to convince you that you were being framed by us and that you had no chance of returning to Box 77. I just played along."

"And Sebastian?"

"Sebastian Mathers, a.k.a. Sebastian Mathers, is what is known in some quarters as a Soldier of Fortune, or more commonly, a murderer for hire. In other words, human garbage. I gather he felt his soldiering days were reaching an end and he wanted a bonus to tide him over into retirement. He won't have to worry about being taken care of now."

"I guess that about covers it," Brad said.

"Well, apparently the Mexican authorities are a bit upset about a lost bag of peyote. But after all, she was a *real* Mayan princess."

Brad heard her chuckling to herself.

"Oh, there's just one more thing," Grace said. "Don't say I told you so, but try to enjoy the rest of your vacation. Relax a little. You've earned it."

"Right," Brad. "As if I could relax now."

He snapped the cell phone shut and turned to Zach. "I can't tell you how much I've missed you," he said. "But it's been a pretty exciting time, all told."

"Certainly sounds like it." Zach's eyes flashed the colour of the sea behind him. "I had an exciting time myself, while I was gone. Not to mention busy, what with trying to break in and fake those messages on everyone's cell phones."

"I take it your Vision Quest was a success?"

"Oh, big time! My chakras opened up completely in the desert. The peyote was a real help, though I won't make a habit of it. The visions were incredible. At one point, after not eating for two days, I saw a trail of smoke rise in the sky. I followed it with my eyes and watched it being joined by other trails until ultimately there were billions of them, all concentrating and connecting with something at the far end of the universe. A voice in my head told me it was the birthplace of creation. I was being shown the interconnectedness of all things."

"Wow!" was all Bradford could say.

"Oh, yeah! And Grace gave me my code name." He grinned. "Say hello to Agent Kong."

"As in 'King'?"

"I was thinking as in 'Donkey,' actually."

"Symbolic of anything?"

Zach shrugged. "You tell me. Just let me know when you want a test ride."

Brad smiled. "I'm just wondering," he said. "If Esmeralda pointed at me on the rooftop and said I was doomed, how come I'm still here?"

Zach cocked his head. "Are you sure she was pointing at you?" he asked.

Brad reflected. He recalled the swinging finger. Little Wing had been standing right beside him. "You're right!

She meant Little Wing." He shivered. "Somehow she knew."

"At least you were there for his final moment," Zach said. "It's a good thing you were able to get down the mountain so fast. That was very brave of you to parasail from such a height. Probably very dangerous, too. Those things aren't that reliable for such long distances."

Now he tells me, Brad thought. He related to Zach his vision of the blue butterfly arriving just as he wondered how he was going to escape his would-be killers.

Zach reflected. "I'll bet it was around the time I was trying to send you a message to give you courage," he said.

"A message?"

"Right after I sent the note about the ransom. I decided to send you some little sign to let you know I was with you."

"And of course it happened to be the same colour as your hair," Brad said. "Coincidence?"

Zach shook his head. "No such thing."

Brad nodded. "I can't help remembering how you saw me flying in one of your Remote Viewing sessions," he said. "I was sure it would never happen."

"That's not all I saw." Zach winked.

Brad looked down. "You also saw me as a lion when you touched my heart chakra. But I wasn't exactly loyal in love," he said.

"Sure you were," Zach reassured him. "But it was tricky, because you were trying to be loyal to more than one person. I know you love me, but you also felt strongly for Little Wing. You just needed time to think it through. I never doubted you."

"So I guess in the Buddhist view of things, I had a fairly strong karmic tie with Little Wing," Brad said.

Zach nodded.

"Will he come back to haunt us in our next life-time?"

"Probably not. You made the right choices this time, so you'll have paid off any debt you had. Not him, I'm afraid. Suicide's a terrible karmic choice. When he comes back he'll be paying for that, so he might not be in a position to bother you again."

"How do you mean?"

"He threw away a perfectly good life. My guess is he'll be fighting difficult odds to survive the next one."

"So you mean if you throw away this life, you're forced to fight for your next one?"

"Until you learn the value of what you have. It may sound like punishment, but it's just the balancing effect of karma."

"The meeting of self."

Zach nodded. "What you give to the world is what you get in return—but in another life."

"You're terribly wise," he said.

Zach grinned. "I do my best."

Brad watched him curiously for a moment. "What kind of karma gives you blue hair?" he asked.

"It's from all those Atlantis lifetimes when I lived underwater."

"Right. So how did those Atlanteans build the pyramids exactly? It's one of the great mysteries of all time. I'm sure if you have the answer, scientists everywhere would love to know."

"Actually, it's quite simple," Zach said. "They used electromagnetic currents to levitate the blocks of stone into place."

Brad's eyebrows shot up.

"Even after they destroyed their civilization, they

were still far more advanced than us," he said. "Everyone knows that."

Everyone but me, Bradford thought. He wrapped his arms around his blue-haired lover. "I don't know what kind of karma brought us together, but I'm extremely thankful for it."

"The good kind," Zach said. "We're connected in the best possible way."

"I feel that way with you. It's like we're part of each other, and we're also a part of everything else beyond us at the same time. It feels like a force running through us and reaching out to everything." He paused, as though the grandness of his thoughts eluded him. "I can't explain it too well…"

"I think you just did…"

"…but I can feel it," Brad said.

"So now that you've conquered your fear of heights, does this mean you'll come zip-lining with me?"

"Uh, maybe?" Brad said hesitantly.

"Good. I've reserved two spots on tomorrow's jungle tour. Then the following day we're all set to go bungee-jumping…"

"All right. But only if we can do a little break-and-entering later, Agent Kong." He winked.

"Deal."

Brad turned and looked out over Banderas Bay. The sun was just beginning to set behind the mountains, sending a golden glow across the water and over the rooftops of Puerto Vallarta. The wind was coming up, bringing with it strains of music, the sound of laughter, the scent of cooking, and even a hint of jasmine. It was the beginning of another perfect evening in Paradise.

Who would want to miss it?

ACKNOWLEDGMENTS

Thanks to Shane McConnell, John Davison and Enrique García-Pereña. Thanks also to Beach Christina and her bag of magic tricks, Diva Devine and the Dirty Bitches, Blue Chairs Resort, the much-missed Descanso del Sol, the late-Larry McConnell who resides somewhere in Orion's Belt, Celine Dion, Barbra Streisand, Cher, *et al.*, as well as the genius of Peter Bogdanovich, the wisdom of Black Elk, and the infectious enthusiasm of Sally Miller. I tip my hat to Red Cruz and David Tronetti for their helpful suggestions on the cover photographs. It's time I mentioned the inspirational Hardys, Frank and Joe, two of the best friends a boy could have, and my ideal reader, Oscar Wilde. As well, my gratitude and admiration goes out to the brave people of Mexico and beautiful Puerto Vallarta as they struggle for a better, fairer life. *¡Muchas gracias!*

Coming soon:

An excerpt from BON TON ROULEZ

The fourth Bradford Fairfax Mystery

1

New Orleans was as unrepentant as a drunk come sunup on Sunday. A thunderstorm hovered in the distance, making the horizon dance with ghostly flashes while the sky glowed with a feverish hue. From nearby came the moan of the mighty Mississippi wending its way past Louisiana's shores. Cajun music spilled from bars and shanties along the river's edge, spilling out onto the streets where the occasional reveller stumbled home in the pre-dawn darkness. Here and there, a stray dog howled to unsettle the night. After all this was the Deep South, where nearly everything sang the blues.

A bonfire burned brightly inside an abandoned warehouse, the orange flames stretching to the ceiling. A tribe of near-naked young men moved restlessly around the makeshift blaze. Shadows flickered and grew, thrown high against the walls. Bradford Fairfax, a.k.a. Agent Red, crouched just outside the circle of light and watched.

Brad counted twelve boys in total. Too many to challenge directly, but that had never been his intention. From what he could see, the pack was comprised of every discernible race—black, white, Asian, Semitic, Indian. Each was a superlative specimen of manhood, making for a gathering of the finest humanity had to offer. Or possibly finer than anything humanity had to offer.

Brad had been careful to enter the warehouse downwind of the tribe. He knew to be wary of these boys. They sensed things beyond the range of ordinary humans. It was as though they possessed a sixth sense that tickled their noses and prickled their skins.

Twenty feet ahead, a sentry leaned against a wall. Gras's younger gayer cousin, Southern Decadence. America was still recovering from the shock in the 21st century.

Since that fateful August when Katrina laid waste to the city, however, all rules of play were turned on their heads. No one knew for sure how many former residents were relocated elsewhere and how many had simply died in the storm and their bodies been lost. By the following spring, one thing was clear: the New Orleans of the past was gone and would never return.

Picking up the pieces in those devastating months after the hurricane, the remaining residents were faced with a choice. They could reconstruct their beloved town and make it a better place than before or they could turn down a road leading to something few wanted—a city for the elite, where no one got along. The scales already seemed to be tipping in favour of the latter. Just recently, New Orleans had been proclaimed the murder capital of North America.

Just then another of the boy beauties ducked in under the arches, brushing the rain from his limbs and shaking it from his hair. If Brad hadn't known better, he might think they were just ordinary boys out for a bit of fun. But he knew better. There was a wildness that distinguished them from regular boys, as telling as the difference between dogs and wolves. At first glance, they looked the same, but somehow they weren't the same. Whatever they were, Brad knew to stay as far away from them as possible. There was no way he was letting one of them get close, with their cool touch and faint blue colouring, as though an ink stain had spread beneath their skin. Still, he was determined to do whatever it took to find Zach and free him from whoever was holding him prisoner. Because Zach would have returned by now if he'd been in any way able to do so.

The drummers continued their frenzied beating. Others had taken up the rhythm, clapping hands and shuffling feet. Sinewy muscles gleamed in the fire's glow, while ecstatic cries filled the air like the howl of dogs catching scent of prey. It had just begun to dawn on Brad what the sticks were: bones. And they were long enough to be of the human variety.

A drop of sweat rolled from Brad's brow and down his nose, clinging for a moment before falling. He reached out a hand to swipe it away, but he missed. In slow motion, he watched the drop fall to the floor where it was absorbed by the dust.

That could be bad news, he knew. It was exactly the kind of thing these boys seemed to sniff out, as though they had some sort of built-in lust-o-metre marking the cravings of ordinary mortals. He feared what would happen if one of those prowling creatures caught his scent.

Just outside the ring of fire, a trapdoor led to some dark netherworld beneath the warehouse where ships once docked to offload their cargo. Since Katrina, however, none of the piers were operative. Every now and again, one of the boys descended briefly into the unseen cavern below, soon returning with an exultant cry.

Clearly, something was going on down there. Brad wondered if that was where they were keeping Zach. If Zach was even still alive, that is. It was the first time he'd allowed himself to contemplate that possibility.

Over the past four days, Brad had made his way

around these warehouses searching for clues to where his partner had gone. Not surprisingly, the police had written off his claims of a roving gang of renegade killers as lunatic fringe or maybe just a wildly exaggerated description of the thousands of refugees currently living in tents beneath overpasses or in derelict buildings.

To the NOLA cops, another random disappearance wasn't exactly news and with the soaring crime rate they already had plenty to keep them occupied. Moreover, Brad had no proof of his lover's disappearance in an area heavily marked as a *No Trespassing* zone. Nor was he at leisure to explain that he and Zach were actually secret agents working for a nameless security organization that recognized no official government body. Even if he had, that organization, known as Box 77 after a post office number, would have disavowed all knowledge of their existence, as well as its own. As far as the world was concerned, Box 77 didn't exist, so it was no surprise the police had fixated more on what two tourists were doing at an abandoned warehouse in the dead of night rather than the fact that Zach had disappeared while Brad lay unconscious after being attacked by persons unknown.

During the first few days of his search, Brad found nothing. It wasn't until the fourth day that he came across the same tribe of boys he'd seen the night Zach disappeared. He followed their wild romp along the coastline, past the dark eddies of the Mississippi and down into the heart of the warehouse district. Eventually, they'd led him right back here, where he'd been knocked on the head by an unknown assailant the last time he'd seen Zach alive.

The whoops and cries grew louder. Brad peered from behind the coiled rope. The tribe's antics were getting more frenzied. It seemed like the prelude to something, but he couldn't tell what. Nothing about these boys made much sense. All he knew was that they were to be feared.

The rain continued to beat a tattoo on the tin roof overhead. Brad crouched in the shadows, waiting for a sign. It could come at any time and he needed to be ready.

Just then the trapdoor lifted and a figure began slowly to emerge. A frenzy erupted. The boys let out a collective howl, as though greeting a long lost friend. It seemed to Brad as though he was witnessing some sort of initiation ceremony. And this would be the new initiate.

The trapdoor fell back with a resounding thud. The new boy stood before them dressed in a plain tracksuit. His body was lithe and muscular; a hoodie covered his head. Apart from being slightly overdressed for the crowd, he seemed much like the others. Here was yet another exquisite specimen of manhood.

A sharp *crack!* resounded from the parking lot, followed quickly by a second. This was the sign Brad had been waiting for. Now it begins, he thought. He hoped Harlan was already far away by now.

The boys stopped dancing and focused their attention on the sounds from outside. Almost as one, they were off and running in the direction of the parking lot. All but the new figure, who seemed unaware of what was going on. Eventually, he too began to follow the others, but his footsteps were slow and unsteady, like a tagalong kid brother trying hard to keep up.

Once the boy in the hoodie had gone, Brad dashed to the trapdoor and tugged on the latch. It was heavier than expected, but eventually opened with effort. A set of uneven wooden stairs descended to a dank, narrow corridor beneath the warehouse. River stench permeated the air. From the other side of the wall came the rumble of rushing water. Brad pulled out his penlight and followed the passage to a metal door. It opened at his touch.

Inside, the walls gleamed with a blue-white light. Brad looked over a bewildering array of tables and machines of unknown provenance. At first glance, it appeared to be a mortuary. Certainly, some kind of scientific or medical work was performed here, but what exactly went on was impossible to say.

He skirted the room, searching for hidden doors or access routes that might conceal a human being. A set of watery footprints seemed to lead from a standing metal cabinet, trailing directly across the floor. Curious, Brad opened it and peered in at a row of hanging white gowns that might have served as laboratory smocks. There was nothing else inside. Whoever or whatever had been inside was gone.

The chamber itself was little more than a sealed underwater cell with just one entrance. Whatever its purpose, whatever it might once have held, Zach wasn't here now, if he ever had been.

Brad made his way back upstairs, gently closing the trapdoor behind him. The bonfire still burned at the centre of the warehouse, while outside the fireworks continued to explode. The smell of cordite drifted in through the open doors, along with the startled yips of the tribe. Brad slipped back across the open space and into the shadows. Just then he heard a distinctive sound, like the slither of footsteps gliding over a slippery surface. A heavy grunting followed, as though something massive were being lifted with sheer brute force.

In the darkness, Brad could just make out the towering coil of rope toppling toward him. He leapt aside as it landed with a thud, reverberating through the warehouse. A flare from the bonfire showed Brad he wasn't alone.

The boy in the hoodie had returned. And while he may have been slow-moving, he was certainly strong. Strong enough to topple a massive cog-wheel. At least he'd come alone, Brad noted.

The two stood facing one another in the dark, each listening to the quiet breathing of the other. Brad wondered what to do. These boys were formidable. The prospect of hand-to-hand combat with one of them offered what would almost inevitably be a losing proposition.

There wasn't much time to think. The boy let out a sudden howl. Whether it was a battle cry or a signal to alert the others didn't matter, because there was no way it wouldn't have been heard. He approached warily, like an animal circling its prey. His eyes gleamed in the darkness.

A metal hook dangled overhead. Brad's eyes followed the rope to its trajectory. The pulley was intact. If he could reach it, he might be able to climb up to the rafters. Then what? The place would soon be swarming with these diabolic monkeys. He couldn't stay in the rafters forever. The climbing quadrupeds would eventually get to him.

Before Brad could decide, the boy lunged. Clammy hands gripped his throat. Instinctively, Brad reached up, smashing the hook into the boy's skull. An inhuman sound rent the air as the grip on Brad's throat relaxed. The boy went limp and fell to the floor. Bradford stepped back and waited. The body twitched for five, ten, fifteen seconds, before it finally stopped and lay there unmoving.

Shouts came from the parking lot, but these were different from the earlier cries. Brad cocked his ears. A shot went off and then another. He heard whistles. The police had arrived.

He knelt and put a finger to the boy's jugular. No pulse. His neck was broken. He hadn't intended to kill the boy, but if he hadn't connected the first time it would have been Brad who was lying there dead right now.

"I'm sorry, pal, but it was you or me," he said, pulling the hoodie from the boy's head.

Blue hair tumbled from beneath the garment. Brad cried out as he stared down at Zach's lifeless face.

Also in this series:

THE P'TOWN MURDERS — **the first Bradford Fairfax Mystery**

In a place that's "to die for," no one expects to die for real. So muses undercover agent Bradford Fairfax after an anonymous call reveals that his ex-boyfriend, party boy Ross Pretty, has died from an ecstasy overdose in "the gayest place on earth" — Provincetown, Massachusetts. But as the body of another overdose victim washes up on the shores of P'town, Brad becomes convinced that Ross's death is no accident.

DEATH IN KEY WEST — **the second Bradford Fairfax Mystery**

The rich really are different from you and me. On a New Year's vacation in Key West, special agent Bradford Fairfax and his blue-haired sidekick Zach meet an improbable "heiress" to one of the world's biggest fortunes who is convinced his own father wants him dead. When an infamous group of drag queens are found poisoned, Brad and Zach find themselves embroiled in yet another tantalizing mystery!

Dear Friend:

When I am gone remember that I was once like you, with all the same passions, hopes and dreams you are experiencing now. If this book can do anything, please let it give you reason to strive for a good life, inspire you and your friends to love one another better, and maybe even leave you with a few laughs. Is that too much to ask?

Jeffrey Round
Sama Martini Bar
510 Olas Altas
Puerto Vallarta
12/17/2013

www.ingramcontent.com/pod-product-compliance
Lightning Source LLC
Chambersburg PA
CBHW051504030726
47592CB00006B/2091